11/23/90

To the Original
Flying Cooper!

Happy Birthday —

Kate

Cooper

Cooper

HILARY
MASTERS

ST. MARTIN'S PRESS
New York

My thanks to the University of North Carolina at Greensboro, Denver University, the University of Jyvaskyla, and to Carnegie-Mellon University for their support as this book was being written.

Design by Claire Counihan

Library of Congress Cataloging in Publication Data

Masters, Hilary.
Cooper.

I. Title.
PS3563.A82C6   1987   813'.54   87-4370
ISBN 0-312-00011-1

First Edition

10 9 8 7 6 5 4 3 2 1

In memory of
Mollie Coyne
who gave me her wings.

. . . where bitter joy can hear
the sound of wings.
—AMELIA EARHART

CHAPTER

ONE

THE clock on the kitchen wall had not reached seven, but the headless bird predicted the hour. Jack Cooper had always meant to glue the head back on; it was still around somewhere, but that would mean going through the whole file of *Hobby & Craft* to find that article on the repair of cuckoo clocks. The bird was stuck on its little platform beneath the eaves of the miniature Alpine *hutte,* as if it refused to return to its cubby without its head; and so it perched, a strange omen to any hour. He would want to fix the whole mechanism all at once, Jack Cooper thought, for there was no point in giving the bird back its head without also restoring its mobility.

"I'm forty years of age," Ruth had been saying. "What's to become of me?" Her face had suddenly grown small as she spoke, like an illustration painted on a shrinking balloon. He wished a car would drive past the house to boil up the dust of the road so he would have to get up and shut the kitchen window, perform a task that was necessary yet also outside their argument—a reminder that even during these arguments there were matters that had to be taken care of and which both could agree were necessary to do.

But nothing stirred. The oak and maple leaves and dust lay quietly on the dirt road that went down into Hammertown. Except for Clay Peck's place, there were only two other cottages on their road and these had been closed up by the families from Queens who used them just in summer. The window beside the kitchen table was shut most of July and August.

But their argument had also settled down and he was glad, because he could almost feel them being listened to. These summerhouses had been built to amplify joyful sounds, and he worried that the eavesdropper would take the talk of suicide seriously, would not have clearly heard the whole sentence in which it was used only as a figure of speech. Actually, Ruth had talked about separation: how she knew what it was like to make such a grave decision and what order it would give a life.

"It's truly amazing, Jack," she had continued. "I'm almost grateful to you for this feeling of calm. I know how Ethel Knox must have felt when she decided to do it. All the towels folded and put away. Bills paid up and the dog put into the kennel." She had poured herself more wine and picked up a small rib bone from the pork roast to play a light tattoo on the rim of her dinner plate. "Why don't you say something? Talk to me. I tell you I'm leaving you and you say nothing."

She resembled one of her students: thin, pretty. The violet circles beneath the prominent brown eyes, as if she had been studying hard for one of her own composition exams, suggested a voluptuous weariness. The dark hair had been pulled back so tightly into a ponytail that the pale skin on her doll-sized face looked ready to crack like porcelain. Large gold hoops swung from the small round ears.

He sometimes thought she dressed this way on purpose so as to put less distance between herself and her students. He could remember her dressing more severely when they had married and lived in the City but she had been younger then. One day he had to find her at the college, and finally, after an hour of awkward search, discovered he had been staring right at her as she sat with students hunched over cokes and coffee cups in the student union cafeteria. He had not recognized her, but she saw no humor in this and told him not to come there again, no matter what the emergency might be.

"Say something. Why don't you say something?" Her eyes swelled, ready to burst with the amusement within them.

"But there's your work," he said finally.

"My work," she almost shouted. "What do you know about my work? *Here?* Is this where you think my work is? *Here?*" she demanded. He knew she referred not to their kitchen nor their house nor even the community college over in Green River. What she really meant was *not here,* not anywhere but New York City. "Say something!"

"Shush. Keep it down," he had motioned, palms against the tabletop, and then looked up. Her eyes also turned toward the ceiling but she had shrugged, almost shivered, and then looked out the window. The field across the road was completely dark, but the hill-side beyond the valley still blazed with sunlight.

He had been afraid to say more—right then—because if he had tried to answer her, or even pacify her, it would be like throwing dry tinder on the spark of her rage. It was not the first time she had talked about leaving them. These sudden angers reminded him of the blackened meadows left after farmers had deliberately set fires to burn off stubble and chaff—the whole countryside looking like a perverse spring on some other planet—but how quickly that blackness would become a lush green; so he had learned to say nothing that might prolong her wrath because the next day's calendar would always take over and give a semblance of order. Her unhappiness would not be forgotten, he knew, so much as it would be overgrown.

"I forgot to make coffee," he said. But this wasn't true. He always left something for her to do and even on this night, after her angry words, she had risen from the table, carried some plates to the sink, and begun to measure coffee into the basket of the percolator. They had worked silently, side by side; the trips took them from the table to sink to refrigerator and back like volunteer kitchen help at a church supper in Irondale, their strangeness joined together in camaraderie to benefit a cause explained in another room and beyond their hearing.

It saddened him that the pork roast had hardly been touched, the orange sauce had hardened like rock candy to cement the meat to the platter, and he put the whole solid affair into the refrigerator. He had enjoyed the different preparations, the ritual of bastings, that the complicated recipe had demanded, taking pleasure most of that afternoon in creating this unusual dish for her, though his satisfaction was augmented by the knowledge that the Volume II issue of *Gourmet* that had provided the recipe continued to increase in value—even as he turned and basted the roast—and would continue to germinate its own worth as it lay safe in a heavy, plastic envelope in the COOKING section. It had filled Jack Cooper with a flush of excitement to think of how an old thing, such as this recipe for *porc rôti à la orangerie,* could be put to use as if for the first time, made brand new and with all its juices fresh.

But even the excellence of the meal had soured her, or if not soured her, had whetted another appetite that he could never satisfy. There was a strange inverse ratio at work that always puzzled him; the better he did something for her, the more despondent she became. But he was never one to do anything in halfway measures.

"Do you have much schoolwork tonight?" he had asked.

"The usual one hundred and ten papers to grade. I'm still trying to write that piece for the MLA." She had put water into the pot and plugged it in. "He's been fed?"

"I fed him before you got home. I made a small cake. I'll leave some out here so if he comes down while you're working, he won't disturb you."

"You're going down to the store?" It was more of a statement than a question, as she rinsed dishes and put them into the dishwasher.

"There's a few orders to fill." He had looked away from the smile that pursed her lips, but he had been grateful for the routine questions and answers. The homely chores absorbed them. Anxieties and frustrations were sponged up by the same familiar moves that put table and countertops right, so the kitchen looked like a magazine layout, a neatness that implied nothing, not even a meal, had ever taken place there.

When the coffee was ready, she withdrew into her study, a coffee mug in one hand, portfolio in the other, her lips armed by a ballpoint pen held in her teeth. Jack Cooper fixed some coffee in a thermos and checked a list stuck to the refrigerator door by a magnet in the shape of a kitten. It was somehow reassuring to review the next day's needs, as if the list of ingredients were enough to guarantee the day's success; but he had also looked to see if Ruth had added anything and, in fact, the tiny printed letters of her hand spelled out two items. Vitamins. Tampax.

Then he had slipped out the back door to walk across the small backyard, around a bed of chrysanthemums, to the graveled parking bay beside the woodshed. An early frost had bruised the blooms. The old Buick Skylark was parked next to her VW Beetle. Venus was a cold, acetylene point in a sky of dark blue tin. He would remember all these details later. He had walked as if half asleep, following the route by rote, for part of him had tried to put away all this talk of separation but especially the mention of Ethel Knox taking her own life—this had been new. Ruth had sounded serious this time, about leaving.

The crossroads, still called Hammertown though the village of that name had disappeared long ago, were only about a mile from their house. Jack Cooper usually walked down to his business, but on this night he got into the Buick and had taken a deep breath. The stale, detained atmosphere within the car seemed better than the open air outside. It was like being in a space capsule, he thought, as he coasted away from the house and watched the lights of Ruth's study in the rearview mirror, and he had been overcome by a strange emotion; rather like how an astronaut must feel; a combination of estrangement, sadness mixed with exhilaration, as he pulls away from the lights of earth, knowing a set of those tiny lights belonged to a place he had put together himself.

When they moved to Hammertown full time, he had fixed over the old side porch, enclosed and insulated it and even put up pressed wallboard that looked like walnut paneling. It was a snug corner and more comfortable in winter than any other part of the house. Ruth's study. He liked to think of her in there, one leg folded under as she sat at her desk to grade papers or read or put down the tidy, meticulous lines of her poems. Even after the angry scene, she had taken all her materials in there and closed the door, so he looked upon these lights in the car's mirror with some tenderness, for they suggested warmth and satisfaction though he also knew the actual terrain might be hostile.

The crossroads laid down a pattern of the village that

once stood there. The last house had been bulldozed on the very day the Coopers had moved up from the city, ten years before. Sometimes Jack Cooper visualized the intersection of the two county roads and one state highway as the meridian lines of a mid-ocean chart, featureless and infinite save for the old one-room schoolhouse in the north quadrant. He had saved the building and its green asphalt roof lifted above the vacancy of the place like the breast of a sunken continent.

BLACK ACE
BACK-ISSUE MAGAZINES
Bought & Sold

On the other hand, he also liked the way the roads suggested the old community, like a template that could be used again, if anyone so wished, to ressurrect Hammertown. Sometimes, on fair days, he would leave his store— the door open should the phone ring—to trace the foundations that lay like shadows beneath the weeds and moss and sod. Here was the multicompartment outline of the general store. Across the road, the shoe-box shape that had been, he had been told, a butcher shop, a bicycle repair, and at last, a barber shop—in that sequence of business. A series of blurs squared off against each other farther along the road: the dwellings of Hammertown. Beyond, the embankment of the old railroad bed took a course around the town to the north, like a protective wall or even a levee put up against the flood of vegetation, but good-sized birch and swamp maples had already burst through its sloped sides. There were other outlines that puzzled him.

"What in hell are you doing?" Ruth had surprised him one afternoon. He had not heard the VW pull up to a stop near him. She had caught him squatting in a lot overgrown by thistles and burdock and facing away from the road, looking toward the railroad cut. "Is this how you spend your time while the rest of us hack a living?" Large round sunglasses, the diameter of their rims extending beyond her small oval face, gave her a sporty look; but when he thought of the circumstances, he also had to admit she resembled a huge bug that had come upon him lost in weeds.

"What's so funny?" she asked, momentarily a little unsure.

"I was thinking this must have been the back of the house." He had come to her car, and turned and pointed. "There was probably a back porch, usually put on the east side of the house, and I was thinking how it looked across that field and down the railroad line and how they might have sat here in the evening or afternoon in the shade and watched the late train come up the track."

Ruth had said nothing nor could he tell what expression her eyes held, because of her glasses, though the black mirrors of their surface showed him his own expression: the guarded eagerness framed within the squared lines of cheek and mouth and the visored scrutiny of his own eyes behind the rimless glasses that were more clear but no less penetrable than hers. He was always surprised by the way he looked when, unexpectedly, he would catch his image in some reflecting surface, not that he had any grand image of himself, no vanity to be exposed, but he carried no image at all and was always taken aback when this vague mixture of dreams and thought and reason was given substance: a vessel, as it were, suddenly fashioned in glass.

Then, "The hobbyist." Her voice was the smoke of smothered scorn. "Why don't you clean up this dump and put up little signs? You could make it into another Williamsburg?"

He did not always know what to say to her when she

spoke this way. Her gift of language, her mordant wit, had delighted and attracted him to her from the first; now, it only puzzled and hurt him. He sometimes felt her anger and sarcasm was directed at someone else and not him, or at least not at the Jack Cooper who one summer afternoon stood patiently beside the idling VW, but perhaps toward an alternate Jack Cooper who existed side-by-side with him through every season, like the two of himself in her sunglasses, but which only she could see and respond to angrily. Nor were these gusts of scorn usual, for she was generally polite if not indifferent, respectful of his needs, as she often put it. Sometimes at a party, or when they had gone to dinner at Ron and Ethel Knox's, her face would flush and her eyes would flash, become glassy, and she would look like the young graduate student who rushed up the steps of the old store on 23rd Street, wild-eyed and greedy for words and charmingly clumsy as she handled the old copies of *The Dial* and *Poetry*. More than one magazine had lost its value by her careless handling but it had not mattered.

"I have to go," she had said and let out the clutch, shifted gears. He quickly removed his hand from the car's door frame. "I have conferences with students all afternoon. By the way, he got out of the house before I could stop him. He's up in the woods."

"He'll be all right."

"Oh, sure, *he'll* be all right," she laughed dryly and pulled away. She gunned the VW through the intersection without stopping; but no one obeyed the STOP sign, not even strangers who after a wrong turn would find themselves at the vacant intersection. He remembered the guttural sound of the VW Beetle's engine chew its way into the distance, suddenly disappearing as if it had fallen through the hole it had made in the countryside.

But this evening when he parked before the old school-house, the air was still; the night's insects had paused in their drowsy conversations. It had been a warm day for October. The single mercury lamp, installed by the county to acknowledge Jack Cooper's enterprise, set the pitch for cicadas and crickets. The man disturbed nothing; he was part of the place.

He was often tempted to ring the old bell still hanging in the square belfry set above the building's entrance. It needed a pull and was probably rusted solid but the idea always teased his fancy, so on this night he had stood on the top step to contemplate the village site, imagining the tardy ghosts such ringing might call up. He would have to fix the bell someday as well as the cuckoo clock.

He needed no light inside, but turned on the small wattage bulb that hung down in the enclosed entry as a signal of welcome to anyone who might pass by. The pale light barely illuminated the interior of the large main room, but he knew his way between the racks of old magazines; he could have done it blind. The magazine business was another reason they had moved up from the city to live year-round in Hammertown, though Ruth sometimes made it sound as if it were the only reason.

The corner building where his father had run the business for thirty years had been torn down. Another location was difficult to find. New York City rents were going higher every year. Also, Jack Cooper had worried about the safety of the inventory: fire, pillage. Relocating outside the city had no great effect, because the major amount of business came from mail orders and the old store, on a second floor walk-up, had never been that accessible to browsers. Actually, in Hammertown he would have more counter sales on a few rainy days in summer than a whole month on 23rd Street because bad weather would bring summer people to the store, driven by the rain from their damp, musty lake cottages, to stand elbow-to-elbow among the racks of old *Cosmopolitans, Gourmets* and *Boy's Lifes*. The Black Ace Magazine Store had become a local custom, one of them told him.

He had reached the end of the central aisle and faced a door set in the center of a plywood partition erected across the width of the building. Inside, he flipped a wall switch and two long fluorescent tubes of great brilliance blinked and settled into a steady hum. He turned on a gooseneck lamp that arched over an old Underwood standard typewriter. The desk seemed to be an open file, wire baskets stacked three deep rose from two corners, and there were also large file cabinets bracketing the desk. The desktop, the baskets, the partially open drawers of the files were awash with paper: cascades of receipts, pools of letters and cards, a run of invoices. On the other side of the room, all was neatness. Every tool above the small workbench was in its proper place. The surface of the workbench was cleaned off and ready for the next project, the jaws of a small vise primly closed. It was like the miniature of a full-sized shop, or as if only small things were worked on in the backroom of the Black Ace Magazines, as indeed that was the case, for suspended on black thread from the ceiling, like the ingenious leaves of some exotic tree, were about a dozen brightly colored airplane models.

Fixed landing gears and bi-wings placed their designs in a bygone era, yet they attacked, spun, and climbed with a panache so dauntless that not even the unnatural silence of their maneuvers could dispel the illusion; this free-for-all was happening far up in the sky, too far for the sound of battle to carry.

Jack Cooper looked away from the display, removed his glasses and held them up to the light and cleaned them with some tissue. He had not lied to Ruth; there were some or-

ders to fill. He replaced his glasses and began to slip magazines into padded envelopes already addressed and
prepared. Then he sat down at the desk and rolled a post-
card into the Underwood. There were several letters to the
right, incoming mail, and he took each one, carefully reviewing the request and his own notes. He typed with two
fingers and thumb of the left hand and one finger on the
right.

Dear Madam:
The *Teen Romance* you request is currently out of stock.

> Yrs to serve,
> Black Ace

Dear Sir:
We have some issues of the *American Mercury* you request, all
edited by H.L. Mencken. Feb. thru Sept. 1935 and March
thru Nov. 1938. All in good condition, some water spots.
Our price: $250, incl. ship & hand. Money order or bank
check. No personal.

> Yrs to serve,
> Black Ace

Dear Sir:
The *Spicy Western* you ask for is unavailable. We do have a
May 1939 issue of *Sizzling Bar-X Tales* in fair condition. Back
cover missing. $25. No personal checks.

> Yrs to serve,
> Black Ace

That had been the last request, the last piece of business,
all of it taking him about twenty minutes to complete and
none of it so urgent that it could not have been done the
next morning, before Red Schuyler came by with the mail.
This is what had made Ruth smile. She had guessed he

would work on another plane model or occupy himself with the contents of the bottom drawer of the file beside his desk. She had known about this drawer, her curiosity drawn to it because it was the only one he kept locked, and suspected it contained materials similar to those pornographic magazines he kept behind the store's rear counter, out of sight and available only to those old enough to purchase them. She had implied these suspicions more than once.

He had unlocked this drawer and lifted out several heavy folders to place them carefully on the desk top. A business-type envelope lay within the top folder. It had already been opened, and the letter read twice since its arrival that morning. Cooper seemed to loosen himself, prepare to take a particular pleasure from what had been inscribed in a large hand on the thick packet of legal-sized yellow paper.

Cedar Homes
Alexandria, Va.
12 Oct.

Dear Mr. Cooper,

Thanks much for your letter and the copies of "Flying Aces," which I'm enjoying a good deal. Yes, old Arch Whitehouse asked me to contribute a few memories of the old days and you see the result. He was my wing leader in the old 34th Pursuit. I was a Raggedyass Cadet, that's what they called us who were the first American pilots to be trained in France. Old Arch has gone West and my motor sputters now and then, and I think that any day now I'm going to break ground.

You got the right idea about that war. What you read and see in these movies is true. We were all scared to death and drunk most of the time because we were. No parachutes, bad ignition systems, and those crates would sometimes come apart at 5,000 feet for no reason at all. Also, the castor oil they put in the gas gave you loose bowels. The exhaust would blow it out in your face all the time, and you'd blow it out the other.

No, I never met Capt. Eddie. Once when I was ferrying a plane from some field, I saw him coming in for a landing. All I ever heard was that Rickenbacker was a gentleman at all times, a fair shooter.

I saw a lot of those Bredas in Spain, but I can't tell you too much about them as I was flying for the other side. That caused me mucho problems later on, but forget that. The Russkies had given us a bunch of pursuits. I wish I had had a few old SE-5s. Now there was a sweet little ship! But I saw a number of those Bredas. They used them for everything: fighters, bombers, observation. They were fast (for their day) and durable. Not much on tight turns but they could fall like a brick on you if you weren't looking out. Also, that gunner in back gave a sting to the tail you might not expect in a fighter. And don't believe all this talk about dago flyers; they were goddam good. As good as the Germans, any day—in my book.

I also thank you for this story you sent me. It's very entertaining. I don't quite understand how your pilot has trained this ape to be his tail gunner. But on television the other night, there's a chimp that's painting pictures that museums are buying. So I guess a monkey can learn to fire a twin Browning. Anyway, it's just a story and very entertaining. Write again sometimes and if I'm still here, I'll answer.

Happy landings,
Roy E. Armstrong
Capt. Army Air Corps, Ret.

P.S. It just happens I've been knocking together an account of my wild days as a flier. Just in case you know of any publisher, *interested.*

When Jack Cooper had put the letter to one side, he had been overpowered by silence, a rush of nothingness where there had been clamor and din. Armstrong's letter had been accompanied by the clatter of machine guns, the whine of wire struts, and roar of engines, even the chair seemed to roll and press against him as he had read the old flier's words. Armstrong's first letter, about a year ago, had had the same effect; though it had only been an inquiry about back issues of the old magazine, *Flying Aces*. A postscript in a large, shaggy hand boasted, "I'm an old cloudbuster and flew Nieuports, SE-5s and Pups in the First War and then flew for the Loyalists in Spain." That single line had switched on Cooper's imagination! Armstrong must have some real stories to tell.

He had pushed up his glasses to massage his eyes. Comets fell in the dark space, a limitless void that always frightened him, so that he quickly cleared his vision, reset his glasses, and took a comforting measure of his desk's perimeter. The night noises had stopped and in their silence, as if a curtain had been pulled back, he heard something moving outside the building. The slight shift of gravel underfoot. The rustle of dry weed stalks being pushed aside. He rolled some fresh copy paper into the Underwood and began to type quickly, automatically, and without any thought to composition or idea.

The controls of the Breda 65 became sluggish as Winslow held the big ship in a tight turn, not its best attitude but the crack pilot had a way with aircraft. He could feel the tail fish but he held it in, tapping the throttle so the big Pratt and Whitney power plant crooned like a Kansan baritone at La Scala. "It's okay, old-timer," he spoke into the mouthpiece. "Just a little turn around . . ." His hairy colleague in the observer seat, who still thought flying was unnatural, drummed his hands against the Plexiglas canopy and bared large yellow fangs. It was a hideous visage, one that had stunned more than one attacking pilot, making him an easy victim of the twin Browning 50s that swung on the scarf-mount at the orangutan's elbow. . .

The door had opened at the front of the store. It squeaked closed. Cooper waited for more sound, his fingers and thumb poised above the keyboard of the old typewriter. He could imagine the figure in the front doorway, silhouetted by the one bare bulb.

"Da?" The voice was heavy and childlike, and sounded frightened, "Da?"

"Ho, there," Cooper responded jauntily. He continued to type, almost randomly hitting the keys of the machine to let the words spatter the page,

> The wing tip pivoted over the empty blue field of the China Sea . . . the horizon came up . . . Winslow eased up on the throttle . . . the plane slipped neatly into a groove in the sky known only to its handsome, carefree pilot . . .

The footsteps approached, each one put forward with a slight hesitancy after the other, as if the person were not sure of the path between the magazine shelves or even feared the floor might give way under the weight of each step. Cooper kept typing, concentrating on the paper in the machine, the cool recessed keys beneath his fingers, even when he sensed the figure take up the space of the open doorway and occupy it completely. He felt his feigned busyness being observed, though not recognized, he knew, for the sham it was. Cooper could even sketch in his mind as he pounded the old Underwood, imagine with a sweet sadness, the contemplation that graced his dumb show to give it a legitimacy it did not deserve.

"Well, old-timer, how's it going?" he finally had said, and pushed in his chair.

The boy always startled him, his great size. Cooper looked upon him each time with effort as if within the interval some new growth had taken place; the hands had become larger, the arms longer, or the shoulders even more of a beam on which the small finely shaped head was set in some monstrous parody of a physics diagram. The face that had regarded him this night had remained the same, had never grown away from the sweet cliché of its magazine cover innocence: the same plump cheeks, clear gray eyes, and shaggy black hair that sometimes could move Copper close to tears, as it had done the first time he looked upon it.

"Good, Da," the youth had said. His voice seemed pressed, ironed of feeling. "Are you good?"

"Yes, I'm fine, Hal." A small tongue tip had poked between the cherry red lips, and the gray eyes had shifted quickly to one side like a cat that had heard a mouse draw breath. But the object of this glance was a large box in the corner of the room by the workbench. "There are new ones. They came in today," Jack Cooper said.

The youth passed behind Cooper, his steps no less certain in this full light as they had sounded in the darkened store while his hugeness cast a faint shadow across Cooper, his desk, and typewriter. "Mums mad at us, Da? Mums going to leave?"

"No, no," he assured the boy. "Mum is just tired. She's been working hard lately. Doing her job. Like each of us must do. Did you have a piece of cake?"

"It was good, Da," the boy had said as he sorted through the handful of comic books in the box. Ruth had been angered by these names the boy used. They also made her nervous; there was something threatening about the way he called her "Mums" she had said—an ominous sarcasm though she had been as quick to mollify her own fears; his mind turned too slowly for such irony. It was just a fad he had picked up from television, Cooper had told her, one of those comedy shows from England that came on after midnight. When he wasn't in the woods, or at the back of the store reading comic books, the boy would be in his room watching television. He thinks it's a grown-up, sophisticated form of address. Sophisticated, Ruth had snorted.

The youth had sat down on the floor, his long legs straight out before him, the large, square-toed work boots pointing straight up—a stack of old comic books had been placed in the vee made by his spread legs—like a pack of playing cards. He opened the cover of the one on top carefully and with a curious reverence. "Suicide, Da," the flat voice rumbled. "That's when a person kills himself bad?"

"Yes."

"Why?"

"When they think there's no way to help themselves out."

Cooper stared at the copy paper in the roller of the typewriter. The thumb of his right hand pressed the space bar, then again, and then once more as if to stitch the unbridgeable silence between them, sew it up some way into a common articulateness both could wear. The words he had just typed had suddenly become silly, toys that deserved the sarcasm Ruth would throw upon them. Even sillier when compared to the kind of history the old flier referred to in his letter. There was the sound of mucilage being poked about and without turning around, he had said, "Don't do that, Hal. Nice boys use a handkerchief. Do you have a handkerchief?"

"It's dirty."

"Use it anyway."

The room had remained quiet. Outside, peepers sipped and tasted the cool night air. There would be a ground fog. Cooper heard no movement behind him. He looked up above his desk to an old poster for the film *Hells Angels*. Jean Harlow smiled a little crookedly, just enough to suggest that she was really a good girl, a real pal with pointed breasts, underneath all the makeup. The faces of the film's heroes shone down upon her like moons of high-mindedness, valor, and sacrifice. What nonsense. What crap. Ruth was right to mock him, to laugh at this obsession; yet there had been the letters from old Captain Armstrong with the intimations that all the old stories had been true. It had really been like that. Over the sounds of the tree frogs and crickets, Cooper heard the faint drone of an airplane. It was high up, a transcontinental flight maybe.

"Da? Where's Flip?"

"Where's Flip?" Cooper had repeated the question, as if he knew the answer but was hesitant to give it. "Flip is over the South—" he had begun to type the words slowly, "China—S—e—a."

"South—China—S—e—a," the boy had reproduced the sounds, the same pauses between letters.

"The South China Sea," Cooper repeated slowly. "Far away." His fingers rested lightly on the keyboard on the Underwood. When he continued to type, he spoke simultaneously, dictating to himself not so much for the benefit of the large youth sprawled behind him but as if he were transcribing the information from another source.

The lush green subcontinent of French Indochina lay to the west, on their left, far out of sight and beyond the range of the Breda, but Flip Winslow had an unobstructed view of the blue-green ocean below them. The plane's cockpit was perched high and ahead of the thick leading edge of the wing. The ocean looked like a huge chart on which someone had forgot to print the lines of latitude and longitude.

"But we'll find her, old-timer," Flip Winslow said into the speaking tube. He could not hear his jungle companion's grunt over the heavy throb of the radial engine. "The fair Elena, we'll find her." The red ape in the back seat hooted and howled over the roar of the powerful radial.

Terrence 'Flip' Winslow, recently cashiered from the U.S. Army Air Corps on trumped up charges of insubordination, let the sleek Italian fighter-bomber find its way through a canyon of high cumulus clouds. The ex-Captain, test pilot, and decorated war ace had been given the most difficult assignment of his life. Find Elena. Elena. Elena. Un-der-wood.

(The typewriter almost typed the name by itself.)

Down there somewhere in that vast, blue vault that was the China Sea, the daring aviatrix had made a crash landing on an island so unknown, so small that not even wily old Colonel Smith who had briefed Winslow in Singapore could give him exact navigational bearings. Some part of the Anambas group. Just over the horizon. Probably just a tiny, green patch big enough for her to set down the trim, powder-blue Curtiss Hawk 24 with the black lace pattern on its wing tips.

"She is one of the best," Winslow said over the roar of the big power plant just inches ahead of him. She had beaten them all: Cochran, Dover, all of them. He had seen her win the trophy in Cleveland the same year he had chased Roscoe Turner around the Thompson pylons.

The Breda emerged from the thick cloud like an ominous black dart in the white and blue of God's heaven. "Hallo, sport, what's that down there?" Winslow banked the Breda slightly so his colleague could see over the wing. Far below, a silver Gloucester Goshawk was taking a ferocious beating from a pair of Suki-Yakis.

With a crash the rear canopy had been thrown back. The giant breeches of the Brownings were cocked. The orangutan pounded the sides of the plane and grunted excitedly. The ape's long arms embraced the fuselage. Winslow knew that if he turned around, his friend would have bared huge, yellowed teeth to the slipstream, a grin of anticipation.

"Settle down, old fellow," he said. "It's not our fight." The old bi-wing scout had been neatly triangulated by the attackers and a blade of flame had sliced through the sides.

Terrence "Flip" Winslow raised his right hand in grave salute. The British Navy plane headed down to a watery grave. Some of His Majesty's bravest, Winslow thought to himself as he set his rugged good looks grimly.

"Let's put a little blue between us," he said and pulled back the control column and upped the throttle. The heavy ship responded like a sleek, black thoroughbred and leaped into the sky. "Let's just see where those little buckets came from, shall we? Notice anything strange about them?" Sometimes Winslow half-expected the ape to answer him. "They've got no markings. No rising sun, nothing on them. They're renegades like we are, old-timer."

At twelve thousand feet he leveled off, and keeping the sun behind him, he followed the pair of Jap fighters. They were painted a dull gray that—there was a snorting sound in his ears, coming from behind him—maybe those little buckets were making sure. . . . What was all that snorting behind him? Was his observer warning him? Was it a warning, an alarm given by his rear observer? The only way he knew how. . . .

"Harold, use your handkerchief. I've told you to use your handkerchief. . . ."

"It's dirty, Da." The gristlelike sound continued.

"Goddamn it, Harold, I said for you to use your handkerchief. Now use it. Where is it?" Cooper had sprung from his chair and spun around. The boy in the corner cringed and folded his long legs against his chest to press against the comic book now held like a piece of armor. His eyes were fearful yet canny.

"Let me have it?" Cooper had stormed over him. "Take it out. Here, I'll do it! Let me have it."

"No, Da . . . please."

"Here," Cooper said as he had thrust his hand roughly into the boy's rear pocket and pulled out the handkerchief. His hands became sticky with the wetness; the blood had not dried yet. "What is this? What is this?"

"I cleaned my knife with it," the youth said fearfully, as if this were an even greater crime than picking his nose.

"Cleaned your knife?" Cooper had asked, the wind going from his lungs. A blackness lifted behind his eyes. Not again, he thought and felt as if he had suddenly dropped thousands of feet. He saw the handle of the long knife sheathed in a scabbard on the boy's left side.

"I've done a bad thing, Da."

Once the problem had been diagnosed, doctors told them that the boy would probably not live beyond the age of nine or ten. He remembered the prognosis had seemed to relieve Ruth, not so much relieve her of the burdens such a child would make on them but relieve her somehow of the mistake she had made in adopting the baby in the first place. She had been given a chance to take it back, as it were, and to start over again. With astonishment, Jack Cooper realized she would have felt this way even if Hal had been a normal child—the whole thing had been a mistake—one more lure she had struck at because of her own barren childhood. From the first days of their marriage she had populated the walls of their Greenwich Village apartment with old photographs, facsimilies of adopted kin, she found in junk shops. Only later the idea came to him that when Ruth had urged the adoption—the doctor of a friend had delivered a baby that was not wanted—it had not been to satisfy any material urge but to fulfill a peculiar sense of form, another picture to hang on the wall.

"I am a failure," she would almost shout. The tears would spring from the curvature of her bulging eyes. "I can't have children. I don't want children. I am alone. Leave me alone!" she would scream and it had been a warning.

"Now, now," Cooper would comfort her. The music on WQXR was turned up so the neighbors could not discern their exact words. "You have your poems. Those are your children. How many people can do what you do?"

"Really?" she would say, a child herself now suddenly. One arm rested on his shoulder, and her reddened eyes would study him, searching for insincerity. "Do you believe that, Jack? D'you?"

"I do. I do," he would reply and she would look at him closer, ready to catch a flicker of deceit, but there would be none. Even her own maudlin expression became clarified, filtered through the lenses of his eyeglasses. Then her other arm would come about his neck and pull them together. The radio programs would change from baroque quintets to Andean shepherd songs as they made love on the day-bed beneath the canopy of bogus ancestors.

Cooper fashioned a large pen out of accordion wooden gates, the kind used to close off stairwells from invalids, and placed it right next to his raised platform at the front of the store in New York. Hal would play there, near the encyclopedias where few customers browsed, happily all day. His first toys were books from the old inventory—before Cooper switched to magazines only. First used as blocks to slip and slide over each other and to be lifted with great effort and set down with a solemn judgment. Eventually the books fell open and the pictures and blocks of type attracted the child's interest. Jack Cooper's heart would twist within his chest as he would hear the baby's clear laughter shaft the dark corners of the dusty store, as if the sun had begun to rise or set differently, its light streaming through the large windows on the north that overlooked 23rd Street. The old sign hanging beneath the windows, the old stationery and bill heads took on new meaning: J. COOPER & SON, USED BOOKS AND MAGAZINES.

"You're doing a wonderful thing," a woman once told him. She stood beneath his perch at the desk and he felt like

Rev. Dimmesdale, looking down from his pulpit, tongue-tied and unable to tell the truth to one of his congregation. "Your wife is in one of my classes. If more men did what you're doing, we'd all be happier."

Little Hal would stand and rattle his flimsy wooden barrier, as if to second the opinion or at least prove its merit, and the woman, as so many would, knelt before the child, caressed him, and cooed to him though probably happy for the fence between them. Hal's cheerful gurgling would pick at Jack Cooper's heart, even more than the sounds of delight and wonder, a double wounding, as the child responded to the pictures in old magazines or books and these sounds became a vocabulary that Cooper would sometimes answer, talk to but expect no answer, with the awful comprehension that it was a dialogue that would soon end. But here—a gratuitous turn of pain—maybe there was hope that it would not end.

The store acquired a celebrity it never had had. It was featured in a neighborhood weekly with a picture of little Hal. Then *New York* magazine picked up the story and made it officially smart to browse COOPER & SON, USED BOOKS AND MAGAZINES, and it became a hangout for a whole new class of customers. Even Ruth spent more time there. Usually they would meet at home, or sometimes she would call to say she had been invited to a social function at the home of an influential magazine editor or a poet—someone who had met with her creative writing class—and would he mind feeding and putting Hal to bed?

Man and boy would hear her quick step, could identify it all the way up from street level to the top, and Hal would begin to rock back and forth in his pen, the large, round gray eyes bright with a glee that seemed maddened by its own purity. "Ma-ma-ma-ma," the boy would chortle and reach out with such desire that his whole body would stiffen and then fall over backward, or sometimes the whole eager essence of him would vent and run in brownish rivulets down his legs.

"Oh God, Jack. Oh God," Ruth would say, the set smile on her face growing hard as she turned away. "What did I do? What did I *do*?"

However, by the time he would have cleaned Hal up, carried him back to the front of the store and his pen, she would have regained her composure. He sometimes found her talking to a customer, another poet or a member of her English Department—some of the new people who had discovered the store. Especially one.

"This is Donald Jacobs," she'd introduce them, ". . . my husband. And here's old Hal. Prince Hal," she'd say and take the baby from Cooper to nuzzle the fat neck. The child would become a thing of waving legs and arms in her embrace, gurgling and rubbing his large face against the front of her blouse. She would smell good, her body giving off that peculiar cinnamon aroma that had cast Cooper's fancy adrift years before; even her breath had grown fragrant, minted, as if she had just returned to them having breathed the air of an undiscovered island.

It seemed only natural to start holding poetry readings in the back of the place, to use its celebrity to help Ruth and her friends to a forum their fledgling work might not otherwise claim, and also to invite more celebrated authors to read their poems. Jack arranged for these poets' books to be on hand, especially if a new one was just out. There was wine and cheese. The old store took on a new life, one his father might not have approved of—for the old man, there was no social side to books or their contents—but Jack Cooper was happy.

He liked being around poets and writers, liked to hear them talk about writing, and it also meant that he and Ruth had more to talk about when they were alone, something to plan. There were flashes in her eyes, a barely contained wildness that he hadn't seen since those first days when she would take the stairs up from the street, two at a time, and clamber up on the high stoop to sit in his lap, whether there were customers in the store or not, and act the unruly girl.

"The language must be charged," the poet named Jacobs had been saying. "Charged, do you understand?"

"Yes, charged," Ruth would answer, her eyes almost closed and her slight torso humped, caved in as if by a blow, the attitude of a martyr in an old painting. Cooper would remember this much later: the way she looked, how this Jacobs seemed to lean over her like a conductor waiting for the right note.

But during the readings Cooper would remain at his elevated stand in front of the store; he felt more comfortable there, and he could see and hear all the proceedings just as well from there than if he had sat among the poets at the rear of the store. It was an audience made up largely of poets, each member carrying a notebook or a folded typescript that contained contributions for the symposium. The poems were solemn and accompanied by narratives that were sometimes longer than the poems they introduced. More interesting, too, Cooper would think; but then his tastes ran to adventure stories and fanciful tales, so he withheld judgment. Ruth's poems were like that, too, long lists of things, items, as if the itinerary were a substitute or an outline for a particular emotion.

"We've got to be realistic," she would say to him, and her poems were like that, a strict rendering of the subject that left no possibility of a different interpretation. In the same way she had filled the walls of their apartment with the images of found ancestors, she stocked her poems with brand names and the trademarks that produced them, as if to reassure herself that she belonged to the times, to an even larger, contemporaneous family. By contrast there was something old-fashioned about her appearance, made more dramatic by heavy jewelry, dangling earrings, and beads of rough-cut pebbles: accessories so heavy it seemed they might pull her slight figure over as she swayed behind the small podium to the rhythm of her own incantations. Her large, brown eyes would turn up toward the ceiling, turn to the old, yellowed plaster busts of Shakespeare and Dickens and Dante that Cooper's father had set on the top shelves above the medical section, and now turn back, lowered by the weight of their own luminosity to the page before her.

> *The backseats taxis*
> *Mete out*
> *To Lovers is not fair . . .*

The vulgar sweetness of her voice could thrill him. Refined and made thicker perhaps by the long distillation of her elegant throat, it raised phrases that seemed ready to fold back on themselves like syrup, and sitting at the front of the store hunched over a journal or dealing with a customer, Jack Cooper would remember how that same honey-eyed huskiness had poured over him other times. He would catch himself staring at the small head tightly bound in its shiny, black helmet of hair pulled into a severe knot at the nape so only the lobes of her ears were exposed and then just enough, no more than necessary for the hooks of the long, dangling earrings. The part down the center of her skull gleamed whitely in the light of the bare bulb that hung down from the ceiling; ruler straight, it looked sometimes as if it marked a fault, and her head would split apart neatly along this line so that both his hands would have to hold the halves together in order to kiss her face, study her close.

"What's going on?" A customer had just come up the stairs.

"It's a poetry reading," Jack would say.

"A what?"

"Poets. They're reading their work."

The man would nod without interest. "Say, I'm looking for a copy of . . ." and then the customer's eyes would be drawn to the wooden pen beside the front desk where the boy would be standing, holding the sides of his stockade as he rocked to and fro in time to the sounds of the woman's voice at the rear of the room. The counters and racks of books walled him up, so Hal could not see the person who read; but he could hear her voice, and his eyes blazed with a fierce loyalty.

Eventually the fence was removed and replaced with a small desk and a chair with its own lamp—a cozy corner in REFERENCE for the boy who struck the unknowing customer as being somehow too large for the short pants he wore though they did fit him. When he was not in the special school a colleague of Ruth's had arranged for, he would sit here beside Jack and read what books he could comprehend or study others with pictures: Brady's photographs of the Civil War or the sets of Audubon lithographs.

"Hal helps," he would say suddenly.

"Hal is a good helper," Jack would reply while going over his mail.

"Hal the helper," the boy would say, suddenly amused by the arrangement of words he had fashioned and his laughter boomed like a sunset cannon. His voice had deepened soon after he turned eight.

"I can't stand it," Ruth would say. "Would you mind putting up the rest of these? I'll go home and start supper."

"Ma-ma go home. Take Hal."

"No, you stay with Daddy," she would say. "Daddy has pretty new books for Hal to play with."

"Okay, toots," the boy would say merrily.

"Where did he get that from?" Ruth asked suspiciously.

Jack would shrug. "He reads a lot. A wide range of interests, you might say. Doesn't always know how they apply, but he tries them out."

He would catch her sometimes looking at the boy with a peculiarly speculative expression. At night she would whisper in his ear as they lay in bed, as if the boy might be listening to them, could hear them talk in their bedroom, that she sometimes felt that Hal was making fun of them both, that it was all an act and that he was as normal as any child.

"Here's one of Mama's pretty new books." It was a chapbook of about a dozen pages, one of a handful she had been setting up on the counter below Jack Cooper's post. Her poems. Don Jacobs had got them published; some of the bookstore poets had started a cooperative venture. As Cooper watched from above, the boy reached out and took the pamphlet, almost looking embarrassed it seemed by the joy his eyes revealed, and then, as if to demonstrate a new skill for her, he opened the booklet in both hands and tore it apart.

"Ruth. Wait!" Jack had shouted, but it was too late. With a cry, Ruth had thrown the other chapbooks—*Pigeon Wings*—on the counter and rushed down the stairs. "Wait," he called after. But she was gone.

"Hal fix," the boy had said. "Hal fix ma-ma's book." He held up the torn pages and then fit the ragged tears precisely together. It would have been an amazing show of dexterity for anyone.

With that same strange precision, the endearing effort to do the thing right because he was being observed, Hal licked the lollipop the doctor gave him. He sat on a stool in the corner of the room holding the candy upright, a military rigidity about the pose, and lowered his mouth to the sweet with a decorum that must have seemed exaggerated to Ruth, for she dug her nails into Jack's hand and gestured with her head, *See what he's doing,* her huge eyes turned to him. *He's making fun of us again.* Then the doctor began to review his findings.

He told them that the original diagnosis had not been wrong but that sometimes there are human factors that cannot be appreciated, that are eccentric to scientific evaluation. "We just don't know everything," he said and leaned back in his chair to regard Hal, who probably for the doctor's benefit, dipped his head to sip carefully at the rim of the lollipop.

"You mean—he will—survive," Ruth said. Her voice had choked on its own richness.

"There are cases that respond positively to their environment, if it's one that gives them an assurance to live. Looks like you two have given this little tyke a lot of old-fashioned love and attention."

She had walked right through the lobby, out through the building's door, across the sidewalk and onto the street with her arm up and in a stride that seemed ready to take her across the continent and probably would have if the taxi had not intercepted her at that point in the street. She got into it, closed the door. She was late for the rally at Washington Square; she had been invited to read with other poets—some nationally famous—to protest the Vietnam War. Jack took the boy to an Army-Navy store and bought him some long pants.

What if the original prognosis had been correct? For sure, they would not have come to this ruin of a village where he now followed Hal around to the back of the schoolhouse. The night still buzzed with insects. The one mercury light projected azure shadows upon the lapstrake wall of the building like a scene from an old horror film; two monsters moving—tall and short—among old tombs. And, in fact, it was to a kind of grave Hal led him, only a slight cover of the dry earth had to be cleaned away by the enormous hands deft as feathers; just as carefully the oblong parcel was lifted up. The body was wrapped in a curled sheaf of birchbark and tied together with a strand of English ivy. The bird lay inside on a bower of pine fronds; the resined fragrance coated Cooper's breath, stinging his eyes, for there was already another smell coming off the feathered carcass, a dustlike smell somehow inappropriate to the crisp, white package Cooper held in his hands.

"It's all right, Hal," he had said for the boy had begun to sob, anxious clots brought up deep from despair. "It's one of Clay's pheasants?"

"Yes." The tall youth put one hand against the side of the building and hung his head. Not looking at Cooper, he related what had happened.

"I'll take care of it," Jack Cooper said at last. "Don't worry." This time the smaller shadow led the way back around to the front of the bookstore. "I'll turn the lights off and lock up," he told Hal, who stood by the Buick.

The boy would not ride home in the car but had run ahead of it like an animal trapped in its headlights, unable to escape the luminous shafts that held him like carriage traces. Cooper drove carefully, slowly, the birchbark coffin on the seat beside him. Hal ran as if to demonstrate the way to run or how *he* could run: the arms held just so to move back and forth, the feet squarely put down and the knees lifted precisely, the spine stiffly erect. It was correct but awkward, yet an awkwardness that somehow hoped to be called graceful; and Jack Cooper could see the boy's eyes turn backward in his head, like those of a fox, to see if he were being watched, being singled out, perhaps, for approval.

Most of the house lights were out and Cooper felt a tinge of desire swell in him as he parked the car, turned off the motor. Ruth, perhaps, would not yet be asleep, only half asleep in a drowzied, humid state he might stir to a quick flash point.

"North star, Da," Hal had said. He stood by the flower bed and pointed up.

"Where?" Cooper asked, not being able to find Polaris. He knew nothing about the night sky, but Hal had developed a workable knowledge of the stars, enough so he could roam the woods all night and never become lost. Even now, he had put his arm around Cooper's shoulder, so the man felt like a child, and directed his attention to the different planets and clusters of stars. "Just below Mars. See, the red star. And there, that's the Plaids. They are sisters, but they only come there now. Halloween."

"Plaids?" Cooper asked. "Oh yes." In his mind he straightened out Hal's pronounciation. Pleaides.

However lost to each other they became during the day, he and Ruth could still meet at night, almost anonymously, on the familiar ground of sex. It had always been that way. "Wow," Ruth would gasp. The blue veins stretched taut over her hipbones as she arched her back, leaned away from him. "In the bookstore I used to watch you. Imagine you. Wonder how it was. I was right. Jack the Hammer."

"Size is not all that important."

"Sure, that's right," she would reply and then laugh huskily and throw herself upon him like someone who had fallen forty stories, had just made contact with the pavement, "Gawd!"

It was not that he had been unknowing. Growing up in

New York City when he did and where he did had provided him with experience, but Ruth had seduced him. This tough, small elfin woman with the strikingly large brown eyes, who could speak so elegantly of Rilke and Roethke also could become possessed by a cold lust, quickly and anywhere it seemed, to pull his own urgency to hers in a contest of breath and pulse touched also with a strange sadness, he would think later; for it would be as if she had this fierce ambition to be sensual, as hard driving and matched by her ambition to be a poet; yet she never quite made it, was never soft enough, or easy enough with her body so that at the last moment he sometimes felt, just as she fell away from him or when he would reach to cup her head in his palm, that her mind had already turned to name the parts of the nova just exploded.

It had happened first there in the old store, in the narrow aisle between *M* and *N* of the FICTION section—it was a rainy morning and no other customers were there. She had been showing up at least once a week, breathless and wall-eyed at the top of the street stairs. A couple of times they had eaten spaghetti and meatballs at the Italian restaurant around the corner on Lexington Avenue. His father had died two years before; she had broken with her foster parents. He liked having her in the place, enjoyed the serious use she made of it and the sober way she would set up camp in the poetry section. But this morning she had barely nodded to him and had gone directly into the ceiling-high fiction cases that jutted halfway athwart the store's interior. A light was turned on. Then her muffled cry, an oath muttered to herself. Was she all right? No answer. He called her name. Nothing.

When he came to the aisle, her back was to him and then she turned with the smile and lowered eyes of a madonna, holding up an index finger as if to show him a cut, and it had looked pink, maybe she had pinched it on the old ladder used to gain the top shelves, but he had been unable to get a close look, for she had continued to push it forward until the finger slipped between his lips and into his mouth. Then it hooked and pulled his mouth down to hers, and he reached out, more for balance than to embrace her, and felt that she had been naked under the flimsy vest and blouse and skirt. "Anything," she had said simply. "You can do anything you want."

It was only later that he wondered what she had meant by *anything*—what possibilities were there beyond the basic geometries—moreover, the circumstances had imposed some limitations; the act performed, for example, within reach of *The Complete Works of Somerset Maugham,* but the idea of unlimited access, of total abandonment, the idea of *anything* passed like a quick fever from her imagination into his so that he had been very rough, had bruised her and, afterwards, apologized almost formally. She had straightened her clothes and returned to the poetry section. Only much later would he understand that she lived in constant fear of her own imagination, that her mind was sectioned into areas of frightening possibilities through which she moved like a comic-strip heroine sending up balloons of alarm and self doubt. Am I pretty? Is he looking at me? What does he want from me? Are my poems dull? Commonplace? Anything?

"Good night, ladies." Hal had just spoken in the dark to the stars.

"Good night, old chap," Jack Cooper squeezed the boy's waist, and they walked this way to the house and into the dark kitchen where the youth went up the back stairs to his room as the man found his way through the living room without turning on any lights. Frog peepers expired long trills, paused to begin again, and Cooper wondered how deep the breaths taken must be, what large lungs their tiny bodies must contain. The house smelled musty, the same smell they had never been able to eliminate and that came up from the old root cellar. When they arrived to claim and clean out the house, they had found shelves of canned preserves neatly ranked against the walls of the cellar: jars of peaches, pears, cherries and several vegetables. Ruth had thrown them all away, would not allow him to even taste any, and had even gone with him to the town dump, as if she were afraid he would open one of the jars in the Buick's trunk and taste it. They might poison them, she had said.

If the boy was going to live, they would have to move to Hammertown. They had only just bought the cottage for summer use, and Ruth had planned it as a retreat for her work, as she called her poetry, but it would have to be fixed over now for a year-round place so that Hal could be protected from the city dangers his own innocence incurred. Even the children on Tenth Street had begun to tease him about his size, about wearing short pants, and about the curious way he talked and looked. It had made her very angry. She was bitter about leaving New York; she had just begun to move in a society of writers, a group that was congenial, helpful.

"It's only two hours by train from Green River," Jack would say.

"Two hours! Two hours—two light-years. These things happen in seconds. You have to be there, on the spot— *there*," she held out one arm, the long fingers extended in the direction of the city. Though her hand actually had pointed to a field marked by worn cedars, ledges of quartz.

"But can't you send your poems in by mail?" he would ask. They were in their side yard, where they had all such discussions, so the boy wouldn't hear. "I can fix up the attic, make a guest room so you can invite people up. They might enjoy a weekend in the country." Her eyes became huge, as if they tried and failed to incorporate the fatuity of his suggestion.

Jack Cooper would have already had suspicions about Don Jacobs or others by then; that her need to be "on the spot," as she termed it, was to answer something more than a literary calling. Or maybe her poetry was determined by the other, a symbiosis composed of inspiration and acceptance. He would never know. In the year before they moved to Hammertown, she would often be late from school and Jack would have to feed Hal and put him to bed. It's just a stupid workshop, she would call him from school, but she had to go to it. Or Professor So-and-so could only review her thesis after his last class—at six o'clock. Or Stanley Spielmach, Jack would remember him signing his books at the last reading, wanted to talk to her about her poetry. Or Jacobs is having a boring party and she would have to go. It would be a *bor-ing* party, her voice emphasized all the arduous and boring things a young, unknown poet had to put up with, but Don is starting this magazine and he might use a couple of her poems.

Cooper would be amazed to find himself excited by these deceptions, what they probably concealed, and he would often meet her at the apartment door, aroused. She would smile ruefully and ask for a few minutes in the bathroom, where he would hear her undress, use a washcloth, and then come find him in the dark apartment—the boy quiet as a stone pillar in the back room. "I'm ready," she would say hoarsely, and as he would enter her he could tell that she was not only ready but had been already prepared. He was certain she had been recommended to the English Department in Green River because she had been "on the spot" in the city, the chance coming from a man Cooper sometimes saw Ruth almost set upon at the rear of the store. She would have intense conferences with this older man, conspiracies it looked like, as the professor's bifocals flashed little alarms this way and that during these informal conferences. Come to think of it, Cooper had noticed him in the store before, before Ruth had introduced him as her favorite teacher; he used to spend a lot of time in the Psychology and Women sections.

The night sounds have stopped. Jack Cooper listened intently. Out by the edge of the small swamp, there is a flurry of leaves, a soft scramble and a sharp cry, then, everything sinks once again beneath the wheezing pool of insect noises.

She was a good teacher, he had been told that. Her position at Green River was her place and separate from him, apart from their life in Hammertown. That's why she had been angry when he came to find her once or twice. That's why she also forbade him attending the poetry readings she gave there or elsewhere in the county. She said it made her nervous for him to be in the audience, but he thought it was somehow mixed up with the way she had divided up her imagination; for him to appear at the college would be like the character in one novel showing up in another.

"Yes?" The young faces turned to each other around the table, the expressions suddenly gone formal.

"I have to speak with you," he had said. Close-up she could still pass for one of her own students.

"This is my coffee break," she had said but got up and quickly led him out of the lounge. They stood by a large billboard in the hall with notices of lectures, films, houses to share.

"Well, what of it?" she said when he had told her about the state trooper bringing Hal back. The boy had begun to roam then and had been found in Boston Corners, in an abandoned garage where he had made a sort of den for himself complete with candy bars and comic books. "I knew he'd be all right."

He tried to ignore the resignation in her voice. "I just thought you'd want to know. I had tried to call your office—"

"I've been in class all morning. Many conferences," she replied. He watched her mouth shape the words. Her mouth should have been large to balance the effect of her eyes, and the lips were too thin and gave a severe, old-fashioned primness to her expression. Cooper sometimes thought it ironical that she resembled one of the daguerrotypes she collected, those she had brought from the city to hang on the walls of the cottage in Hammertown, a peculiar migration of pioneers. Put a high-necked dress on her, put her hair up instead of the usual ponytail, and she could pass for one of those old-maid aunts, the school marm from Indianola, Iowa. "Is that all?" she had asked, the pointed toe of a black patent leather shoe tapped against the polished tile floor.

But like the imprint on a kissed mirror, the image of her mouth lingered in his mind as he had returned to Hammertown. Just before he had found her in the coffee shop, he had stepped into a student washroom. There were three urinals, two stalls, and four sinks. RUTH COOPER SUCKS GREAT COCK: The notice had been penciled over the urinal he had chosen, the centerpiece of an elaborate tryptich of numbers, sketches, slang expressions—the work of an *ecole,* perhaps. It was an ambiguous statement. Was *great* used as an adjective, applying to the member, therefore suggesting she was interested only in a premium quality, perhaps size was important after all? Or was the qualifier meant to be an adverb, to honor her technique? Maybe both were intended. More likely the true message was one of revenge, a libel put there to slander her independence, her assertive manner.

But the idea is put into Cooper's mind, like a cry in the night; ambiguous and with no known authorship so that it could be either an expression of ravishment or of hunger, terror or joy. He sometimes wonders why these single sounds, single acts can only be given a meaning afterward, that he can put them together into a pattern only later like a collection of old photographs or old recipes or the plans for old airplanes. He can reconstruct them in every detail except the fervor that gave them their origins, without the appetite or anger that distinguished their happenings. Like the models hanging over his workbench down at the store, the prototypes had become miniaturized.

"Say something," Ruth had said earlier. "Why don't you say something?" She had asked the same question many times, her eyes looking for a response he could not fit together.

The house was quiet. Jack Cooper turned his imagination to the search for a woman waiting to be rescued in the South China Sea, a harmless place, no longer found on any map and where one could always be a hero.

CHAPTER
TWO

O NE afternoon, soon after they moved to Hammertown, Ethel Knox had arrived. She bore a jar of
green tomato pickles, though the way she sat down by the
kitchen window suggested that her appearance among the
boxes and packing crates of the Coopers's possessions was,
really, gift enough. The couple continued to unpack, putting dishes and utensils into cabinets and on pantry shelves
as the older woman dispensed information about the village—hints about stores and handymen, most of which they
already knew. They had already spent several summers in
Hammertown, though this would be their first full year. She
was a tall handsome woman with young-looking skin and
thick puff of white hair, and she reminded Jack Cooper of
pictures his father used to keep in worn portfolios: old
prints of eighteenth-century court ladies.

"Hang the clock over the stove," Ruth told him. If they
had been alone her tone would not be so sharp—she might
even have asked his opinion—but she sometimes spoke this

way before others, particularly before other women. Jack wondered, as he drove a nail into a wall, if all women did this or whether it was only Ruth who was afraid to show him any softness before another of her own sex.

In fact, only a few minutes before Esther Knox's intrusion, Ruth had been treating him to considerable tenderness. They had been opening the packing cases the movers had delivered the day before, piece by piece transferring every article, every book and all the pictures, everything they had used in the city, to a new and permanent place in this summer house. "Permanent tomb," Ruth had cracked, as she fit her books into shelves. "It's like *The Cask of Amontillado*." But her spirits had been pretty good and she had gone about the chores with a cheerful determination. Hal had been put out to play in the sunshine, and they had been alone in the familiar yet still strange interiors of this small cottage. Ruth wore jeans and a T-shirt, her hair pulled back tightly and up in a ponytail. She resembled a sprite, he thought, an image in a children's book about "little people" playing among the artifacts of full-sized human beings.

Then, as if to follow his thought, she half bent over to peer into an open box, her hands clasped together and between her knees—an appealing, expectant pose that gave them both the same idea. "Ah, you Turkish devil," she cried when Jack pressed against her. So, when Ethel Knox arrived with her green tomato pickles, they had been on the bare mattress in the bedroom, and the idling, dying sounds of the woman's car made their frantic buckling and buttoning even more ridiculously difficult.

"Oh, it's a cuckoo clock! How charming!" the white-haired lady said. "Ronnie has just restored a wonderfully funny one for a client in Connecticut."

"Are these yours?" Ruth asked, holding up the jar of

pickles. "We inherited a whole basement of preserves. They came with the house." She laughed and looked at Jack.

"I didn't know the lady very well," Mrs. Knox said vaguely, finding and reattaching a strand of pure white hair. "But I guess, like the rest of us around here, she put up a lot of things."

"Not me," Ruth said as she put out coffee mugs on the table. "You won't catch me doing any of that stuff. Hope you don't mind instant. We haven't unpacked the Chemex yet."

Ethel Knox seemed about to reply; a twinkly light in her eyes indicated she was prepared to argue the point, but the sternness in the younger woman's expression discouraged her—for now.

"How's that?" asked Jack, stepping back from the stove. All three regarded the clock, silent as if waiting for the little door to burst open and release the wooden bird.

"Good, but don't set it," Ruth replied. "I'm not ready for that dingbat popping out at me. Your husband is a clock maker?" She turned back to their guest.

The older woman's comic-opera prettiness flushed with pink; a small floodlight had come on to introduce the soubrette's solo. "Ha, ha, ha," her laughter was light, tinkly. "Ronnie is just one of those self-taught geniuses, I'm afraid, who can do anything. He's an architect, mechanic, designer—just everything." Her arms had been thrown apart as if to share him with the world.

Jack Cooper took off his glasses and polished them, looked through the lenses, and rubbed them once more with the tail of his shirt. The Knoxes had moved to Hammertown when Ronnie—she pronounced his name as if he might be a youth—retired from advertising. He had been an executive vice-president, but he always did these other things on the side. Now, there was a long list of people in

Connecticut waiting for him to renovate their old house. Ruth's attention has slipped away, Jack could see. The linear narrative always bored her and Mrs. Knox seemed to have made the form her own.

"Well, as you see, we just have a simple place here," he interrupted, to make conversation. "We have no need for an architect. Maybe later."

"Oh my," Mrs. Knox replied with an amused *moue*. "You've misinterpreted me; Ron is only interested in . . . well, at the moment he's redoing a gatehouse on the Wallace estate in Sheffield." She paused to look around the kitchen of the summer cottage. "Ha, ha." The comparison made her laugh. "But you might need a carpenter, and there's Clay Peck. He lives at the end of your road, at the top of the hill."

Just then a car went up the road in that direction and Jack lowered the kitchen window to keep the dust out. It was May, and the dust was already a problem, one they will never solve. Ethel Knox talked on, undisturbed. Ronnie used Clay Peck. The carpenter had been brought here by a developer a couple of years before to redo some old buildings in Irondale, and he had stayed on. The way she told the story, it sounded as if Clay Peck had sawed and hammered his way through the valley, redoing barns, furniture, houses, whole villages. "He's a superb carpenter," she said, "but of course, he needs direction."

"Jack is pretty good with a hammer," Ruth said. Her round eyes turned on him with a deadpan look he returned.

"Oh, I'm sure," Mrs. Knox replied. She looked at Ruth intently. She has missed something. "What do you do?"

"I am a poet," Ruth said simply. Jack felt his senses tingle; he always felt this way when he heard Ruth announce her profession. "I will be teaching at Green River."

"How wonderful! Ronnie almost went over to see if they had a place for him, but then he got so busy."

"It's a very professional place," Ruth sipped at her cup. Only a few nights before, she had screamed and kicked about the provincialism, the state college's lack of distinction. Now she gave praise. She was still bitter about Don Jacobs not getting her a position at New York University, particularly bitter since she had slept with the magazine editor, Jack was pretty sure. Say something, she had said one night, coming back to the apartment late, bruises on her thighs. But he had only kissed them.

"But you'll have to meet Clay Peck, anyway, just to meet Grace and her dog," the older woman continued. "She keeps this dog that seems to be in perpetual heat, or is it in heat perpetually?" Her laughter once again gifted their small kitchen. "She keeps the poor thing in a cage in the backyard. It never gets to run around. She's never bred the dog. Never lets it in her house. Just keeps it in this cage."

"In heat," Ruth said and laughed.

"Yes, but the bad part is that all the male dogs in the area come around and then Grace calls their owners and screams at them on the phone. You'll see."

"But we don't have a dog," Jack said. The screen door on the small woodshed that adjoins the kitchen slammed, and the sound was like a lash across Ruth's back.

The boy entered the room, his face round and red, and a fist clutching wildflowers and weeds, some with their roots hanging in clumps of wet earth. "Flowers," he said and thrust them at Jack.

"This is our son, Hal," Jack said, taking the flowers quickly and putting an arm around the boy. Hal pressed his head into his father's shoulder.

"Charming," Mrs. Knox said, her expression a practiced benevolence.

"Knock, knock," Hal said, suddenly bold.

"Who's there?" Mrs. Knox replied quickly.

"Albert."

"Albert who?"

"Albert Hall is full of crap." The youngster's laugh was deep and joyous. His hands clapped together once, twice. Mrs. Knox smiled, little gray lines around her mouth, and looked at Ruth with different eyes.

"Have some milk." Ruth jumped up, went to the refrigerator.

"Milk-mummy-milkmummy-milkmummy." It was a march and his feet stamped in cadence to the words, around and around.

Jack caught Ruth's eyes. "Hey, buster, grab some cookies and let's see what's on the old boob tube."

"Ho, ho, hah," Hal responded. "Boobie tube," as he followed Jack into the next room. The boy carried cookies in one hand and the glass of milk carefully in the other, like a drunken guest going to another part of a house party, uncertain of his steps and his reception. The television was the first thing they had hooked up when they had arrived. It was in a corner of the living room, not its eventual location but a quick, comfortable place for Hal to sprawl among the debris of their moving. "Only three channels," Ruth had said the night before. Jack felt more comfortable about that move, more convinced of its rightness as he watched Hal take up his post before the shimmering screen. Even the boxes around him seemed to protect the boy.

When Jack returned to the kitchen Mrs. Knox was standing, ready to go. They escorted her outside and to a big Ford station wagon. "Well, we're just obstinate," she explained. "Everybody's going small and we decided to go big. Just to be ornery," she said defiantly. "Ronnie has one, too. We're a pair," and she gave that bell-like laugh. She backed the large vehicle into the road and swung it around and forward, the maneuver done with a flourish, a demonstration of some sort.

The still warmth of the May afternoon settled upon the couple as the car passed down the road. It would be a very hot day and there was yet much to do. "Guess what?" Ruth said. "She writes poetry, too," and she picked up a stone and hurled it with a special gracefulness high into the air over the swamp.

The swamp looks almost the same this October morning as Jack Cooper waits until after Ruth sputters off to Green River and her class, waits and then takes down the small wrapped thing from the rafter in the garage where he had put it last night. He unfolds the mangled form in the crisp light, his breath hovering above it like a cloud in some primitive painting. The dead bird lay surprisingly heavy in his hand, too heavy to fly; yet he has seen these golden pheasants of Clay Peck's rise and ascend over hummocks and stubble, lift away from the earth effortlessly and with powerful release.

It is only about a mile up to the carpenter's place, the walk would have done him good, but he did not wish to carry the carcass, and anyway, he would go down to the shop afterward, then go to the store. He did not look up at the window under the eaves as he starts the car, did not wish to acknowledge the boy's anxious face. To look would be to chastise, he knew, and there was no need for that. So, he turns around and heads up the hill.

There had been another drought this year so autumn has run quickly through its color, and the leaves, as if to protest the outrageous exertion, have fallen to the ground quickly, almost overnight. It was Jack Cooper's favorite season, even this bare framework that sat upon the landscape like a wicker screen. He liked to see the design of the limbs, the faithful construction that lay beneath the fickle abundancy of leaves. Once, when Jack was a boy, his father had handed him an old volume of Michelangelo's figure drawings and made him look for the hard bones within the flesh. His first set of plans, he thinks this morning and pulls off his glasses to polish the lenses with a handkerchief.

Clay Peck's place was set among red pines. The plantation was about fifteen years old and the trees, grown from seedlings purchased from the State Conservation Department, completely hid the house and outbuildings from the road. It was like coming upon a dark, green island in a gray sea, and the narrow road onto which Cooper turns the old Skylark could be a channel into an uncharted bay. But after a hundred yards the thick forest opened up into a large clearing, an island within an island, and a frame house with a large porch sat there, a small barn and two smaller buildings; these last two, the carpenter's workshops.

Just as Cooper parks the car, Peck comes out the backdoor and walks quickly toward one of the workshops, as if Cooper's arrival had been a cue for the action. But the burly figure did not pause or even acknowledge his presence, save for a sidewise shift to look back over his shoulder, and then he opened the door and went inside his shop. Because he fed them every morning, he has already counted the pheasants and found one missing, Cooper figures, and he has been waiting for him to show up. Nor was this the first time the count was down. The carpenter has decided to receive him at his workbench, surrounded by his tools and the aromas of wood and glue.

"Morning," Peck says. He was removing clamps from a chair, and he continued to examine the mortised joints even when Cooper puts the small package on the counter. "I just wanted to check these joints, see if they dried right."

"Hal came on one of your birds last night in the swamp."
Carefully, he unfolds the cloth. The two men look at the
bird. Its plumage looks false, too colorful, and the open
eyes are without light, no time to squeeze them shut against
the dark. The feathers around the neck were discolored
and stiff. "He thinks a fox may have got it, thinks he scared
the fox off. But the bird, by then, was badly hurt—in pain,
so he . . ." Peck has begun to nod, never looking up, "so it
wouldn't suffer."

"When I came home yesterday, he was playing with them,
cooing to them through the cages." The carpenter's stubby
fingers prod the bird on the workbench. Sawdust and resin
smells mix in the air, and Cooper half expects the older
man to take up tools and restore the pheasant to life. His
hands are kin to the wooden handles of the chisels and
planes arranged in neat rows on the shop's walls; they are
fashioned and polished from usage. All hands should look
like that, Cooper thinks.

But Clay Peck picks up the bird's carcass and without a
word turns toward the door. His manner is so brusque as to
seem angry and Cooper follows him out the door and into
the side yard. "We just can't keep him penned up," he says
to the man's back. "He's at home in the woods around here.
That's why we came up here, so he would have space."

Without saying anything, Peck has walked toward the
woodshed in that peculiar sidewise manner, Cooper thinking he would turn to speak over the left shoulder; but he
says nothing, continues with the bird held easily in one
hand. At the end of the woodshed is a fenced-in compost
heap, and Peck takes up a spade with his other hand and
with one straight thrust opens up a cleft in the mound, de-
posits the pheasant, and pats down the earth. Nothing remains. "What can we do?" Cooper asks.

"He sometimes don't know his own strength," Clay says

and leans the spade against the woodpile. "You see that statue over by the backdoor." Peck pointed with his right hand and Cooper noticed, for the first time, that the first joint of the index finger was missing. The stump was smooth, long healed. A cement birdbath stood angled by the back stoop. "That must weigh better than hundred pound, but he just put his arms around it and lifted it right off my truck. Set it right down there, easy as nothing."

"Where'd you get that?"

"A job Knox has me on over in Sharon. The new people didn't want it, so I took it. But they're the sort that don't know what they want, which is why they hire Ron Knox." When he laughed his mouth opened wide and his teeth looked varnished, set in his mouth at odd angles. "Oh, to be sure, Ron Knox will tell them what they want and it will only cost them a little. Yes." He shakes his head as if amazed by his own words.

Though what could still surprise him about Knox's deft fondling of the wealthy, Cooper could not imagine. Perhaps his own employment in the architect's schemes yet bemused him. Maybe Ruth was right. "That's why Grace Peck took off," she had said one evening. They were coming home from dinner at the Knoxes'. "Clay would never loan his tools to anyone, would he? Not to someone like Ron Knox especially. But he loaned himself."

Cooper had driven the road carefully; there was a fog that night and deer were moving into their feeding grounds. He picked his words carefully also, what not to say. During the evening, he had recognized a restlessness in her, almost a heat given off, that usually signaled sexual desire; but there had been other nights when he had said something, a wrong word that had chilled her. "But his craft . . ." the word was poorly made but he could think of no other. "He's still the same good carpenter."

Ruth said nothing. The tires gossiped over the wet pavement. Then, "She was an angry woman. She had been betrayed and she was angry."

The birdbath becomes more distinct as Cooper walks with Clay Peck toward the carpenter's house. The cast concrete in the center of the cement tray takes on the rough idea of a dolphin, though it looks more like a fat porgie. The face of the small boy on its back has been rubbed smooth by weather. He raised a chubby arm, a gesture intended to be of delight, Cooper thinks; but the expressionless countenance suggests a bland, indifferent attitude toward his conveyance. Two scraps of wings sprout from the cherub's shoulders.

"I'm very sorry about the pheasant, Clay. Can I pay you for it or—" The carpenter waves him silent.

"He's a good kid. I don't care what anybody says. He comes up here a lot, you know. Likes to help out. Likes the birds. Watches them a whole lot. I give him chores. I even showed him how to make a few things—nothing much. You don't mind?"

"Why no," Cooper replies, his turn to be amazed. Hal, of course, would be shy about talking about this.

"Oh, yes. Well, he's good company for me, don't you know." He makes no move, not even a nod of the head, but Cooper automatically looks back toward the woodshed. Cordwood was stacked neatly within the shelter. The handles of tools, axes, and shovels lay in parallel bundles waiting for Clay's careful salvage. He never threw anything away. But it was the kennel in the back corner, a kerosene can, and two oil lanterns on top of it, that has drawn Cooper's attention.

Made of one-by-two lumber with heavy metal screening fastened to the framework, the joiner work of the cage identified Clay Peck's hand. A hinged door hung open not so much as to accept an occupant, Jack Cooper knew, but to release one, and, it was the suddenness, as it were, of that open door that still startles him, as if the dog that had once been inside had only just bolted out and rushed past them and on up into the woods behind the house. He even looks around.

Clay Peck has cleared his throat and spits to one side. "It's not easy for me to believe that I miss that old lady. She might be the meanest woman to ever make a bed, but it's damn quiet around here without her." He spits once more, to the other side.

"Have you heard from her at all? No card? Nothing?"

"Oh, I get this letter from her. Somewhere in New Hampshire. Has to get away for a spell, she says. Then, one of her cousins writes me that she's taken up with some fisherman out of Portsmouth. Even goes out on the boat with him, works the nets. Think of that." He looks toward Cooper and grins. The teeth have changed around in his mouth.

Clay has stopped talking and looks toward the green mass of conifer that seems ready to overwhelm them from all sides. In this quiet between them, almost like the lull that might precede such a tumult, other sounds press themselves upon the air. Someone chopped wood. Late corn was being harvested and the sound of the tractor drummed and waned as the farmer passed and turned down the field. A screen door slammed. His house, Jack Cooper thinks, and he imagines Hal coming out the backdoor and into the sunlight of the small backyard and then into the mottled shadows of the swamp. He often marveled at his son's movements, how they went from clumsy to fluid as he entered the woods, almost smoothed out by the gloom, until the boy became one with the quilted light. He hopes Hal has something on his head. The air has a chilly dampness about it.

In all the conversations he has had with Clay Peck, Jack Cooper could never remember how they ended. Usually they just stopped. The carpenter would turn away abruptly, as he does now, walking back into his house as if he had taken the measurement of the talk once, maybe twice, and then just cut it off. The Skylark's rusted door hinges screeched; the door has to be slammed twice before it held closed. Cooper sits without turning the key. A dog barks down at the crossroads near his store, the sound pulled like taffy into a sweet croon. The old kennel in the woodshed, its door open, seems to catch the sound, entreat it.

Had Grace Peck left before the dog escaped, or had the dog fled the coop first? He can recall Ethel Knox on that sunny May afternoon, sitting in their kitchen and telling them about the the dog—in perpetual heat, she had said and blushed—but had the Doberman disappeared before Ethel had taken her own life? He would have to ask Ruth. He starts the car down the driveway. He hoped that had been the case, it seemed important that she had known about the dog's escape. She would have enjoyed that. Some thought it had been Clay who unfastened the kennel door, but the list of suspects was long, people who had had dogs destroyed or who had been pestered by Grace's phone calls. Sometimes Cooper wondered if Hal had given the Doberman her freedom; the boy had begun his nocturnal wanderings about then. People would meet at the Agway or at Bomberg's in Green River, and they would say, by way of a greeting, "Well, we had a call from her last night." Everyone had a story, everyone who owned a male dog that is, and it was always the same story but always of interest, as if the woman's sour belligerency preserved their astonishment and kept it fresh.

He and Ruth would collect the stories. They all started the same way. About supper time, a farmhouse phone would ring. Grace Peck would begin speaking immediately. No need to introduce herself; her voice was enough, a flat, plain bran of sound ground from the corner of her mouth. "You better come get your dog. He's up here making a disturbance and doing his business on our lawn." On some nights she'd make three or four calls. Sometimes there'd be no calls but dogs would disappear, never return home, and the owners would know why.

Occasionally, a farmer would admit he had made the mistake of trying to talk to her. Why didn't she have the dog spayed? Why didn't she breed her? What good was the animal just locked up in her cage on cinder blocks in their backyard? Was it fair? Humane? There'd be silence on the line after that, but not because the questions had stumped her. Cooper though it was more the silence of a profound amusement, an absolute pleasure those very questions seemed to set flowing and, as the long pause stretched across the telephone line, the questions finally lost their energy and fell back upon the person who had asked them.

Whenever he had gone to Peck's to bring Hal back home for supper, two or three male dogs would always be standing guard by this cage set on cinder blocks in the center of the yard, open to the various airs as it were: courtiers waiting recognition, hoping for a favor from the tongue-whipped, stiff-legged Doberman locked inside. She was a lithe, handsome animal, built for speed and sport, Ron Knox would say.

Then Clay Peck was alone; people became aware he was by himself about the same time they noticed the phone calls had stopped. About then, the Doberman must have got loose, too, Cooper figures. She was reported everywhere at once, an ebony dart that streaked across the countryside.

She was seen in Irondale, on remote hilltop farms, at the crossroads in Copake and even on the outskirts of Green River. Sometimes a movement would catch the eye, a speck that moved across a far hillside, from dark to light to dark, and it would be the sleek Doberman, racing like a greyhound, accompanied by several male dogs who galloped after her like grenadiers escorting a monarch hellbent on some emergency of state. She was making the rounds.

"Maybe she kept track of them," Ruth said and laughed. Had it been possible that the dog remembered all the morose animals who had kept vigil outside her cage and, once free, she had made visitations to reward them for their devotion, bestow a beneficence that was unexpected as it had been joyously employed. Others speculated that the dogs had even talked it over, planned the whole thing as they gathered around her kennel in Peck's yard. In any event, once liberated it seemed her first and only desire was to join a canine witches' Sabbat.

The lower part of the county became one large rutting ground. Now the phones rang for a different reason. "She's here!" Panic, pity, wonder, and scorn made for wordless response. There was no time for salutations. "She's headed your way!" the alarm would be sounded. The phone would dangle from its wire, thump the kitchen wall as an owner would rush outside just in time to witness the last giddy convulsions behind the toolshed. How did she get there so fast? How did she get it done so quickly? *The Green River Sentinel* published a whole page of angry letters. There had been a sermon at the Irondale Presbyterian Church. The sheriff was pressured to hire extra deputies; local dog wardens had already used up their budgets; and mothers waited with their children until the school bus arrived, met the return trip in the afternoon.

One morning Jack Cooper heard a ruckus behind his magazine store. Two large mongrels were going at each other's throats while to one side and in the shadow of a sycamore a black labrador solemnly humped Grace Peck's dog. Cooper noted how the male's expression became more and more sad and then, like a signal of some sort, the tip of its pink tongue popped out to one side of the black muzzle. But that seemed to be the only fight to take place; it was in the first days of her freedom, and the word apparently passed that there was no need for such combat, that there was plenty to go around and it would get around as quickly as her four slim legs could bring it around.

One morning Red Schuyler nearly wrecked his car on the mail route to avoid the Doberman as she trotted down a back road carrying what looked, he said, to be Miller's German shepherd along with her. It was a ludicrous sight, as Red described it, with the male dog hung up and jiggling along as fast as he could on his two hind legs; but the Doberman didn't seem to be concerned about him or his enjoyment, the look on her face already set as she pursued a commitment elsewhere. Most of the men laughed, but some of the farm women thought something had to be done. The rest of the women said they weren't sure.

Over in Boston Corners the Taylor's Irish setter was found strangled on the very chain that had been meant to preserve his chastity, but which apparently had tightened around its windpipe at the critical moment. He was found dead in the barnyard the next morning, tongue hanging out one side of his mouth and, some said, an all-knowing look in his eyes. Something had to be done, people said.

Other dogs just disappeared. Nothing would keep them home; something made them run away. Plates of the most extraordinary food, pork guts and beef testes, were left to rot untasted in the empty sunlight. The tears of children, the calls of old masters—even letting the dogs sleep indoors at night— nothing worked. Tie ropes were broken and collars slipped. Fences tumbled over and kennels mysteriously undone, some even chewed right through. The area was in turmoil, put into a heat like a pressure cooker. Families began to come apart. Attendance at PTA and Grange meetings fell off. Veterinarians stopped answering their phones. Children began to look at their parents in peculiar ways. A beer-and-bitch posse sponsored by the volunteer fire company in Irondale was successful financially, but one of Ike Vosberg's barns burned to the ground while the firemen were out chasing Grace Peck's dog. The slim, swift animal slipped through all the roundups and sweeps, all the stratagems and nets, like a sliver of tortoise shell disappearing through the coarse knitting of an afghan throw.

Oddly, no one blamed Clay Peck. It wasn't his dog; it had been *hers*. In any event, he continued his work and routine as if nothing unusual were happening. He drove through all this chaos, his tools neatly put up in steel cases in the back of his truck, toward a house, a piece of work—endeavors that required precise measurements and perfect fits.

One evening Ruth looked up from her books. "She's gone," she said as if she had heard the news on the evening television. Maybe the same statement was made all over the valley, the idea occurring all at once. Nothing dramatic, no bellow and yammer trailing off into the distance. Nothing like that. She was just gone. Dogs, sitting stiff-spined at the taut radii of their tie ropes, suddenly went limp, turned, and ambled back toward their water dishes to drink a little, turn around once, twice, and then lie down. Some of them slept for days.

The same dog Jack Cooper had heard barking when he pulled out of Clay Peck's driveway is still yammering at the crossroads of Hammertown. The little dog continues to bark as Cooper pulls up by the magazine shop. It is a stray, and Cooper is amused to think it might be a progeny of Grace Peck's dog returned to defend its mother's old territory against the incursion of this maroon and gray sports car, the top down, parked by the building. The car's radio crackles and pops in the archival quiet of the deserted village. The music comes and goes in the sunlight as if from the dark side of the planet, like a sampler from a large album of nostalgia.

On some mornings, Jack Cooper's bare feet would be warmed by the same sunlight but coming through the windows set under the eaves of the east side of the house. Ruth had thrown off the covers while making love, kicked and ripped off the sheet and blanket as if they restrained her from reaching some higher plane of pleasure; so they had dozed afterward, naked in the morning air.

Without opening his eyes, Cooper could feel his feet laved by a warmth that crept up over the ankles and then began to rise on his legs, a tide quite opposite in effect to what old Socrates described to everyone after he drank down the hemlock; now why did he think of that? "I feel the cold creeping up from my feet," Plato reported him saying, or some such phrase, and the idea made Cooper chuckle so that Ruth stirred a cautionary sound deep in her throat, a warning not to disturb her while she played out the last line of her own sensations.

But he had not intended to disturb her, because his own reverie came without a language. This feeling warmed and filled out his body, like a draught taken, and the two became one for a moment only, just as the poison had worked its way through the old philosopher's body so that when the deadly synthesis came together there had been time to say only, "Listen, friends, I still owe a cock to so-in-so, would one of you pay off for me." Jack Cooper had laughed to himself once again and was made dizzy by an absolute wisdom that was beyond language—perhaps best it was, he would think later—he had raised up on one elbow and leaned over Ruth, was about to touch her, when she said, "Whew! We smell like a couple of pigs," and she had slipped out of bed like wet soap off a basin and flitted from the room, a thin ghost to his sun-drugged eyes.

Down at the store as he cataloged magazines and answered orders, he would sometimes go through the different possibilities as to why he never talked about her affairs. He was a coward. He did not want to lose her. Hal needed both of them *together and under one roof.* There were several more ideas; all made sense but none came close to the real reason. Her work. Ron Knox had helped him find this answer, and for his assistance, Jack Cooper had almost hit the older man.

One day the architect, a large white and pink counterpart of his wife, had been moving through the racks of used magazines speaking in an easy, almost enjoyable way about the clients who paid him huge sums of money to put fancy weather vanes on top of their split-level roofs.

The man's cynical anecdotes amused Jack Cooper, composed a background for his own work, like a radio program that one didn't actually listen to but which lent a beguiling atmosphere to the most ordinary preoccupation. Meanwhile, Knox had made, as he always did, a complete survey of the store's merchandise to end up, as he always did, at those racks at the rear, beside Cooper's high counter, which kept the back issues of "skin magazines." It was as if someone had asked Knox to inspect the complete merchandise of the magazine store, section by section, and—by golly—here's a section that he had *almost* overlooked. Sometimes he would even grunt with surprise. He did so this morning.

The dodge amused Jack Cooper and he continued his own inventory while listening; the man's different exclamations were spaced by intense silences. Even in this, Knox could not be straightforward, nor even original, but piled mannerisms upon a banal obsession like the curlicues he directed Clay Peck to include on cabinets in Connecticut. The ramble toward the rear racks was a familiar pattern. Old John Cooper used to nudge his son and say softly, "Another disciple." And father and son would watch a man studiously browsing through the home decoration and then on to the philosophy sections, finally toward the racks that held *Sunshine and Health* and other nudist publications of that day. The bodies were the same, but modern photography had transformed them into something inhuman and unbearably touchable.

"My God," he heard Knox gasp. "This is the sort of thing a man could eat with a spoon." Cooper turned around, though he already knew what he would see. Knox held out the centerfold of a magazine. The photograph of the female nude had been so filtered and colored that the torso looked like a piece of fruit ready to burst. It was no longer a human body, at least not one that had been born the usual way, but something that had been grown from a particular hybrid seed. But Cooper's amusement was tempered by the look on the older man's face, a stricken, almost quizzical expression.

Now that he had Cooper's attention, Knox had started to talk about women in general and Ethel in particular. There were sly references to her aging and how it affected their sexual life—nothing wrong with him, by golly—and Cooper turned away, embarrassed for both of them, but then the man's talk shifted and he found himself listening as he went over some order forms.

"She's taken up photography now. I had Clay put in a

darkroom for her off the downstairs bathroom. You remember the sculpture bit?" He laughed. "Well, now it's to be photography. Flowers and sunsets, I suppose. Maybe a hummingbird, if she's lucky. Well dammit, what is there for them to do around here?" He had put the magazine back on the shelf, lined it up with the others—the inspection over. "We have our professions, our business to keep us going. But what is there for them? I suppose Ruth's poetry serves her the same way."

The air seemed to be sucked out of the room by the same heavy blackness that replaced it. Ronnie Knox's lined handsomeness still kept its superior mode, but the eyes had gone flat, uncertain, when Cooper turned on him. "Well, I mean . . ." his voice had lost its manly poise.

"What do you know about her poetry?" Cooper demanded. "What do you know about her work?"

"Hey, golly, Jack—I—"

"It's . . ." but his anger just as quickly cooled, stoppered not so much by the alarm on Knox's face, but by the words that had been lining up in his own head. He had been about to say that Ethel Knox's hobbies could not be compared to Ruth's poetry, but to make this distinction would be to punish Ethel Knox for a risk she had never taken, had somehow failed without taking it. So his hands dropped to his sides and he turned away.

Only minutes later he felt a peculiar gratitude to Knox for bringing his pride to the surface, for catching up this special passion he felt for Ruth, so that the two men parted on easy terms, Knox inviting the Coopers to dinner as he said good-bye and Jack accepting with a smile. The moment had explained much to him, more than he could actually understand, but he accepted the sense of its truth.

The truth came in splintered frames of light, snippets, like the old cinema cards that, for a penny, he used to crank past the metal aperture of the peep shows—a jerky prize fight or a dance of many veils—still to be found when he was a boy in an arcade on Third Avenue, or it came sometimes with Ruth as her pale, slight body crossed his vision in the bedroom, his eyes slitted against the bare bulb of the sun as she returned from the bathroom, slim loins and small breasts in segments, yet all coming together into a single image, one he would never understand even as its light and shadows mesmerized him. Why had he never been jealous of her body, of the uses other men made of it? That day in the shop, Knox had given him the answer. Ruth's discipline, the obligations she made for her words—writing and crossing out once more, all to find one word sometimes—her devotion was a chastity, a vow taken. Her integrity was inviolate; it dare not be tarnished. But the body was different. Its wrongs could slough off like old cells, everything replaced by the new ones, everything fresh. It seemed to him the body could suffer innumerable violations without harm, but the soul of a poet once hurt, could never be mended.

At times, his eyes blind and dazzled by the morning sun, he would feel the weight of her small, retrievable body press down the mattress beside him and he would force his lids apart, a painful sensation at once eased by the look of her kneeling beside him, looking down upon him, her hair pulled and falling over one shoulder. She resembled one of those figures in a Maxfield Parrish print. "I have to talk about Hal," she would say. Then she'd look down at her hands clasped before the round swell of her breasts, a look of pious attention in the large, round eyes as she studied cracked nails as if a breviary shackled her fingers.

"Hal?" He had shifted to his side, a more conversational postion.

"I try so hard with him—to be easy with him. He reaches for me and I turn away. I can't help it, Jack." He stroked and folded her hair. "It is wrong. There is something missing in me. I feel like a cripple." Her voice had been low, the words whispered though no less intense.

"He loves you."

"I know. That hurts even more." Her face pressed against her hands and she rolled to lay against him, curled up. "His eyes rest upon me and I want to run away. It rips me apart." She reached back and took hold of his forearm, the strength of her grip almost painful. Her fingers released then squeezed again then relaxed, as if to assay his presence next to her, the muscle of it. "What am I to do, Jack? What am I to do?"

"He feels wanted and cared for with us. He's happy with us."

"What are you doing to me?" Her voice had gone high, the sound going beyond sound. "What are you saying? Of course he feels wanted and cared for and he's happy. Why? Because of you—fucking earth-father." She had snorted but tucked her feet up to rest against his thighs. "None of it is because of me, but I can't help it. It's like when they gutted me, they also took out this other thing."

"Nonsense."

"It's true. If he had been all right—normal—I sometimes say I could be normal too. I could do things for him, touch him, hold him. Be a mother. But it would make no difference—that's what's wrong." She had turned to face him, her brow against his chest. "It's not that I'm selfish, not that I'm repelled. There's just nothing in me to give. Even if he were normal. It's true of my poetry."

"Your poetry is wonderful."

"My poetry is shit." She collapsed upon him, surprisingly heavy for her size. "It's a jerk-off. What do you know about it?"

"I know," his voice was smothered by her hair but also

stifled by the dumbness that always overcame him when he tried to put his feelings into words. It was a cruel trick of his mind that could carry ringing phrases, which only tarnished, turned dull in the air. "Your work," he began again, cupping the back of her head with one hand. "It is true." She had shrugged. "It is honorable."

Her voice tickled his chest. "Why doesn't your goodness pass into me. Dickens says it happens."

"What did he know?"

Her left hand, which had been blindly touching him, a hard testing of his body, had relaxed, exhausted or satisfied that his hip and thigh were actually there. "I feel so barren."

"Clay Peck has a set of wood planes that must be sixty or seventy years old," he said. "The handles are made of chestnut, and the box that holds the blade is of some other wood, maybe yellow pine. He says they were his grandfather's. But the swirls and grain of the wood are polished and gleam from all those years of being taken up and used. The handles give off something more than the natural oil of the wood. It's as if all the hands that have used these tools so well have left their mark on them, imbued them somehow with their life's work. I think of your poetry that way. How you put all of yourself into it, how it moves and gleams with your . . ." He had paused to think of another word for *devotion,* for Ruth would have laughed at that. Then he sensed her heavy breathing, and weight loosened upon him. She had fallen into a deep, quick sleep without hearing what he had said, and, in fact, he even wondered if he had spoken the words aloud.

Or other times, her body would block the sun as she sat cross-legged and leaned to use his torso for an ottoman, one elbow so sharply set into his ribs that he would have to reposition it. Her skin would be sticky with soap (did she do these postcoital scrubbings with other men or just with him?), and her manner made him reach to the side table for his glasses, to put them on. The two small moles below her left breast formed a range with the childish pucker of the navel. The coarse pubic hair glistened as if varnished. The soles of her feet were soiled; the toes tiny, pink dots.

"What would happen to Hal if something happened to us? I guess what I really mean is what would happen to Hal if you were not in the picture? If I died tomorrow, it would make no difference."

"That isn't true." These had been days of melancholy. Ethel Knox's suicide had not surprised them, but the pretentious memorial service her husband had designed, her body had yet to be recovered, had saddened them both, for the man had put together without knowing it a fair tribute to his wife's awful life. There had been something else. "You are important to both of us," Jack told her.

"To you, maybe. Yes, I know that. But not to Hal. Not Hal. Without you, he would die too. It would be fearful." Her eyes had become glazed, farsighted. The look frightened him, as it had before; it filled the rounds of her face and eyes with a light that lifted and pulled her away from him, from solid ground.

"Ruth. Ruth." He shook her gently by the arm. Ethel Knox's suicide had upset her. The older woman had almost told them in the poetry workshop what she had planned. "It was in her work all along," Ruth moaned, conferring a status upon Ethel's verse withheld until then. Which is why he could never understand Ruth's reaction to the cuckoo clock. Theatrical, he thought and probably standing for something else. When he had heard her scream, he thought a rat may have crawled into the kitchen. She sat like stone at the table. Hal stood by a chair next to the stove. The boy's posture was stiff, his arms at his sides and fists clenched. His back to them, as if waiting for them not to see him, to go away so he could move. But the chair by the stove. That was out of place and Jack Cooper put what had occurred into order. From the boy's tense back his gaze moved to the chair and then up the wall to the clock which had been stopped—was still now—and then to the small wooden bird on its tongue of a platform. The head was gone.

"He did it when I came in the backdoor," Ruth's voice had come from far away, from wherever her eyes looked. "One twist. It was horrible. He just tore it off."

"Hal," Jack had begun softly, a coddling chastisement, and he raised an arm, but Hal shrugged away as if he had had eyes in his back and took two heavy steps to the corner of the kitchen, where he stood face to the wall under the open shelves Jack had put there to hold canned goods. The boy had to bend his knees slightly to fit beneath the lowest shelf.

"Ooohhh." The sob had made Jack Cooper shiver. "Hal's bad. Bad. Bad Hal. The birdie was—was—was—" The sounds in his throat drowned his words. They were un-domesticated sounds, not housebroken nor trained for the decorum of any room, leastwise this small kitchen.

"Hal's not bad," Jack had continued quietly while he moved carefully toward the trembling figure in the corner. "Hal's curious."

"Curious?"

"Hal wants to know."

"Hal wants to know," and the boy cried more heavily and pushed his face into the right angle made by the oak-streaked walls. Ruth had groaned and put her head into her arms.

"It's a pretty bird and Jack can fix it. Make it go." He was now standing right behind the youth. He could not escape. "Give Jack what you have. Can I have it?"

"Yes," Hal had almost shouted, the relief loosened his

voice so that it ballooned toward the ceiling. Simultaneously, one of the clenched fists at his side slowly opened. Jack Cooper reached out and plucked the spiny, wooden head of the bird from the boy's palm as if it were a priceless gem. Ruth remained at the table, motionless, face buried in her crossed arms like a figure in a painting.

Some mornings Cooper would rise halfway off the pillow and put his arm around her. "Ruth," he said softly. "Ruth." Almost with an audible click her eyes turned to meet his worried expression. She smiled, a rare gift that filled him with celebration; then her eyes became very solemn.

"How lucky . . . how lucky." She had put her face close to his so he could not look away, for that had been his impulse as it always was when she looked this way at him; it embarrassed him. There was a sudden sad evaluation in her look, like someone who had come across a rare thing they could not keep. Her lips took his as if she were afraid to bruise them.

"This isn't fair," Jack Cooper said. His voice had gone ragged. "You're not being fair." Then she had moved to make love to him, to treat him with a slavish impulse, but he took her by her shoulders and pulled her upright, a little roughly for she winced. "If we are to settle this business, this is not the way. I want no payoffs. It can't be evened up that way."

She sat beside him and nodded, the pose of a penitent; yet he suspected she regarded his rejection as ridiculous. He could not be sure because of the light, but her mouth even seemed to turn down. If he wanted to deny himself this pleasure—this pleasure for which she had already been immortalized, it would briefly occur to him—then that was his foolish business, but he did not have to turn it, at the same time, into a gesture that might pile a little more guilt upon her. He knew this was what she would be thinking, a rationale she had picked up in the city, in the literary circle she now cried for in exile, where even the simplest behavior was judged in terms of its motivation. And this always a matter of endless speculation. So he found himself apologizing.

"It's all right," Ruth shrugged him away. "But do this one thing for me."

"Anything," Jack Cooper said and meant it.

"If something should happen to me, if I should die, destroy all my poems. Jack?" She looked at him when he had not answered. "Promise me. That would be the worst thing you could do."

"What?"

"You would want to put out a collection of my stuff. Save me that. Don't do that to me. I know I deserve a lot but not that. I don't deserve that. I'm not Ethel Knox."

"Yes," he said. "I promise."

"What time must it be?" Ruth would then bounce off the bed to rip through the clothes hanging in the closet. The bell jar of sunlight that had enclosed their morning, that had somehow suspended the day's sequence, suddenly cracked and fell apart.

But it wasn't a matter of running out of time, not an apt phrase Jack Cooper would often think; it was just that time had been set going again after having been stopped, or put into a parenthesis, perhaps, as the earth took a slight turn about the sun. Depending on one's place and luck, this sort of hiatus might even last for days, months, maybe even years, but eventually, the gears would engage and then came the sensation of time slipping away.

This was why he never repaired the cuckoo clock. It was a conceit, a metaphor worked over and over by novelists of different perceptions, different temporalities; but he liked the idea of the still clock in the kitchen containing their lives, not marking them down with a fall of weights. Nor was it to preserve this time of their lives because it was so benevolent, so felicitous; quite the contrary. It was to suspend the time. Just maybe, lying outside the far perimeter of this becalmed equinox—the crossroads of this deserted village—an entirely different season waited for them, joyous and full of fine weather and slowly floating toward them like Atlantis, risen and about to appear on the horizon.

CHAPTER

THREE

You'll find what I'm going to tell you next hard to believe, but it's the God's truth. It's no stranger than that story of yours with that monkey shooting machine guns. It was in '18 just before our boys gave old Ludendorff a bloody nose at Château-Thierry and at a terrible cost, you'll remember.

We had been assigned to Spad 600 of Group 29, flying out of a little field near Villeneuve. A month later the skies would be dark with Fokkers when the Germans made their last big push of the war. But we knew none of this then, of course. We were a happy bunch. There was Swanson from Harvard, Locke from Cornell, Putnam and Reynolds both from Yale, and yours truly, a tiger from Princeton. We would take our little ships up on patrol and fly the sector of the Marne, take what came, and be back at field for tea. There was an inn about five miles from the field, set at a little crossroads. It was run by two women, mother and daughter. The daughter was married to a *poilu*, a French infantryman who was at the front.

So we go to this little tavern when off duty and the mother would invite us to have our cognacs upstairs, in their living quarters over the inn. There was no funny stuff. It was just that this French lady had a class distinction about things; we were flying officers so it wouldn't do for us to drink with the noncoms and grease monkeys in the main tavern. To be truthful, the arrangement had some appeal for us, too.

Anyway, after about two or three weeks, the mother and daughter joined us. Usually we were left to ourselves, they being busy with the crowd downstairs. But this night, they come in and sit down. Very formal. Swanson had a little of the parleyvoo on him so we got along pretty well. Then, the mother starts talking a long streak, very serious. The daughter stands behind her. Swanson's expression gets strange and his face turns red. Then his ears. What's she saying, we want to know? Wait a minute, wait, he motions with one hand, rather like what I had seen him do on patrol, pointing down to something beneath us. Then the woman has stopped talking, and both women look at us expectantly. Well? I can still remember the sounds of the mantel clock. Swanson put it into English.

To be brief, the mother was asking one of us to get her daughter pregnant. As she explained it, they had no hope of seeing that French soldier boy alive. The French were taking horrendous casualties in the trenches. They were to lose almost four million by Armistice—think of that. Anyway, it was these ladies' belief that more sons and daughters had to be got someway, somehow to make up the difference. *Pour patrie, pour patrie,* she had repeated a phrase familiar to all of us because we'd see it on the casualty reports tacked up in the ready room. They had made the choice, one of us who resembled the *poilu* the closest. *Pour patrie* turned out to be Putnam of Yale. Now you may want to know what this young French woman looked like, but I cannot tell you for I do not remember. If you want to make her look like one of these movie queens, so be it. I can't help you. I can't even remember what Putnam looked like; all those faces are about one to me now.

What I do remember was how we argued—debated is more the word—all the way back to the field as to whether Putnam ought to do it. It was adultery, pure and simple. Another man's wife.

Somebody, probably Swanson of Harvard, brought up the idea that the Frenchman might already by lying dead in some muddy shell hole so it wouldn't be adultery. But someone else, can't remember who, said we must assume the man to be alive until proved otherwise, so it was adultery.

It was June I remember. Quiet. The big battle was a month off, though we didn't know that. I would have just graduated from Princeton if I had not enlisted, but here I was risking my neck every morning and arguing at night about whether one of us should have sexual congress with a foreign woman. The world had gone nuts.

So we took a vote. That was the democratic way, wasn't it? President Wilson would have approved. And it was a secret vote, too. Back at quarters we made up slips of paper—yes or no. Putnam said he shouldn't vote, but that would have left only four of us voting and maybe there'd be a tie. That would get us nowhere. Every candidate is allowed to vote in his own election, someone said. So we all voted. It came out three to two for him to go lie with the tavern keeper's daughter for the greater glory of France, *pour patrie*. I always thought that Putnam voted against himself, he was that sort of fellow. I know how I voted, but I'll never tell. It was a secret vote after all.

Anyway, Putnam went about the business with the same even, steady way he flew his Spad. He was a book pilot if you know what I mean. Not inventive nor crazy like Tommy Slater over in the 602. Just dependable. A good man to have on your wing. He performed his duty for about a month and then old Ludendorff tried to push through the French lines east of Rheims and all hell broke loose.

So that shows you a little difference between that war and all others to come, probably some of that difference came out of that big battle that started on July 15th. Other battles after that, too. Swanson went down in flames over Verneuil. Putnam was brought down by Archie, but landed in a tree behind German lines and spent the rest of the war as a prisoner. The rest of us made it through but were moved to another field nearer the front. We never found out if anything happened *pour patrie*.

I want to say, I've enjoyed and have been thankful for your letters. I'm about the only cloudbuster left on this aerodrome. Keep writing until you hear otherwise. Also, does that pilot of yours ever find that lady flier? Crazy as it is, that story of yours has me interested. I've been putting down more of my memories, like the above, too.

> Happy landings,
> Roy E. Armstrong
> Capt. Army Air Corps Ret.

"Some beautiful ladies. Those were some beautiful ladies back then." The man's voice is soft and padded like a piece of furniture. Cooper tries to remember his name—when Kelly Novak introduced them she had begun to sort through her mail—but he suspected that it made no difference, that the man would answer to whatever name the woman cared to use. Cooper had met the editor and her companion, up for the weekend, in Irondale, where he had gone to put some magazine orders into the mail. Kelly Novak had invited him to follow them to the old barn she was doing over as a summer place.

Clay Peck had talked about this renovation taking so long and costing so much, and now Jack Cooper could see why. Ron Knox had had the carpenter make up the oversized windows especially. They had been cut into the barn's west side, eliminating several hand-hewn chestnut posts in the process. None had screens so had to remain closed because of the great insect population in the Hollow. The fixed panes of glass magnify the sun's heat inside the room as they seem to diminish the landscape outside; fields and woods, only partly seen within ordinary windows, were framed completely within the huge casements. A newly harvested cornfield of around sixty acres on Stickles' farm, Cooper noted, takes up the lower, right-hand corner of one panel. It looked like a small rug eaten down to its fibers by moths.

He had not wanted to share the old flier's letter with Kelly Novak's companion, but she had urged him with such a winsome manner that he found himself pulling the envelope from his back pocket even though he guessed it was a stratagem to keep them both occupied while she went through her mail. He had been watching Ernest Miller weigh and stamp his packages when a car pulled up and stopped outside the post office. Cooper recognized its soft murmur, the purring ticks of a high-compression engine that articulated in his mind's eye the instruments set into the sport car's walnut dash.

Now Captain Armstrong's letter is safely back in his pocket. The man across looks at him with sweaty anticipation, the pink, blue-eyed expression of a coach who had just finished a pep talk and confidently waited its effect. "Don't you agree?" he finally asks.

"What?"

"That our Ms. Novak is some special lady."

"A specially broke lady if these taxes around here keep going up." The woman saves Cooper the chore of answering. She turns toward them, carrying the few pieces of mail salvaged from the pile of pennysavers and circulars on the floor. It is a fairly long walk from the far end of the old granary. The way was strewn with lumps of foam furniture and other odd pieces. The furniture was all covered in the same oatmeal-colored material so the chairs and sofas looked like stage boulders or, maybe, large mushrooms that had seeded themselves in the floorboards and grown to enormous proportions because of the old barn's rich detritus.

"How come my school taxes took a fifteen percent jump?" She moved with wonderful grace despite the obstacles or maybe because of them, the same way as that first time Cooper had seen her, as he stood by her sports car parked by his store. As he chased off the stray dog, she had appeared near the railroad embankment, as if stepping out of one of the houses that was no longer there, but the long length of white silk scarf looped between her hands was not the usual accessory for the country woman who might have lived there. She had driven up from the city with the top down and had used the scarf to keep her hair, which was almost the same color as the silk, in place. Cooper had seen deer move similarly across a field thick with sumac and hawthorn and apple trees gone wild, look away briefly and they would be gone, and with this same grace, she seemed to take distance by surprise.

"It's the local custom, I'm afraid," Jack Cooper tells her. "The same thing happened to us. They always reassess property when it changes hands. If you're from the city a small percentage is tacked on."

"Small?" Her mouth curls. "Look at this dump. They must have super schools around here to levy taxes like this." She looks at him quickly, as if peeking at him from around a corner. "What *are* the schools like? Your boy's in school."

"Hey, got a boy in school? What grade is he in?" Her companion takes the question and genially plays catch with it. "Nothin' like having a son, is there? I have a couple."

His interruption annoys Kelly Novak. "Here—" she says quickly, pauses as if trying to remember what to call him. "Here, take this list and go to Green River. We need milk. Get some eggs. See if the greens are fresh. Use your judgment. But I don't want iceberg lettuce. And forget the endive, even if they have it. Get some ice. Tonic water. Limes. Want some money? Here. Take this money. Is that enough? Do you want more?" She hurries him across the floor and out the door, her questions like prods though he seemed ready to run errands.

Nor was she done even after the man got outside, for she shouts more instructions through the screen door. "Get some fish. Not frozen. Go to that store in Connecticut. Oh, what about my bags? They're still in the trunk. I can unpack while you're gone." Again she turns back toward Cooper, only to wheel about once more, but the throaty mumble of the departing convertible brought her up short. "Oh, damn. He's gone. Do you think he'll get some fruit?"

She sounds hurt and strangely defenseless. The same quality of voice had urged Cooper to share the letter from Captain Armstrong. "Whew. You could bake bread in here. When is Mr. Knox going to get my screens made?"

One boot has been kicked off. She takes three steps, stops, and removes the other and raises her arms, hands before her face—a quaint parody of a pugilist—to unfasten the buttons at the cuffs of her blouse. Each sleeve is fastened by four or five small pearls: as she unfastens each one meticulously, the material falls away from white arms; then, her hands move to the front of her blouse. Here there were larger pearl buttons. One, two, three, and four, and the blouse hangs open; but she is indifferent to her dishevelment before Jack Cooper.

"What do you think? Knox is doing a number on me, isn't he?" Cooper shrugs, a preface to his opinion but she goes on. "Let me get out of these clothes."

She has pulled the blouse from the tight waistband of her skirt. She passes behind him, probably continuing to undress as she goes toward a far corner of the old barn where bathroom fixtures have been roughly installed.

"So tell me about that letter?" she asks. Cooper hears drawers opening and closing, the squeak of an armoire's door, the rattle of metal hangers. "What do you think of that letter?"

He had forgotten her eyes, how they looked that first meeting at his magazine store. The pupils were large and

· 75 ·

gray and set within elliptical openings, outlined in coal black like a child's drawing of eyes and the skin around the eyes was fresher, he thinks, and different from her complexion. The long blade of her nose ascended into the high arches of her brow, again as if drawn but this feature drawn by a fine artist. In fact, all these aspects of her face had a sculpted look in that they were too regular if not perfect, and with a strange newness about them as if they had been modeled out of some material that would never change, never age with the rest of her.

"Hello there. Anybody home?" She continues to move around behind him, changing her clothes. "Calling Flip Winslow . . . calling Flip Winslow . . . come in, Flip." Her voice had flattened theatrically.

"What do I think of the letter? I think, like Armstrong says, it shows how different we've become. I can't see soldiers in World War II or later debating whether one of them should . . . go ahead. There was still a sense of chivalry then, I guess." She did not answer. Cooper looked out the windows. The large island of a cloud launched its shadow on the green swells of the Taconic Range. A box was closed and pushed across floorboards, maybe under the bed.

"Well, it's different but also the same," Kelly Novak says. "You think it's different simply because they took a vote before one of them had her. But it's all the same fucking whether they voted or not. It's the same idea: women kept in the pasture to be—what do your farmers call it around here when they inseminate a cow?"

"Sweeten."

"Yes, sweeten. How's that for a male euphemism? Sweeten. No, that story doesn't say anything new to me."

"But the French women did this on their own. No one was forcing them." The island has disappeared.

"You don't understand," her voice comes nearer. "It wasn't voluntary. *Pour patrie?* What is that? A man's concept? Being shot to pieces for the greater good of the national compound. Being made pregnant for the greater good. It's all the same thing."

She holds a large brown envelope, the same one he had used to send her his manuscript. "Look, I want to apologize for my remark about school, asking about your son. I hope that didn't upset you."

"No problem." Perhaps she wears contact lenses, Cooper thinks. "Hal goes to a special school the school district runs here. He doesn't like it much. Sometimes plays hooky. Actually, that day we met, I thought you might be the truant officer checking up on him."

Hal would get on the little bus that took him and the other "exceptional" children to their special classes, but then he would sometimes elude teachers and counselors to melt into the surroundings, over the closed fence and away like a breeze rippling a forest fern bed. That first time it had happened; they found him in that empty garage in Boston Corners, and Cooper had gone to the college to tell Ruth Hal was all right.

So when he returned the dead pheasant to Clay Peck, Jack Cooper had expected to find the stray dog barking at the sort of plain automobile truant officers are given to use; but the dog barked at a maroon-and-gray convertible, the driver seemingly vanished into the growth around the store, as the radio music from a New York City station also seemed about to disappear into the thicket of Hammertown. Then far down the road, just where Cooper imagined the row of village houses to have been, this figure steps out from the weeds and onto the road. She stood there for a moment and removed the scarf from her head and shook out her hair. It was the color of white silk and fell and coiled against her hand with a syrupy heaviness. On first sight he had thought her to be very young, but as she walked down the middle of the country road, she seemed to pass through a long history. She had begun talking while still a way off, but Jack Cooper hardly heard her words for he was thinking, she is much older than I thought. She's much older.

"This," she had repeated, as she walked toward him. She had taken the small manuscript from her shoulder purse and shook it before his face. "I asked if you were responsible for this story? I was up for the weekend on Labor Day and bought an old *McClure*'s magazine you had here. Remember? And this story was in it. Maybe you were reading something there, doing research, and forgot this manuscript, something like that? Yes?"

She was now squarely in front of him, and he caught the heavy scent she uses as she ruffled the typescript under his nose, apparently wanting to be sure he was its author before she surrendered it. "This is yours," she said with a demanding tone that both chided him as it teased his answer. He had hoped Ruth, someone, would drive by right then.

Yes, it was his, he admitted. He recognized it as an episode he had been looking for, and he *had* been doing some research, as she called it; there were ads in the old magazine showing the kind of formal dress worn in the Palm Beach of the 1930s. He was writing about a meeting between Winslow and Colonel Sandford, in Singapore; their dinner jackets had to be right. Something must have interrupted him.

"Great stuff. Great stuff, this guy and his ape. Do you have more of this?" She flashed the pages once more, and again her perfume filled his head. It didn't seem to be pressed from any flower Cooper could recognize, something with vanilla. "If so," now she returned the pages, "I can make you a lot of bucks. You are a natural, Jack. That's what they call you, isn't it? I've heard others call you that. Jack, you are a natural storyteller. A Jack London but with poetry."

Then she had just as quickly introduced herself, saying she was a senior editor at Wilson Bean and that they and been looking for just such a story. "It's the kind of time when people are seeking Utopia. The big market in science fiction, that sort of thing. But what you have there," a finger reached out and tapped the rolled manuscript with a perfect, untinted fingernail, "what you have there is something very special. The old code, honor and heroes."

The moment, thinking about it, still makes Cooper tingle; even now as he sits in this old barn and hears her fuss about. Could this be happening to him? Novak has changed to shorts and a T-shirt and runs water at a sink set into one corner, takes ice cubes from a refrigerator. The equipment was plumbed and that was all, like the elements of a rude base camp.

"I haven't told you," she continues, "but old man Bean is about to retire, and I'm going to take over the house. I can do what I want, but I want you to read what this other reader has said about your manuscript, Jack." She brings his attention down to the envelope that lies on the Lucite coffee table near him. "I'm fixing some iced tea, okay? It's instant. It's a negative report, but I want you to see it. I think you should see it, Jack. It was just a formality to have another reading, and I gave it to this editor who I knew would be hard on it. Now who's this?" She leans over the sink to peer through the open window. "Bruce can't be back already." Cooper hears a car come down the driveway and stop. "Oh, it's you." Kelly Novak says through the screen door.

"Your servant, milady," the voice outside replies. It is Ron Knox.

* * *

Ethel Knox had parked the big station wagon halfway across the Rip Van Winkle Bridge and, by habit, had rolled up the windows and locked the doors. So she had taken the keys with her when she jumped off the bridge into the Hudson River. It had been March, after a long winter. Crusts of snow and ice still followed the banks, but the main channel ran deep and wide. Her body was never found. "It must have been so cold," Ruth had shuddered.

Because there had been no witnesses, and no *corpus,* it took a little while to declare her officially dead, and Knox himself prompted the idea that she had only wandered away, that she was still alive somewhere and would come back after she had punished him enough. It was locking the car and taking the keys that supported the idea she had intended to return. "You know how women get sometimes," he had said to Jack Cooper. "There's no explaining how they act." Punished for *what* he never explained, though Ruth would say a man like Ron Knox should be punished on sight—for just being in sight.

"There was no way I could get out of the invitation," Jack told Ruth, as they dressed to go to the Knoxes for dinner one time.

"I can put up with him," Ruth had said. "It's her I can't stand. I can't stand seeing her. Her eyes are so defensive. A permanent flinch."

"Well, we have to go," he said.

And in fact they both welcomed the evening out, for they hardly went out together except for an occasional movie in Green River or supper in one of the country restaurants over in Connecticut. There were few people they could visit as a couple. Ruth's relationship with her students constituted a kind of social life and she had been spending one evening a week with the writing workshop she had started, but neither of these included Jack and she did want to go places with him. He could tell that she wanted to go out with him by the way she put out a particular shirt for him to wear or would make a fuss over his glasses, polishing and cleaning them and then carefully putting them back on his nose and fitting the earpieces just so. "There," she said, close to him. "Sexy. It was your glasses that turned me on."

"Just something more to take off," he said.

"You got it," Ruth barked, her laughter more like the cough of a fox. He could tell when she had had a good morning working on her poetry. Her spirits would be high.

"Here're some new books for Hal," Jack told the boy. That day Cooper had received a box of old comic books, cartoon adaptions of classics: *Treasure Island, Jason and the Golden Fleece, Robinson Crusoe, The Count of Monte Cristo.*

"O-boy, o-boy, o-boy," Hal said doing a slow jig and clapping his large hands together, but he took the worn magazines from Jack carefully, to prolong the gift.

"We'll be home early," Ruth said to him and even kissed the side of his head. Hal did not look up from the comics but blushed a dark crimson.

Though what early or late meant to the boy was never clear. He seemed to observe a timepiece of his own invention, directed by his instincts or his reading of the night sky. When the school authorities notified Jack that Hal had disappeared, he would find him sometimes in a hollow behind their house curled up in a ball beneath ferns and swamp maples sound asleep. Maybe that's why he played hooky; it had been his time to sleep.

Naturally, Jack and Ruth Cooper would look back on this and other evenings at the Knoxes' for a remark, some look, or gesture that might have predicted Ethel's suicide. The review was not made to blame themselves for missing a sign;

but if there had been clues, these would retain their mystery, always. They could never think of any.

Curiously, Knox had not redesigned the old tenant cottage they lived in, and the rooms promoted the same harmony with the human figure that had been chalked off two hundred years before. Large paned, six-over-six windows looked out on this corner of the Livingston Manor and framed the identical landscape for several generations of viewers. "The shoemaker's children," Ethel Knox said merrily more than once, and it amused the Coopers to watch the tall, white-haired architect turn impatiently within the unmolested näiveté of his own house. That had been Ruth's description, *impatiently,* and come to think of it, Jack could never remember Knox sitting down except to eat at the round table near the kitchen. The rest of the time he prowled the living room, paced about the hearth as if he were measuring an angle or corner—His metal tape was always within reach—before it was torn out.

Before dinner the Coopers would each nurse a single glass of white wine while the older couple drank several large whiskey sours. Jack associated their heavy drinking with an earlier time, and in his imagination, he could place Ron and Ethel Knox in the advertisements of old *Collier*'s and *Vanity Fair*s with other tall, elegant couples. The women always seemed to droop within heavy draperies, standing on terraces and porticoes to sip cocktails from long-stemmed glasses while regarding the year's new Packard.

"Where did they come from?" Ruth asked him after one these evenings. "I mean, what did he do before he retired here."

"Advertising," Jack replied. "There was a phony quiz show on television a while back. Some of the contestants had been given the answers. The champion was crooked, too. Knox claims he had nothing to do with it, but it was his account that sponsored the show so when the thing was exposed he had to resign. Meanwhile, he had put together a lot of stock options."

"I like her," Ruth said. She leaned against him as they drove home from that dinner. "I think I'll ask her to sit in on my workshop."

"Want you to take a look at these," Knox had told them with a twinkle in his eyes. He placed photographs around the chimney wall.

"Just what are you doing, mister?" Ethel Knox said from the pantry. The kitchen behind her was another old magazine illustration; chintz curtains chorused the same blue and white of her cookware and pieces of crockery. Canisters and implements that should have been odd with each other gave off a cozy affinity. Cooper expected the refrigerator to sprout one of those old-time coils from its top. "You put those up," she said. "Right now."

"Naw, I want the Coopers to see them. They're terrific," Knox said as he continued to mount the casual exhibit. "Hey, here's one of that corn lot you used to paint. She used to paint this corn lot over and over," he told his guests. "There must be a dozen paintings in a closet upstairs of that little corn lot." He held the photograph up, as if the light above his head would be better. "Isn't that terrific?"

"Please, Ronnie." Ethel Knox raised the cooking spoon she held in one hand. It had been a futile gesture, done good-naturedly because she knew it to be futile.

Cooper remembers the details as he watches Knox strut around Kelly Novak on this Saturday in fall, a clipboard in one hand and the ever-present tape measure in the other.

"One or two things I'd like to measure," he grins. The metal rule was pulled out a short length and quickly retracted. Knox did this several times. Kelly Novak regards him blankly. "Be careful of this fellow," he looks over at Cooper. "I thought that was your old Skylark in the drive."

Jack Cooper feels out of place, like a delivery man invited into the parlor. Nor did the report in his hand suggest acceptance would take place anywhere, anytime. He had read a few sentences as Knox arrived; it was a very negative report. His story about Flip Winslow was called *juvenile*.

"I thought these screens were going to be in by now. And what about the kitchen?" Novak was angry. "Look at that kitchen. It's like a floor display at Sears Roebuck. You said the interior walls would be up by now."

"My dear lady," Knox replies. His patience, his obvious patience with ignorant clients was apparent. "You would be bored with the details. Problems with suppliers. With the local workmen. Let me spare you the details. These are ancient constructions we are dealing with."

"Let me hear the details. How long is this going to take?" Kelly Novak returns to the freestanding sink unit. Cooper watches Knox watch her walk away. Her shorts were frayed.

"I've made some new sketches—I don't have them with me—but I wanted your approval. First." He goes toward a blind wall. "I think we should cut through right here and build you a dandy little breakfast-pantry. We can make up a pretty little bay window right here. . . ." he has begun to measure as he talks.

"Wait a minute," the woman stops him. "What about that post there?"

"Oh, we can just cut that out. It will be no problem."

"But that's another old beam I'm losing. All my hand-hewn beams are being cut out?"

"Oh, they're not so special," Knox pouts. "Lots of them around here. We can put some in wherever you like."

"But I don't need any more space. Look at this barn. Do you think I need more space?" She asks Cooper, who took his cue from the question. "Where are you going? Sit down. I want to talk to you about that." Her eyes glisten and he sits back down. "Just get me some screens, Mr. Knox. All right? I won't be coming back until spring so—what's this?"

He has handed her a small envelope. His face has flushed and he seemed to go on tiptoe as Kelly Novak withdrew the folded insert. "What's this bill for?" Her voice became flat.

"You remember the contract we signed," Knox replies. He scratched his brow with the thumb of the hand that held the tape measure. "We agreed to several payments spread over a period of time."

"But nothing's been done."

"A good deal has been done; it just doesn't show. Also, my fee has nothing to do with the actual construction. I can't be responsible for the local workmen not completing the work on time. That's your responsibility. You have to keep after these people around here. I'm responsible for the design only."

"I see," Kelly Novak says. She seems to take some sort of measurement herself and Knox turns away toward Cooper. Jack could see a question form in the man's watery eyes, saw how the speculation amused the questioner. Kelly tosses the bill onto a large table that had had some of the old finish removed. "Okay, I'll send it to you."

It took a while for Knox to hear the dismissal in her words. Then, almost gallantly, he bows toward Cooper and then again toward Kelly and goes to the door. "Of course," he says with a knowing smile. He nearly backs out through the screen. "Of course."

"What a character," Kelly says. They listen to his car pull away. "But he's part of the cast in this little pastoral. Right?" Her lips thin when she smiles. "I forgot the tea." But the ice has melted, and there is no more ice in the fridge.

"But listen," Jack Cooper says. "These stories are just

· 85 ·

something I made up to amuse myself and the boy. They're not to be taken seriously. They're parodies of stories I used to read in old pulp magazines when I was growing up. It's only a hobby."

His feelings caught him unawares, and he heard his voice growing thin. It hadn't been fair. He had not written the Winslow episodes to be read by anyone but Hal. The reader's report had flailed the story, the prose, the idea. He felt spent in the hot, dusty air of the old granary. He hadn't asked for this professional criticism, and his hurt feelings took him by surprise.

"You may think so." Somehow the T-shirt and shorts, the informal pose she took on crossed legs only emphasized her deliberate manner. "I recognize something very special in those stories. Right now there's a demand for romantic stories with a touch of the kinky." She smiles as the gray eyes almost closed. "I think—I know," she leans forward to hold his eyes with hers, "—I know this is dynamite material. Forget about that report. I knew it would be a bad one. That's why I gave it to that particular reader, so we would have some hard questions that would give us something to work on. The bottom line. If we can answer the questions this kind of mind asks, then we have a winner because the basic poetic imagination of the work will carry the rest—as it does now."

Jack Cooper looks away. The view through the large windows is the same. He could understand none of this, but she spoke so confidently that he is convinced. Perhaps he wanted to be convinced.

"For example," her voice draws him back. "Why have you put an American engine on that Italian airplane?"

"Because the Pratt and Whitney was more powerful than the original. Also . . ."

"Yes?"

"Well, I knew someone from East Hartford, where Pratt and Whitney is located."

"Aha." Novak has raised one leg and rests her face against the bare knee. "And why an Italian airplane in the first place? Why does this American fly an Italian airplane?"

"I always liked the looks of the Breda 65. It just looked good to me."

"I see." Her eyes become distant. "Then there's this chimp—"

"Orangutan."

"Yes, the simian sidekick," she laughs at the alliteration. "I like him. I like that very much. There are reverberations coming out of this duo: man and monkey. Maybe some references are needed to show how Winslow met and trained him to do all those things. Fire that machine gun—"

"I only made it a twin .50 calibre because it sounded more formidable. I could change it back to the original Breda 12.7 millimeter single gun. It would be easier for the ape to handle."

"I want to publish this book." Her eyes searched out his doubt, speared it. "I only gave the excerpt to this other reader out of protocol. Her report has no value in the house. Believe me."

"I must go," Cooper stands.

"Now you think of what I've said." She takes the manuscript and threw it toward him. He caught it automatically. "I want to work with you on this book. I'm convinced we can make a lot of money on it. I can do what I want at Wilson Bean." She walks to the door, a hand on his arm, but it was a formal gesture. Cooper imagined her New York office: the furniture, its height above the blur of city traffic. She even accompanies him outdoors to demonstrate the sincerity of her interest. "You could come to New York and we could work on it there. I can set aside a day to work with you. You—" Her nails suddenly needle the flesh of his arm. Her face has gone blank, white, and the eyes glaze.

The snake looks like a thick black belt that has somehow worked its way out of the zippered red luggage to lay loosely coiled around one of the soft, leather bags placed on the grass near the driveway. There is a querulous look on the reptile's face as if it is embarrassed to be caught traveling across the clearing near the old barn, a domain once all its own. Kelly Novak has begun to shiver, to whimper. "Oh. Take it away. Take it away."

"It's just an old black snake," Cooper says.

"Take it away, please." She presses her knees together and puts a hand over her mouth. Cooper starts forward; the snake flowed and curved in the direction of the barn's foundation. Cooper finds a stick to push the snake. The reptile was about five feet long, he guessed, and it turned on the prod. The man quickly pinned it down, grabbed it behind the head, and then, with a motion as ancient as it was graceful, Cooper cast the serpent high into the air. The snake marked the sky like the last letter of an old calligraphic alphabet before it disappears into the weeds below the barn.

"You actually picked it up and—"

"It was just a black snake."

"Oh."

Ron Knox's first commission was to design a social hall for the Union Presbyterian Church in Irondale, so it was somehow natural that the building be used for Ethel's memorial service. The hall was quite large, more space than the Irondale church's small congregation knew what to do with, and then only on alternate Sundays. They shared their minister with another church in Green River, so the exhibit of Ethel's works that Knox had mounted, almost a retrospective it could be said, took up only one corner of the vast space.

"See those dandy stress arches," Knox was fond of pointing up at the ceiling and even did so once or twice during that spring afternoon. "Those are laminated and prefab. The first of that kind to be used in this area."

Ethel's pickles and preserves had been arranged on a long, refectory table covered with a sheet of butcher's paper. The jars were labeled in a squarish style of hand printing: SWEET & SOUR CUKES. WATERMELON PICK. PEACH CHUT. STRAWBERRY PRES. Ceramic plates, the color of baked mud, displayed sugar cookies and gingersnaps. Knox told everyone how he had taken them out of the freezer, and they were just as good as when Ethel had baked them: try some. More ceramics, pots and dishes, held cut flowers and assortments of dried gourds.

Photographs and watercolors were hung on a wall of about eight-by-twelve feet. The subjects were clouds and farm buildings and farm animals. Several of that particular cornfield painted or photographed in different seasons. What had she seen in those orderly rows of corn? Cooper wondered."

"Eat 'em up." Knox recommended the dead woman's cookies, defrosted and rather soggy. "They won't keep." He looked sturdy, jovial, something like a carnival barker, because he had removed his jacket and wore a red vest with brass buttons, a blue shirt, and white tie. His face was the color of his vest, and he ladled punch from a glass bowl.

The Coopers knew few of the people who came by; most of them seemed to be people from Connecticut for whom Knox had done renovations or designs. It was not just the way they dressed that suggested a "foreignness" but their quick affability, as if they were just looking in on their way to another, more agreeable affair. Leaving, they stepped stiffly across the bare floor of the social hall, startled by the sound of their own footsteps.

But the Coopers did know people like Clay Peck and other local workmen. They nodded to one or two farmers. Men and women stood in separate groups like teenagers waiting for someone to ask them to dance. "Drink up," Knox urged one and all. Music played from a phonograph in the corner. The old records reminded Cooper of stories and illustrations in the magazines he traded. The lyrics were either slightly naughty or sweetly sentimental.

"If you do this to me, I'll come back and pull out your tongue," Ruth had said. "I'll come back and pour lightning down your throat and cook your eyes." Then she laughed to clear her sudden fierceness, even put one hand out toward Jack for she had staggered a little.

He put an arm around her. Her hair gleamed like a black enamel cap pulled tightly over the finely made head. It could come undone so very quickly. Jack Cooper reached, touched it, always surprised by its softness.

"Don't," Ruth pulled away from him to put down her punch cup untasted. "I have office hours at school this afternoon." He knew this was not so. He knew her schedule.

"Well, isn't that terrific," Ruth says when Jack tells her about Kelly Novak's interest. "Isn't that just great." Her response saddens Jack. She is grading examinations, looks as if she may have spent most of the afternoon at it, for the living room floor is tiled by blue-paper covered booklets. "How long have you been writing these stories?" Something still vibrates in his chest, in his stomach.

"They're just something I did to amuse the boy. They're not serious."

"All these years, and I discover I'm living with a closet Hemingway," Ruth says and laughs, though it is not happy laughter. "Of course, they're serious. These people don't have time to fool with . . . my, God, Jack, do you know the writers who would do anything, anything, to get a book done by Wilson Bean?" She pulls a sweater close over her shoulders. It's cooler in their cottage than in Novak's renovated barn.

"It's far from being published," he assures her. "It's just some wild stories I put together just as a . . . well, almost as a hobby. It's the airplane stuff, you know. It's not even a book. She wants me to come down to the city and work with her on it."

"What does this hotshot editor look like?"

"Oh, she's tall. Blonde, but that's dyed, I guess. She looks polished. She's not young." The few details embarrass him though they are sufficient for Ruth, and she looks at him carefully.

"How old?"

"I don't know. Hard to say. Older than I am, for sure. It was a mistake, her seeing the manuscript. Some of the pages got mixed up with a magazine she bought."

The silence pours between them like resin to set them up like sculpted figures. Far up in the woods, a chain saw droned—someone cutting wood for the winter. Its sound, miniaturized by the distance, reminds him of the small gas motors that power plane models, some of them controlled in flight by tiny radio transmitters. He had never made any of this type.

"So when you go down to the store at night, you've been writing these stories." Ruth pieces it together. She bends over, kneels, and begins to gather together the student themes. There's something about their disorder now that strikes him as unusual; it's the way she's picking them up, as if in the same order they had been set down. "So how often do you have to go to the city to work on it with her?"

"No set schedule. I'm supposed to go in next week. It's ridiculous." A yellow van has pulled up beside the house. "There's Hal. Maybe I won't go."

"Of course you'll go." Ruth stacks the collected themes on the table. "I think she's right. You'll probably sell a million copies." Cooper remains in the living room as she goes through the kitchen to greet Hal at the backdoor. He has guessed that she has been home for only a little while before he arrived and that the themes scattered about the room represented only a few seconds of stage dressing. There was something about the way she had fixed herself that morning, the way she fiddled with her hair and chatted, idly, about an appointment, a conference, that would keep her busy past lunch.

He hears Hal and Ruth greet each other, and he steps out the door onto the small porch that lies along the back wall of the house. When they first moved to Hammertown, they would use this back porch a lot, sitting here on long summer evenings to watch the western sky go dark. Now it was an open storage bin, a place to keep odd pieces of furniture or tools that had become broken, disused. Several large, clay flowerpots, a tangle of old clothesline, and an electric oven rusted through have been placed on the cracked, plastic cushions of the old glider.

Just in the center of the small yard is a vegetable garden prepared for winter. It is only a sketch of the full-sized garden he used to cultivate, whose productivity used to amaze Ruth. She had never seen broccoli grow, and the way pea pods hung down from their lanternlike blossoms had delighted her. Only ten years back, he thinks as he comes out to check the tomatoes. The high, warm atmosphere that made the afternoon a dividend on the season could just as easily suck up all the earth's heat to produce a killing frost at night.

A row of onions, their withered stalks neatly pigtailed, kept snugly underground and a late stand of kale expanded with a corrugated hardiness. But the tomatoes look very vulnerable, he thinks: the two Big Boys and three Good Sisters raised themselves on the lattices he had built around them, self-contained jungles. In fact, he had named each plant similarly—Borneo, Yucatán, Kenya. It is a secret. He picks the green fruit and places them in an old bushel basket that was nearby; he had come across some unusual pickle recipes in an old *Farmer's Almanac,* and it would be fun to try them out.

"Where did you learn to do all this?" Ruth asked one time. It was their first spring in Hammertown and he had been preparing the garden, turning the soil, putting down onion sets. Her question also included the brick barbecue she perched upon, in cutoff jeans and one of his large flannel shirts. Cooper had come across plans for the outdoor fireplace, one side of it a clever trash burner, in an old issue of *Mechanics Illustrated.*

"Did you learn everything from those magazines?" Ruth laughed and rolled her eyes. Cooper continued to spade the soil, mixing the rotted manure a farmer had given him the day before. She had gotten off the hard perch, and walked to the garden fence, the outline of the brick printed on the flesh of her thighs. It was a little too high for her to step over. Cooper remembered saying nothing, intent on working the ground with his back to her. He should have turned around, maybe, he thinks now; maybe he should have turned around or said something to her, at least told her about the hours spent as a boy pouring over *Country Gentlemen* or some similar publication there on 23rd Street. But she had heard it all before.

There must be twenty-five or thirty pounds of green tomatoes in the bushel basket; the bushes have been cleaned off. About two dozen pints of pickles or relish, he figures. Through the back window placed just over the old porch glider, he can see directly into the kitchen and can see the table between the two windows that face the road before their house.

Hal sits beside Ruth at the table as the two of them look over the school papers he just brought home. The boy is a head taller than the woman, but the careful purse of his mouth and the halting scan of one large, blunt finger over the red construction paper placed on the tabletop clearly defines the relationship. Ruth has been holding his free hand in both of hers, and as Cooper watches, she raises her left hand to embrace Hal's shoulders. Her arm does not quite reach across him. "That's well done, Hal," he hears her say. "You have done well."

They had sat so in the porch glider, cleaned off in those days, the whole porch a pleasant, extra "room" in warm weather; Ruth had even strung part of the porch rail for morning glories, the string slicing the space under the eaves into wedges. "Zoo-oo-oom!" little Hal had crooned, his voice going out of control.

"No, not zoom," Cooper said, "but Monte—"

"Zoo-oo-oom," the boy almost yelled this time and laughed. He had caught on to the game, the joke.

"Shush, now," Ruth said, and coaxed him with the arm around his shoulders. "Listen to Daddy."

"Montezuma. It's a Mexican name," Cooper added as if for the boy's benefit. He could just barely see the round, moonlike face in the deepening twilight of the porch. The kitchen light silhouetted the two on the swing sofa. "Maybe some veterans of the 1848 war with Mexico may have named the place."

"Of course," Ruth said in the dark.

"Montezuma, Iowa. This outfit made marvelous kits of

flying models. I'd order them—write to Montezuma, Iowa—from advertisements in magazines. They had marvelous plans. Sometimes I would just look at the plans for days, maybe even a week or more. They were beautiful."

A flying circus of gnats did giddy stunts against the darkening sky, and Jack Cooper waved them away from his face and continued. "All the parts had to be cut out of sheets of balsa wood. None of this die-cut business where you only pop them out. No plastic either. You had to cut out each rib, each piece, with a razor blade. Sometimes the parts would be so small that the balsa would split, so you'd have to start all over again."

"How long did all this take?"

"Days. All the parts had to be cut out and sanded and then matched against the plan patterns exactly. I'd spend a week on just the formers for the fuselage. The wing ribs would take a weekend."

"Stretching it out," Ruth laughed. The sound was heavy, almost drowsy. She was in complete shadow as she sat on the glider, with only the dim light of the kitchen behind her. That piece of furniture had come with the place along with the jars of preserves in the basement. He had never got around to cleaning the rust off, though he had oiled the pins at its joints so it moved noiselessly on its pivots. "Almost," Ruth answered his silent question. He could see the boy's large head had slipped beneath her shoulder. "A little more," I think.

"Sometimes parts like the nose cowling had to be carved from a solid block of balsa," Cooper continued softly, a seductive tone in his voice. "That would take a long time. I could measure its shape from templates I had cut from the plans and glued to cardboard. Even the wheels had to be made; several layers of sheet balsa glued together and cut round, sanded."

"A lot of sanding, Mr. Sandman," Ruth said quietly. The glider went to and fro easily.

"It took me a long time to carve the propeller, all those reverse and compounded curves; the whole blade balanced. Everything had to be just right." Feet drummed against the porch floor. "Well, not yet, I guess."

"Quiet now, Hal. Daddy's getting to the good part. Put it together, Jack."

"I'd put wax paper over the plan so I could work directly over it but keep the glue off. I always saved these plans, just to look at. I could pin the balsa stringers directly over the plan; they'd be about one-sixteenth square or larger, depending on the size of the plane. Then the braces would be cut and glued. But only just enough glue, if you wanted it to fly well."

"Not make it too heavy," Ruth said.

"Right. So two sides of the fuselage would be made exactly alike—exactly alike—and then these were joined with crosspieces, so you ended up with a long, slender box that usually tapered toward the tail. The angles had to be perfect right angles. Sometimes I'd have to redo this part several times before I got it straight. The formers were then glued to this framework, the stringers fitted into their notches, and all of a sudden, the whole graceful shape of the airplane's body materialized right in my hands. It had changed from the square, boxy rig into a complicated mass of curves and lines. It would be fragile yet amazingly strong. It was abstract yet it was substance, too. It was an idea of something that would fly. Sometimes I'd put an airplane together but never cover the framework with tissue paper. Just hang it in my room to look at."

"A skeleton." He could hear her move and sensed she was looking down to check on the boy. "Ouch. Hal move your head. It's too heavy. Ow, ow."

"Toot," said the boy.

"No, tit," Ruth said with an exasperated laugh. The glider rocked and the round shape of her head moved to the left, beyond the light frame of the window, and disappeared.

Jack Cooper changed his position on the porch railing to swing one leg free. "But usually I'd covered them with tissue—all colors. Reds. Yellow. Dark purplish blues and greens. The scraps of the stuff would float in the air of my room for days like strange leaves. This was a delicate process, fitting and doping the tissue to the framework."

"Dopey. You're a dope," the boy cried out, catching on to part of the game they were playing. "Dopey-dope. Dopey-dope."

"Oh, Hal! Let's forget it." Ruth shifted her arm and sat up.

"That's what it was called," Cooper persisted. "It was made from banana oil and acetone. I used to get high on it without knowing it, I guess. The whole thing had to be doped. The tissue to seal it, protect it from moisture, and give extra strength." Clay Peck's truck passed up the road; he would be the only one using the road this time of year.

"When it was all assembled, I'd take the Fifth Avenue bus," Cooper continued. "It ran both ways then, uptown as well as downtown. It'd be a Saturday morning, sometimes Sunday. Few people on the bus. Everything had a clean, sunny smell to it. But no crush and no one to crush against me and my airplane. Or to take it from me. That happened once on the subway. More than once, the bus driver would pull over to the curb and stop the bus—can you believe that?—and have me demonstrate the model to the passengers. I remember some of them moving from the rear seats to the front, like school kids getting close to the teacher. And it was me.

"Some of these planes would have a wingspread of three feet and took several strands of rubber to power them. I loved looking down through the hole in the nosepiece, down along the length of the rubber motor. The interior of the fuselage was so orderly, so neat. The uprights, the stringers—all the exact parallels I had pieced together, all one now. The tissue, drum tight and like armor. Yet it was so thin, so easily punctured. And the whole thing could be turned to ash in seconds."

"We may have lost him," Ruth said softly.

"So a first few test glides in Central Park. Wings level, nose slightly heavy. Then wind the propeller a few turns and test for torque, angle of turn. Make corrections by breathing on the rudder and the wing tips to warp them. The first real flight. One hundred, two hundred turns on the propeller. There was always the fear that I would make one last turn, one too many, and the whole plane would collapse, like an accordian. But that never happened. There were some models, much larger than mine, where the whole propeller and rubber motor would be stretched way out; it took several people to hold the plane and wind up the motor, using a hand drill fastened to the propeller. But these were endurance models and looked like no actual airplane. Mine looked like real planes. The *Winnie Mae.* The Curtis P-6-E. All the World War I planes. Like that. So then, the propeller tense, the whole plane trembling for release, I'd raise it to the sky—and let it pull away from my hands. Up it would go."

"Up—up—away." The boy's voice was like a frayed line thrown from a raft drifting away.

"That's right, Hal. Up, up, away the plane would fly. It would actually fly. The propeller spun. The rubber motor unwound knot by knot pulling the plane higher and higher. I had made all that. I had done that. I could see every strut, every piece of wood I had cut and glued. The whole plane became illuminated, the daylight came through. It became a pattern flying—all my dreams—flying above my head." There was yet a silvery patch of light lying over the hills. Cooper turned toward this sky.

"I could see my work. I remembered the rainy afternoon I had made a certain part of it. I remembered the homework I had not done to make the landing gear. One Saturday my father asked me to help him with an inventory, and I remembered the lie I told him about homework in order to redo a tail assembly. All the hours, the excuses, the lies were suspended over my head—free. It seemed as if the plane would never come down."

"But it did come down," Ruth said. She had eased off the glider and stood beside him. Her face had been barely defined, the large whites of the eyes almost invisible as she turned to match his gaze. They looked into the darkness where the new garden had been tilled that afternoon. A last glimmer seeped into the night sky.

CHAPTER
FOUR

THE Ansonia Hotel wallows in the gray drizzle. Cooper sometimes thinks the building resembles an ocean liner, a caricature of one anyway, because the domed cupolas and gaudy balconies are too ornate for the bridges and superstructure of an actual ship. Unless, of course, this vision has sailed into the intersection of Broadway and 79th Street from another world where such rococo fancies were the norm for steamships, a companion world that exists beside this one, he thinks, that knows the extraordinary as commonplace. This tall prow wedged into the morning mist is a cruel hoax played upon any shipwrecked sailor, for the towering dreadnought seems ready to run him down where he stands on the desert island of the street median, waiting for the light to change.

Cooper feels adrift also. On the train down from Green River, he had felt part of himself loosen and give way, almost float, and he had been sad. It should be Ruth on the train, Ruth coming down here to meet with an editor and talk about her poetry. This morning, she had gone into her office and closed the door, saying good-bye to him from within, as if her books and manuscripts in there were to insulate her from the why and how of his leaving. But she had a lot of revisions to do, she told him, and had to get busy, get them done, as if couriers waited in the backyard by the circle of faded chrysanthemums, ready to rush her poems to someone like Don Jacobs as she got them done, got them right.

But he also carried with him into New York that sense of loss a former city man anticipates for the places and byways that have vanished and been replaced almost overnight so that walking through a once-familiar neighborhood can make for a peculiar disenfranchisement with each awkward step.

The stores he remembered from his youth were no longer on the lower East Side, their premises transformed into chic shops that sold cheeses or woven fabrics or basketware. The last time he brought Hal to see a specialist—the boy had been having nosebleeds—Cooper had made a quick tour. Once Hal was in the doctor's examination room, he jumped into a taxi and gave the driver directions. A new bank like a large appliance had been set down over the corner where the magazine store had been located.

Down below Gramercy Park and east across Third, the taxi slowly passed the old tenement building where he and his father had kept house, but the building had been restored. The brick face had been scrubbed to an elegant complexion. Window boxes graced every level, and an orderly arrangement of garbage cans sat before each doorway. A few spindly seedlings, captive within tight wrappings, were staked out in open squares of the sidewalk. The street had always needed a little shade, Cooper thought.

But the picture-frame shop still kept business beside the apartment doorway. It had been the one "classy" establishment in the neighborhood, but it now seemed a bit worn. There was a large plastic sign in the window promoting a copying service; the main trade, Cooper figured. Picture frames marked off the dusty drop cloth and Rosa Bonheur's white horses still raced neck and neck within the oval corral of a hand-finished walnut frame. He and Ruth would joke that the main reason she had moved in with him was the convenience of the frame shop.

"You are lucky to have pictures of so many relatives," the framer had told her. "So many relatives."

"Yes," said Ruth. "They were from Delancey Street." The pictures came from a junk store on Delancey Street.

If he stayed on the subway this morning, he would have passed beneath the Ansonia Hotel or maybe it would have thundered overhead like one of those old submarine pictures—all of them in the subway train waiting for the fatal depth charge to explode. He would have gone on to Van Cortland Park, the end of the line, then walked through the park to Woodlawn Cemetery. His father's burial there was only meant to be temporary. Sometimes Cooper felt sorry he had lost track of his father's family in Iowa. He could have moved him there. But he gets off the train at the 72nd Street station and walks up to 74th Street and toward Central Park, toward Kelly Novak's apartment.

"You don't even know where he is in the cemetery?" Ruth licked her fingers clean. They were having pastry and some espresso one time on MacDougal Street. "You can't find your father's grave?"

"Oh, they have a record of it. I could find it, if I had to."

"Don't you remember your mother at all?"

"No."

"What happened to her? Didn't your father tell you anything?"

"She was a nurse. The last he heard she was the school nurse at a junior college for women in New Jersey. Then, he lost track."

"How come you're so straight? Don't you have any hostility at all? Isn't anything buried down deep in that meringue? Maybe your anger is like poisoned sugar. I sometimes don't understand you."

Ruth's eyes had lifted in wonder. But she looked tired, too, and her eyes always got that lighter-than-air expression when she became fatigued. This was the night of her first public reading, a real reading that Jacobs had arranged for her at New York University.

"I'm sorry," Cooper laughed, then took his apology seriously. She had. He took off his glasses, looked through them in the dim light of the café, and polished them with a corner of the paper napkin. "I really would like to come."

"Please," Ruth made a face. "We've talked about this. It would make me too nervous to have you there, listening to me. But come to the party at Don's apartment later. You know the address. Why not?" He had shaken his head. "What will you do?"

"There's a revival of *Grand Illusion* at the Eighth Street Cinema. I may check that out."

If anyone deserved a break it was Ruth. "What's fair?" she had shrugged that afternoon when he returned from Novak's barn. "Listen, I think it's great." But she had swallowed hard and turned into the house to sit and stare at a notebook and at the lines of her small, neat script. Somewhere in that sequence of those words was the secret of her own recognition.

Kelly Novak had tapped a key to send a message that surprised him; his quick response to it had surprised him. It was like a message from another world, out of one of his own fictions. Flip Winslow waiting for a code of some sort, maybe a faint voice coming over the transmitter of his secret airfield.

"Help, help." C'mon, pal, Winslow would call to his simian sidekick, and the big fourteen-cylinder Twin-Wasp C-3 radial roared into life.

"Do you suppose she's really serious?" he had asked Ruth.

"About you?" she responded. "Are you?" A pair of red-tailed hawks reconnoitered over the swamp just then, so Cooper did not see the expression on her face.

There is an obscure configuration chiseled into the keystone of the doorway of Kelly Novak's brownstone, an elaborate monogram of the original builders that still effectively supports the arch over the iron grilled entrance though it is indecipherable. "Cooper?" the woman's voice is distorted by the speaker in the foyer. "Come to the second floor. The door's open. I'm on the phone."

The barrenness of her apartment surprises him. He had thought it would be more designed, not so much in a luxurious mode but more of an ensemble. Tasteful, would be Ruth's suggestion, and there is a transient quality about the furnishings in the high-ceilinged, white living room that some would attribute to an expression of minimalism. Her voice came from several rooms beyond, and it seemed to Cooper to alternate between commands and pleas.

In the absence of color the prints of Mondrian and Klee taped to the walls are even more startling. One is off center. A portable television is on the floor at one corner. A large, leather sofa next to a round table, the legs of which have been cut off below the knee level, are set before a shallow fireplace. The hearth has also been painted white. A bouquet of dried flowers lies athwart the grate, put there a long time ago he thinks, while a vase was looked for; but the search had been interrupted and, then, dropped so the flowers and leaves had turned crisp and brown. The stacks of books and manuscripts on the floor, the table, and every surface top, such as the mantle below the large mirror, are the only details Cooper finds that he expected; their familiarity is somehow trite in a setting that seems to have been slung together while he climbed the stairs from the street.

A flash of scarlet down through several open doorways. Kelly is waving to him, the phone cocked at one ear, her youthful eyes brighten with an unspoken greeting. She is wearing a red velvet tunic that falls to hip length over pressed jeans. Her hair is pulled back and held by a red print scarf tied in a large bow. He follows her beckoning, for she has turned and disappeared from the doorway, the sounds of her conversation giving him the way, though he could have scarcely got lost. Several pigeons fall from the rooftop and then take flight. Their wings clap the air, almost a self-congratulatory sound that goes with the miracle, and their shadows pass quickly down the white walls and into the next room   a sort of study with a sleeping alcove.

"Pigeons applauding themselves!" Ruth would exclaim. This would be the morning after.

"That's what it sounded like," Jack Cooper said and laughed. They were in the kitchen and Ruth was heating some old coffee. "It's just the way it struck me, that's all."

"Not bad," Ruth said under her breath. "So she has all these pictures of her daughter?"

"Or it could be a niece. I don't think she's been married—I mean, had children. Just a hunch. But in this second room, there are these photographs tacked all over. Bulletin board. Walls. She's a fat girl. About twenty, looks like."

"How much you think she pays for this apartment? That's an expensive neighborhood."

"I couldn't guess. Six or seven hundred . . ."

"At least," Ruth said tasting the soup.

"But the bathroom is no great shakes. Tile is cracked. An old tub and a skylight that has been patched with plywood. The kitchen is nice."

"Your room," Ruth laughed.

"No, I mean she's apparently spent a lot redoing it. Everything's taken down to the brick walls and she's got copper pots suspended from a metal frame that hangs down from the middle of the ceiling. The kitchen is where the phone is, but it has a long, long cord. She could talk from any part of the apartment."

"She's probably got an extension by the bed. You didn't see that yet, I guess."

"No. What does that mean?"

He spooned some of the hot, tomato soup that Ruth had put before him. "You think she's after my body? That's kind of insulting isn't it. I thought it's my prose she wants."

"Join the club," Ruth said. She had sat across from him to eat her soup, one leg tucked under her, her back primly straight.

"Then, anyway, she motions me into this back room. It's a dining room, still all white but with a large purplish print on the wall. I couldn't get the name of the artist. There's a terrace off of this; French doors open out onto it. I could see some lawn furniture. A chaise. A stack of flowerpots in one corner. Some of that woven fence around the three sides. It must be pleasant in good weather. What's this in the soup? Basil?"

"Something of this and something of that," Ruth said. She seemed unusually gay and Jack was sure it had nothing to do with his good luck. Perhaps some of her poems had been accepted for publication. Her hair was down, loose upon her shoulders. "So, do you have a contract?"

"No contract."

"No contract," Ruth looked shocked.

"Well, it's different than other books," Cooper would remember just how Kelly Novak had explained it.

"You don't want to get caught up in a silly contract," Kelly says after she hangs up the phone. "Do you want to deal with a stupid woman like that." She points to the white telephone fixed to the wall by its long vinyl vine. "That stupid woman." She gives the word a heavy emphasis, like the last notes of an aria. "That's Bean's administrative assistant and you would have to deal with her if you had a contract. What would that mean anyway? A thousand dollars? Is that that important to you? You don't need the money. Do you want to fuck around with stupid women like that one?" Again she waves toward the phone. Her fingernails are neatly trimmed, polished with clear lacquer. They look feminine and—Cooper tries to think—capable. "Why are you smiling?" Kelly stops short, her own mouth turning up.

"What I want is that you and I work on this book together, your imagination and gift and my expertise direct ing it to the right packaging. Already sold. Subsidiary rights—everything. Can you imagine the movie this is going to make? Baby, I'm going to make you a millionaire. I have someone, a screenwriter, who owes me a favor and I'll have him sit down with you and do the script. You're going to be a quarter-of-a-million-dollar screenwriter, kiddo. See, that's what I want. That's what you want. We can come to Wilson with a finished product and say, here it is—you want it— *then,* we talk contract. See what I mean?" She has talked with both hands in the air.

"It sounds like—aren't you on the same side? I mean with the publisher?"

"Old Wilson enjoys adversarial positions." Cooper almost laughs but sees, in time, that she's serious. Kelly puts herself into the corner of a small sofa and takes up a bag of knitting. It looks like a long scarf in different colored wools. "I read what you sent me. Now you read what you've brought there."

"Out loud?"

"It's just us." The long knitting needles begin to clack. "Let's hear it."

The empty cockpit of the little Curtiss Hawk 24 was immaculate, and Winslow reached down and placed his hand against the panel of the radio transmitter. Hard to tell if it were warm from the China Sea sun or from engine heat— say a few hours before this morning when he had heard that faint message come through his receiver at Home Plate.

"I like that," Kelly Novak interrupts though her knitting continues. "Calling his secret airfield 'Home Plate.'"

The plane's powder-blue fuselage, the black lace design on the pink wing tips, not a single bullet hole anywhere. The fuel gauges were barely half down. Elena Underwood must have landed on this outer beach of this atoll on her own. She was not forced down by those Suki-Yakis he had seen earlier. Winslow imagined how prettily the aviatrix must have set down the little pursuit ship on the hard-packed sand. He had had a little trouble bringing down the much heavier Breda, but the Italian attack fighter was parked up the beach and without a scratch on the glossy black surface that seemed to double the very light that struck it.

"What?" Cooper asks. Kelly Novak had made a sound in her throat, but the knitting needles continue their rhythmic clatter.

"Nothing. We can come back to this when we start the rewriting. But while we're stopped, I want to ask you about this scene you sent me. When he hears the message. When he's playing baseball with this ape."

"They're not playing baseball, exactly."

"Well, okay, he's throwing pitches and the ape is catching. The needles go faster. "I mean, that may be a little too much."

"The orangutan only has to sit there with the big glove; he's more a target than a catcher, and Winslow has trained him to roll the ball back, throw it underhand. It makes his operation of the plane's rear machine guns more plausible. I'm very thirsty."

"Sure." Kelly Novak goes into the kitchen and opens the refrigerator. "Oh, that stupid Bruce never brought my groceries yet. I had some—"

"Juice. Anything," Cooper says.

"No juice. I have a half bottle of Meursault. . . ."

"No, no wine. Milk?"

"No milk." The woman continues to look into the refrigerator expectantly, as if it might produce what's being requested. Should he keep asking for things, he wonders, until he guesses what she keeps there?

"How about? . . ." She pauses and rises a cup to her nose. "Oh, that's awful. It's gone bad. I could fix you some tea. I think I have some tea bags." She raises on tiptoe to reach a tin on the top shelf. "If that stupid man had only brought what I had ordered at the store."

"Just water," Cooper says. The large purplish print on the wall seems to be an Impressionist study of a jungle, humid looking and laden with shadows. "Water would be fine."

"Here's some of the city's finest," the editor says as she brings him a glass of water. "But this comes from up your way, doesn't it? The Catskills? What bothers me about this ape is that you haven't named him yet. He's got to have a name. What would you call him?"

Where was Elena? As if to find the answer, Winslow's simian sidekick had pulled off his helmet and goggles as soon as the blades of the Hamilton-Spencer propeller had stopped turning. He had slipped over the side of the Breda to amble on rear feet and front knuckles across the hot sand and into the dense jungle that grew down to the edge of the water.

Two months before someone wandering into the snooker and trophy room of the Britannia Club on Singapore Beach Road would have sized up the two men chatting in the corner over a pair of brandy and sodas as a well-turned out uncle—something exmilitary in his crisp mustache and erect bearing—entertaining his fresh-faced nephew from America. Their dinner jackets bore the recognizable sharp lapels of Dunhill tailoring. The boy, the stranger would assume, was probably just out of one of those eastern universities that train its graduates for a life of idle snobbery. Little would he suspect that the younger man was the legendary Black Ace whose sable-laquered Breda 65 swept the skies in the cause of justice and that the "uncle" was Colonel Willis Smith, the director of Q-4, the man who single-handedly foiled the rape of Hang Chow in 1922.

"You are to find Elena Underwood," Smith said with a pleasant smile. It might appear he asked the health of a relative. "She's somewhere in the Anambas. We've got you set up near Subi Island. Everything you need. We'll call it Home Plate."

"I like that," the young airman responded. He sipped his drink. Winslow rarely drank, but he thought he recognized the brandy as being a Courgoine '09, probably out of Smith's private stock.

The older intelligence agent's hazel eyes darkened as they carefully took in the room and its occupants. "It is imperative that you find her—and find her alive. Strange things are happening in the Gulf of Siam and we need to know about them."

"I'll leave tomorrow. By way of Sydney?"

"Quite. We've put your hairy friend out as a specimen you're taking to the Sydney Zoo."

"I hope he doesn't find that out," Winslow tried to joke.

"Right. And Terrence," Colonel Smith was one of the few who could use Winslow's given name and walk away, "keep the ball low."

"What does that mean?" Kelly Novak interrupts Cooper.

"The best pitch, the most difficult to hit, is thrown low in the strike zone." The apartment becomes silent, as if a timer has shut down all activity. It's a melancholy silence and Cooper imagines the apartment noiseless each day just like this, not even the occasional clack of knitting needles to disturb it, only the occasional guttural acceleration of a bus on Central Park West outside, moving away. Kelly Novak continues to knit. She had said he was to get "everything down" before she began to make revisions, but obviously she was doing this as they went along. Something was missing.

Cooper gets up and takes his glass into the kitchen for more water. It is more an excuse to move, to break the static quiet that seems to have fit over them like a glass bowl. He counts the dishes and silverware in the rack and wonders if their number represents a supper party for four or five, or whether these have been the place settings of five solitary meals. He always thought she would eat in restaurants with large menus. The sound of her knitting continues and he senses he has been granted the freedom of the apartment while she considers what he has read. He turns into the next room.

As he would tell Ruth the next morning, most of the pictures were examples of that kind of photography in which a watercolor brush tried to overcome the unforgiving exactness of the camera lens. The girl's image was no clearer in the snapshots: a plump little bride in First Communion lace and ruffles; a sturdy teenager beside a bicycle, though a wary look had come into the eyes; and then a hefty highschool graduate in rented baccalaureate gown. These three pictures made a triptych on the top of a Nordic-design bureau, or what Cooper assumed was a bureau because of its place near the sleeping area. It could just as easily be a large filing cabinet. To the right of a mirror was a large, colored print that looked to have been taken the same time as the graduation picture, but with the mortarboard removed.

The arch of neck, the glance over the shoulder, and the head set at a certain angle were all part of a formula Cooper recognizes from old photographic magazines with advice on lighting and settings meant to give spirit to dullness, expectancy to worn acceptance.

"It was then I felt she was pulling me back," Cooper would tell Ruth as they had their coffee. "I had gone as far as she wanted me to go and she was winding me back. Do you think some people can hear another's concentration? Or can concentration become so intense that it sends off—"

"Alarms?" Ruth supplied. She brought a bowl of fruit to the table.

"Not sound as we think of it but something, well, maybe we think of the 'silent dead' not because they cannot speak but because they lack concentration. Or the concentration has gone from the mental to the physical."

"Where in hell is all this coming from?" Ruth asked as she selected a pear. "Where do you get these ideas?"

Her eyes had rounded with astonishment, a sudden intimacy. He did not feel like answering their desire just then. "Well, anyway, she spoke to me as if she could tell I was looking at the girl's pictures. 'That's Mary Novak,' she said. Just like that."

"That's the girl's name? Mary Novak?" Cooper shrugged. "She must be a niece."

"Where's Hal?" Cooper asked. There had been something missing that morning about the place, and it was Hal. The boy was seldom in the house anymore, except to sleep, eat, and do his special skill books at the kitchen table; yet Cooper sensed something different about his absence at this hour on a Saturday. He couldn't quite place it, but it was off somehow. He knew he was spending more and more time with Clay Peck.

"He's up flying his kite on the Knob," Ruth told him. "You haven't seen his kite, have you? He's worked on it up at Peck's. I guess Clay has helped him put it together. It's really pretty good. I went up and watched him fly it yesterday. Now, do you want to hear my news?" Cooper opened his mouth to reply, but Ruth plugged it with a slice of pear and capped this with her own mouth.

"You went up there?" he finally said. "You watched him?" His questions put aside the eager light in her eyes and what she had been waiting to tell him.

What Jack Cooper would not tell Ruth was the actual way Kelly Novak "pulled him back" as he was to put it.

"That's Mary Novak," she says, as if she had heard the hum of his concentration but more likely has assumed his silence meant he was looking at the pictures, the only real objects in the room that could be inspected. A soft plop, and the ball of yarn rolls on the floor and through the doorway like a playful, multicolored kitten. Jack Cooper returns it knowing that he might be joining a retinue of footmen, like the tardy, forgetful Bruce, for example; the idea amuses him, but he keeps this from Ruth because she would recognize the scene, too. So he would not tell her about picking up the ball of yarn and winding up the slack strand, which in effect, pulls him closer to Kelly Novak who knits on the sofa, who has not ceased the rhythmic play of the long, plastic needles.

"So let's hear more," she says without looking up.

He returns the ball of yarn and says, "Is this a scarf for Mary Novak?" The editor only smiles, doesn't even look up, but with a free hand motions him back to the table and his manuscript.

"And that's all?" Ruth was fidgeting, eager to tell him something.

But it hadn't been all. On the train home, he reviews an idea that had come to him when he had left Kelly Novak's apartment. On a whim he had walked west, all the way to Riverside Drive and the Hudson River, then turned south and then back east. Then he had taken a bus downtown, got off in midtown, and gone below to a subway to take a train going south; but he got off in the Chelsea area and then walked east to Lexington Avenue, where he boarded an IRT subway going north to get off at Grand Central Station. His route had been whimsical, devious, and almost like a puzzle that one part of him had laid to test another. He had solved each of its steps with delight, a joyous bounce to his steps as he took the subway stairs two at a time; yet, where was he going? Only back to Grand Central, where he had a ticket to take the last evening train back to Green River. But it was the way he got there, this wandering, crisscross path he made across Manhattan Island. On the train, looking at himself in the black mirror of the coach's window, he sees a whimsical, devilish flash in his spectacled eyes. For years, he reminds himself, his path between their small house and the Black Ace back-issue store in Hammertown has been along one route, back and forth. Even stopping by Clay Peck's or trips to Green River were only extensions of the same straight line. Yet, that afternoon he had gone from point A to point B differently.

That this possibility was urban was the revelation he thinks of sharing with Ruth. Was it likely, say, that the first city man was the guy who, one morning on the well-worn path to the water hole, was distracted by something fluttering in the jungle off to the right, a butterfly, perhaps. He leaves the path to follow the butterfly, gets lost, but eventually finds his way back to the water hole. Meantime, the idea of a city has taken form. The concept so energizes Jack Cooper that he changes seats in the train and spends the last half hour of the journey standing in the foyer between the cars.

But by the time he reaches Green River and takes Roy's Taxi home, it is too late; Ruth is already asleep. In any event, his urge to talk about it has been censured by the thought that he must have read about this somewhere, probably in an old *Scientific American* or *Philosophy Today*, and that the idea can not be original with him.

CHAPTER
FIVE

"WE should have seen it coming." Ruth slices another pear into quarters.

Cooper watches her, takes the piece of fruit she offers without looking at it. "Why think of Ethel Knox?" On a beautiful morning like this, he wants to add.

"I met the workshop last night," she continues. "While you were in New York with your editor"—she can barely say the words straight—"and as I listened to my ladies read their poems, I remembered Ethel at those meetings. Humming to herself, blushing, trying to make us act *like* ladies. That's all."

But that wasn't all. Cooper sensed a resignation in her, a turn of her head on the slender neck, that saddened him. Her melancholy burned his conscience, the thought he had yesterday on the train, that he was the one going to talk with an editor about something he had written and not Ruth.

Meanwhile, she had spent her time with housewives,

shopkeepers, and widows—amateurs in his mind, compared to her, with whom she shared her insights and energies. The workshop initially was a project she had invented to help her tenure case at the college but now it seemed to be a way to keep busy, something to do. Maybe, he was afraid, it had become an answer to the question she asked the other night. "What's to become of me?"

After the first time, he wanted to read no more of the poems submitted at these meetings and brought home by Ruth, shown to him and sometimes even scattered over him as he lay in bed, maybe looking at an old magazine. "Look at these!" Ruth would say fiercely, as if the poems enforced some argument she had been having with him all the way home though, all that time, he had been peaceably waiting for her, leafing through a *Popular Mechanics*. After reading the poems, he sometimes had trouble looking their authors in the face, meeting these pleasant-faced women in stores in Green River or suddenly coming upon one of them buying popcorn in the lobby of the movie house.

Dimpled and plump, gray and lean, young to middle-aged—they shared the same history, carried the same freight of woman flesh that had been possessed and im-pounded by men. Fathers and brothers sexually abusing them. Husbands and boyfriends beating them up. Whole, glistening viscera of female angers had been exposed to him, and he had trouble matching those angers with the smiles he would encounter at the supermarket meat coun-ter. Ethel Knox had seemed different.

"Remember Rosemary Brower?" Ruth is saying. "She with the degree from Smith College." Her mimicry of the woman's pretentions makes him laugh. "One night she asked Ethel, 'Hasn't anything bad ever happened to you? Doesn't anything bother you?' Ethel's poems were like the cookies she brought to the meetings—sugary and half done.

All about good old Ron appearing in the doorway. Birds making nests on her porch. 'Like letters from camp,' someone said. The girl who runs the fabric store in Stout Falls. You know who I mean, I've seen you look at her. Anyway, she said, 'Don't you know letters from heaven are boring, Ethel?'"

"What did Ethel say?"

"Usually, she'd start humming and blush. Then, laugh. She'd sing a few lines of some old song as if that did anything." Ruth pointed a pear slice at him for emphasis. "As if the wisdom of Irving Berlin or Cole Porter could give the answer."

Her remark started an inventory in his head of the sheet music section his father used to keep in the old store. He couldn't remember a single song, in fact, written by a woman, and this evidence for Ruth's argument quickly excited him. She could do a paper on it. Song lyrics written by men that assisted their dominance of women, a subtle brainwashing in three-quarter time.

"I just thought of something," he says.

"No, wait a minute. Let me finish." Ruth waves him off. She tastes her fingers, uses a napkin. "One evening Rosemary submits one of her artful numbers, replete with classical allusions. We were so terribly impressed. This number is about Orpheus looking around at Eurydice, so she goes back to Hades. Right?" Ruth is giggling; her good humor is a sudden warmth like the passing sunlight on the tablecloth. She has raised up slightly and resettles on one folded leg, leans forward.

"So Orpheus descending in Hammertown. Okay? Everyone takes a shot as to why Eurydice turns back to hell. Everyone but Ethel. She just sits there like some old sibyl stoned on her own face powder. Playing with her beads. Ladylike. 'How about it, Ethel?' someone finally asks her.

'Why did she go back to hell?' 'Well,' now listen to this, 'maybe because he didn't recognize her, looked like he didn't know her.'

"Then she tells this long story about one time at Myrtle Beach—she and Ron going around the buffet table. Seems like that's the sport at Myrtle Beach, going around buffet tables. Anyway, she's right behind him, a plate of chicken à la king in one hand and the fruit salad in the other, and he turns around and looks right at her. He doesn't recognize her. Old Ron in his white shoes and white belt and a blank look on his face. Who's this lady with her plateful of chicken à la king? It's Ethel; after thirty years—it's me—Ethel."

Then Cooper asks, "And?" Ruth's eyes have become far-seeing, a luminous pressure within that seems to make her blind to everything before her, to him. "What next?"

"Last night, I wondered if it wasn't right then—talking about Myrtle Beach, how he looked right through her— maybe, right then, Ethel Knox decided to turn back. Make the jump."

Cooper has been studying the headless cuckoo above the stove. The bird, stuck on its platform, waits for them. The kitchen and the two people sitting at the table by the window are a display too, part of an exhibit that represents domestic life in the northeastern United States at ten on a November morning. Keeping his gaze on the clock, Cooper deliberately fits words together, almost thinking he could activate the bird, wishing he could make it pop back into its Swiss *hutte* at the sound of his voice.

"So, this kite. What about this kite Hal made?"

"It's quite wonderful," Ruth replies, still distant. Her mood returns gradually. "They came and got me, insisted I go up to the Knob and watch him fly it. That's when they dropped off that thing in the garden. Did you really tell Peck you wanted it?"

"Did I? I can't remember," Cooper laughs. Last night when he came home, he had noticed the old birdbath. The sculpture rises from the center of the frost-burned chrysanthemums in the backyard. The boy rides the dolphin away from the house in a northerly direction, and the clear, midmorning light magnifies the statue's details. The scraps of wings on the sprite's back seem incapable of flight and the rain-worn slab of hand points toward the still, heavy-leaved woods of the swamp as if boy and dolphin were preparing to rise into the trees, to leave one element for another.

"Maybe I did," Cooper laughs again as he pours more coffee for them.

"You mean we're going to keep it?" Ruth comes to the window by the sink to stare out into the small yard.

"Sure. Why not," Jack says. His tone of voice surprises him, a hard edge given the three words that might come from fatigue, from the late train back from the city last night; but there was something else. Ruth has pulled back, given in quickly and without argument. Certain signals, a pinning and repinning of her hair, a fiddling with the earring loops, suggest that she is returning to what had been pushing eagerly at her earlier, before the memory of Ethel Knox had sidetracked her.

Well, she went back to the table and sat down as if she were an actress going to a certain passage of the play already rehearsed, he would remember Don Jacobs? Cooper would give her credit for looking a bit chagrined when she asked this, though as she turned to one side, the large, round eyes look boldly into his face. Yes, he remembered Jacobs—the poet she used to know, he added. Well, it seemed she had been keeping in contact—just correspondence, of course—and sending him poems now and then for his review and he used one or two in his magazine and sometimes passed others on to friends who edited similar journals. Yes, Cooper nodded, he had read the magazines and seen her poems in them and had seen the magazines around the house, sometimes with her name on the front cover with other names, some familiar to him but mostly not; he knew little about that business. However, he had meant to congratulate her on these publications and never had but did so now. Why not? Why hadn't he congratulated her? she asked. The gold loops circled the question merrily. Why not? Well, she had always been so funny about his participation in her world, never permitted him to come to her readings, and one never let him read her work. Remember the time she caught him looking at a manuscript left on this very kitchen table? That's different, the one leg crossed over the other began to arc menacingly. This is different— this is work that has been accepted, given recognition in nationally distributed literary quarterlies. Look, she couldn't have it both ways, he said. She didn't want it both ways.

"Look," Jack Cooper is saying, "I have to get down to the store, so tell me what this news is."

"Oh, down to the store," Ruth replies. Her laugh is a series of hard breaths. "Down to the old typewriter is more like it. Give him a little smell of commercial success and the boy becomes a regular sausage factory."

"What does that mean?"

"And speaking of sharing work, were you ever going to show me this great opus of yours?"

"It's just an adventure story."

"So is *Nostromo*."

"You'd—well, it's pretty silly, I think." Cooper takes off his glasses to clean the lenses, but it is really a nervous habit, and he puts them down on the table. Ruth's face becomes a blur of concentrics like one of those ring puzzles. Her voice is clear, delicate.

"It can't be too silly if the number-one editor at Wilson Bean wants to publish it." He hears her take a deep breath. "My God, my God," and the expression in her voice sounds like the one he knows must be on her face. He feels he should apologize, but then he puts his glasses back on.

"So tell me this news."

Well, it happened that Don Jacobs had put her in contact with several writers who had been running an MFA program at this small college in Pennsylvania, and they gave graduate degrees in creative writing, poetry and fiction. Just this week, Ruth got the go-ahead from the State Board of Regents and all this might explain why she may have seemed so distracted, so bitchy, the last few months because all of her energies, her anxieties, had been worn by the effort of getting the Quinn MFA Program here in the campus at Green River. That's the name of the college in Pennsylvania, Quinn College, and the MFA program is famous. What a silly question, she looked at him sidewise. Of course, people weren't coming to Green River to take up residence at the community college. People come here? To live in a dump like Hammertown? Or even Green River? Not very likely? Well, the beauty of it is that it is so simple. The students come to them—through the mail—and they were going to put everything on computer disks.

"Like a correspondence school," Cooper says. The clock attracts his attention once again. He has the urge to fix something, to work with his hands, and he might take it down to the shop later and look up that old magazine that had all the instructions.

Ruth is at the door by the window and is looking out the window into the backyard at the cement figure. He can tell by the stiffness of her spine—her whole figure seems to vi-brate—that she is suddenly very angry. "Not a correspondence school," she says.

"Well, I mean it's similar. The students send their work in by mail and it's looked at, graded or whatever, and then sent back to them. A great idea."

"That's not it. We're going to use computers."

"Well, then how—"

"This is serious. Serious," she whirls around, and he is astonished by her anger, by how it has changed her appearance. The eyes push out and her mouth and lips look black. "Don't you see how serious this is? It will be a symposium of poets, apprentices and masters, freely exchanging their views with none of the constraints of an academic atmosphere but with all of its long-range attributes."

It has been an odd recitation as if her sightless eyes read the words off of a circular tacked to the kitchen wall behind Cooper's head. "It sounds great," he finally says. "Come, sit down. You'll be part of it, too?"

"They have asked me to be the program's executive director," Ruth says simply and sits down. She places her hands together and then presses them between her knees and bows her head.

"Well, that's great," Cooper says. "A lot of work, responsibility, I suppose. What about your own work?"

"Oh, my work." She shrugs. "Sometimes, I feel you're holding *my work,* as you call it, over my head like a rock. I am worn out with my potential. I am tired of you waiting and watching for me to do something—I don't know what. I am so worn out by it, Jack. Beat."

Cooper doesn't know what to say; to comfort her would only anger her. He never knew why she became like this, a mood he ascribed to artistic temperament, the obsession to find the right word. Because sometimes when the right word was found, the whole line falling right, her mood would be totally opposite, euphoric. Like a sexual frenzy, almost. Finally, he gets up and goes to the stove. "Why don't I fix supper? I'll fix something really outrageous."

"You're always feasting me," Ruth smiles but her voice is sad. Her pose is of someone just declared guilty. As Cooper gets out pans from the cupboard, he wonders if he is seeing her whole for the first time?

"Listen, do you have to have a bachelor's degree to enroll in the Quinn program?" Her face tells him his attempt to kid around will fail but he must finish the joke. "Maybe, I'll sign up, too, and get some expert advice on this yarn I'm doing."

"Oh, why do you say things like that. Do you know who the people are on this board?" She lists names that mean nothing to him. "These are writers who are seriously engaged with literature, Jack. Besides, this Novak person will give you all the help you'll need, I'm sure . . ."

She has changed, and Jack Cooper does not know how or why. There is something smaller about her, though when he had put his arm around her she fit against him as always, the same petite being that seemed made for his embrace, an embrace not always sufficient.

In earlier times, a man like Jacobs might come to Hammertown to seduce someone's wife, carrying on the seduction within reach, the liaison known to everyone in Hammertown. Even Red Schuyler would know of it, though the mailman would know nothing of this latest seduction even as he must have carried the letters and messages that procured the act, Old Schuyler, Cooper thought—the name "Red" a nomination of his youth and no longer applicable—whose family boasted an ancestry that included the model for Ichabod Crane, made into a minion, unknowingly acting the go-between for Jacobs's long-distance dalliance. It was the nature of this seduction that made her seem smaller maybe. It may have been his trip to New York, his meeting with Kelly Novak in her world that has miniaturized the familiar surroundings of Hammertown—even Ruth—looked at through the larger end of a telescope. But something else occurred to him.

The disparity between Ruth's small body and the huge ambitions that petite physique supported had been Cooper's first and continuing fascination. Her different sexual exploits didn't really matter, he told himself, as long as the poetry was not touched. Maybe one worked on the other. He had never been sure, so had chosen to be tolerant, almost paternal, while he looked for other reasons for her behavior. But now, this Jacobs seemed to want more than just her body, which he had surely enjoyed before they left the city. Now he wanted to seduce her dreams as well. "Do you remember those weighing machines that used to be all over the city," Cooper says suddenly. Ruth starts. "There used to be one in every subway station; every public place had one. Well, they're gone. I didn't notice it until I got off the subway at 72nd Street. There's one still there, upstairs just as you're about to go out the door into the street. One of those tall numbers with a large round face and a needle like the propeller of a plane. But that's the only one I saw."

"What's all this about?" Ruth half laughs.

"Well, you remember them, don't you? They had them in Brooklyn too, didn't they? Of course they did." He sits down opposite her. "I must have had a drawerful of the little cards the machines would dispense. The needle would sweep around the compass of the face, stop at the right figure, then *plop*, this little card would drop into the metal cup in the front with my weight, sometimes even the date, printed on one side. All neatly printed so you could keep a record of how much you weighed on that particular day."

"And your fortune printed on the other?" Ruth says.

"Yes, that's right, or sometimes a whimsical saying like

you find in a fortune cookie. Or sometimes a historical fact about New York."

"But most times, it would be your fortune," Ruth says.

"Yes, that's right," Jack says. "Most of the time it would be my fortune. And all for a penny."

I'll tell you what it was like, Ron Knox would be saying a couple of months later. The year's first snow has covered the old foundation lines of Hammertown. Knox was looking through a stack of *Architectural Digest*s at the Black Ace. "You're not a college man, Jack, so you don't know about blind dates. Once in a blue moon, you'd get one that would knock your socks off, but mostly, they were just plain awful. Here's what I'm looking for." He had begun sketching in a notebook, copying something from the magazine. The design would end up in a Connecticut ceiling, Cooper was sure.

"You can have that one. Take it home," he offered. He wasn't being generous, he only wanted Knox out of the store quickly. The older man had been waiting for him within the entrance of the old schoolhouse, beating his arms in the crisp, wintry air, and his ordinariness stood out in the crystal clarity of the morning. Cooper had done the morning dishes quickly, eager to get down to the store and into the back room, cozy on such mornings, and to continue the search for Elena Underwood.

I fear the Red Tong have me in their control. Flip Winslow had found her note a few days before in the cockpit of the powder-blue Curtiss Hawk. *Only you can help me.*

But it was Knox who waited for him and it was like coming upon a commonplace detail in a masterwork. Even then, the man had put up the *Architectural Digest* and had started to thumb through the rows of *Modern Photography* and *Mechanics Illustrated* casually, on his way to the *Playboy* and

Penthouse files in the rear. Cooper guessed this perusal was urged by the same literal pulse that warmed the man's imagination to copy the shape and arrangement of architectural details line for line. Another morning he might have felt some sympathy for him; but the day had been so brilliantly cast by the net of fresh snow, Cooper had been eager to work on his story. A town truck clanked by, plow up, on its way to Stout Falls.

"But this third kind," Knox would continue, carefully returning a *Popular Mechanics* to its place, "was the worst because there was nothing basically wrong with them. Good dancers. Pleasant. Some even go all the way, as we used to say. But it was a long weekend. I had thirty years of long weekends." Knox pulled in his upper lip and sucked on part of the white mustache. He turned toward the rear of the store.

"I'm closing up," Cooper would say. He had begun to think of the store as a window through which he would climb every morning, sometimes an evening climb into a place beyond Hammertown. Not another world but more like a side road of the same world, and on this morning he found the entrance blocked by the inert figure of Ron Knox. He had almost mentioned this feeling to Ruth a couple of times but he was afraid her response would be sarcastic. But the window had been there all along, only boarded up.

"Closing up?" Knox would exclaim and his dismay made Cooper turn away, smiling. Several packages the parcel service delivered yesterday were still unopened, but he knew them to be a complete and rare set of the *National Geographic*. "Closing up? Why it's not ten o'clock yet," and he has no place to go, Cooper added to himself. Then the designer's expression would become quickly apologetic; he wrapped the scarf about his throat, as if Cooper's announcement had also singled out something embarrassing, say a food stain on his clothing.

So Cooper gave excuses. "Hal left before breakfast this morning and I want to check his school. I may have to go talk to his principal." But Knox would be withdrawing already, a peppy sort of wave of one hand behind as he walked down the main aisle of the store and out the door.

Cooper heard the crunch of the snow as the older man walked to the station wagon parked on the side. The eight cylinder engine started; the exhaust's heavy chortling evaporated into the midmorning silence as the car pulled away. Had it always been so quiet here, Cooper would wonder? He listened. Not even the drip of melting ice from the eaves of the building—the sun not high enough for that to happen. *I fear the Red Tong have me in their control.*

"Why, *I fear?*" Kelly Novak would ask when they next met for lunch in the city.

"Well, it sounds more mysterious, I guess."

"More ladylike," she said dryly. "I fear you're out of the veal Prince Orloff. Is that right, Mario?"

"That is correct Miss Novak," the waiter replied.

"I fear we must choose something else," Kelly continued.

"Okay, I get it," Cooper had laughed and sipped a little water. The goblet was long-stemmed and looked like crystal. He ordered a piece of fish. The restaurant was near her office; they ate before going to her apartment to work on his manuscript.

"You don't get it," she said after she had ordered. "That's a ladylike voice saying such things. Even in moments of danger she's adjusting her white gloves. I like it. Do more with that, when she makes her appearance. When *does* Elena show up? I'm getting eager to meet her. A hunkie like me being threatened is no big deal; we've always been threatened, but white gloves being soiled is always interesting.

Now do you see? Get it?" Kelly Novak spoke sometimes in ringing absolutes as someone would who had made a career of writing book-jacket blurbs.

Cooper nodded but only vaguely understood; the restaurant claimed his attention. All the years he had lived in New York, a native New Yorker, he had never been in a place like this. The first time she brought him, they had paused at the small bar in the front, and she introduced him to several people as her "brilliant, new novelist." She even told them about the episode with the snake—"a green world hero" she had called him—and a couple of the women had shuddered and touched each other on the arm. He fit in at once, or so he was made to feel.

"I'm very grateful," he would say later as she signed the check, "but shouldn't we talk about some sort of a contract?"

"Why do you want to be tied up in a contract? A first novelist gets peanuts, believe me. No, let's get this book in shape and then let me bring it in to Wilson with maybe a movie option already flagged down." She waved off the waiter's gratitude. "Who's talking to you about contracts?"

She knew the answer, the crinkles about her eyes said so. How was his wife's writing program doing? The computer idea is a nifty angle; everything is being put into a computer, why not poetry. She didn't know Don Jacobs but had heard the name.

"Here." Cooper interrupted her and took something from his pocket. Maybe this was the time, rather than at her apartment. He pulled away layers of white tissues as if he picked apart the fiber of a seedpod, but the kernel inside was powder blue. The blueness of the model airplane vibrates against the white linen tablecloth, and the silverware, cups, the espresso pot contribute to the scaled authenticity. The daisies in a green vase could be palm trees. Even the minute dials and gauges of the instrument panel, just barely seen in the open cockpit, could seem to tick in this articulation.

"Isn't that darling?" Kelly Novak had said. Cooper saw he had surprised her. She even blushed. "Did you make this?"

"It's a Curtiss Hawk 24, Series C. Elena's plane."

"You really made this?" Her hand reached out to touch it then pulled back. The fingernails were painted a glossy scarlet. "You made this?"

"Yes," Cooper replied, embarrassed all of a sudden. He should have waited until they got to her apartment. The restaurant's tables were set close together. Laughter sounded at the front, in the bar, probably her friends who always seem to be waiting for a table while telling jokes. "Are we ready?" He had reached for the little pursuit ship and dropped it into his jacket pocket. "Don't worry," he told Novak's startled expression. "It's more durable than it looks."

Nor could Ruth believe in the strength that would come from those wispy stringers of balsa wood, each one fitted into the right notch and glued so that their aggregate number would be as strong as a small tree limb though weigh as little as a leaf. The paradox intrigued her as did this monoplane shaped like a thermos bottle. How could anything so thick and stubby actually fly?

"It was a wonderful plane for its time," he told her as he held the open kit. His breath was still shortened by the surprise of her gift. The colorful label on the box cover pictured the red airplane and its pilot: AMELIA EARHART'S LOCKHEED VEGA 48″ WINGSPAN. It would be the largest flying model he had ever made. "Where did you find it? They stopped making kits like this long ago."

Ruth squirmed with delight; maybe the question had tickled her in the ribs, and her flannel robe came undone.

Cooper caught the aroma of bath oil. "I looked in the back of one of those magazines you have and found the address of that place you talked about in Iowa. And I wrote them." She came to her knees by the tree, the small lights pinked her cheeks and twinkled in her eyes. That first Christmas in Hammertown they had made their own ornaments for the Christmas tree, cut them from coffee can lids, and Ruth had strung cranberries and popcorn on threads to festoon the branches. A star was fixed at the top; the points were uneven and wrongly angled but oddly real. She had guided Hal's hand on the round-nose scissors as he cut the cardboard, and Jack had helped him glue the aluminum foil. "Vega is a star," Ruth said, bending over the model kit.

"Yes, but think of that place still being in business."

"They sell only to collectors now. Old kit models. I had quite a correspondence with them." She had hugged herself gleefully, face flushed with the successful conspiracy. "They said this Vega had been the top of their line. Could use either rubber bands or a small gas engine."

"Just before the War, small gas engines came on the market, so the larger flying models were adapted to either." The kit seemed to contain hundreds of parts: stringers thin as spaghetti, sheets of balsa with different forms printed upon them, wire, small rectangular blocks of the same light wood, and several yards of scarlet Japanese silk tissue. All these parts were laid out neatly on the floor by the tree, beside the tinseled, wrapped packages that Hal would tear apart the next morning, his legs straight out and stiff with excitement. Cooper could see fascination rise in Ruth's expression, a kind of heat familiar to him. How could all these linear, flat, right-angled pieces become a round, graceful, streamlined object that could lift into the air, that could fly? It was a spindly sort of magic but magic nevertheless, and with all the astonishment of good magic when one thing is unexpectedly made from another.

As they took the kit's splendid inventory, Cooper told her a little of the actual plane, about Earhart's flight across the Atlantic—the first woman to do that. Did she know that when she ordered the model? No, Ruth shrugged, she hadn't known. Yes, it was a marvelous plane, stable and fast. Long endurance in that fat, tubular fuselage and something muscular in the deep airfoil of the wings and the heavy wheel coverings that stuck down from the body like teardrops going sideways. More like big lollipops, Ruth mused bending over the plans.

Later, Cooper might frame the plans, for they seemed like a work of art to him; he was drawn by the simple explanation of a complicated idea. Ruth had studied the detail of the blunt, rounded cowling that enclosed the engine (a 500-horsepower Pratt and Whitney, he told her, ahead of its time), how to moisten and shape the paper-thin piece of balsa around the formers that had also been cut from a flat sheet of wood but glued together to make a sequence of rings, volume and roundness coming out of thin, flat planes.

Yes, she understood, she told him dreamily. It had been a long day for her. That afternoon she had taken Hal to see a Santa Claus who lounged in a LazyBoy chair outside the J.C. Penney in the Green River Mall. The hot bath had nearly put her to sleep. He watched as she reached up to repin her hair, still studying the plans for the Lockheed Vega. She always pinned it loosely high on her head when she took a bath like one of Degas's *baigneuses*, a crown of hair casually fastened and about to come undone to fall around her shoulders humid and silky.

Piece by piece, Cooper carefully had returned the parts of the model kit to the box. Ruth folded up the plans along their pressed lines and passed them to him, and he returned them to the box. He fit the cover. The trusting, hopeful face of Amelia Earhart looked up at them. "I made a special kind of eggnog," he said. "The recipe was George Washington's favorite."

"Was it really?" Ruth laughed like a child. She draped her arms across his shoulders and leaned forward to kiss him. "I surprised you, didn't I?" she spoke against his lips.

"You really have," he said. He kissed her again. "Don't you want some of this eggnog?"

"Sure," she said, drawing back and sitting up almost primly against the sofa skirt. "Let's have some."

But what seemed like a rejection, a preference for milk punch over the lips she offered him, had been a pretext to leave the small box in gold paper on the floor between them as they kissed. He had always been shy giving her presents, and she had received them shyly. He knew as he opened the refrigerator, took out the pitcher of prepared eggnog that she was silently staring at the gift, as if it were taking shape, a presence, in her vision. She was like a cat with a mouse, putting off the consumption as long as possible; meanwhile, the small package would be turned around, looked at, turned around again or moved to one side as if to ignore it completely, then moved to another. Perhaps the space around her would be changed by moving the gift to different locations within it. He would never know why she did this. He figured it went back to some deprivation as a child, though her foster parents had been kind to her.

"Go on," he returned with two cups of the eggnog. "Open it." Ruth reached up for a cup, holding the small box in her other hand. They heard Hal mumble something in his sleep, then turn in his bed above them.

"George liked this formula, did he?" Ruth asked.

"Go on. Open it," Cooper persisted.

She sipped the punch, a line of cream left on her upper lip when she put the cup on the floor. Her tongue tasted, then cleaned her lip as she held the package in both hands. She pulled one end of the gold ribbon and looked at Jack expectantly; perhaps that would be enough, she seemed to say.

"Go on."

Almost regretfully, she had unwrapped the package and opened the box. She stared down at its contents, but her look would have been the same if it had contained pebbles. The earrings were antique and Jack had been assured the stones were genuine topaz. When she fixed them into her ears they gleamed in the tree lights like small, pale suns. "Thank you," she had said and helped him to more punch, holding the cup to his mouth. They embraced, moving Hal's gifts to one side to gradually make space on the floor beside the tree. Their breathing joined the boy's earnest slumber and the small house had sparkled.

A piece of ice fell from the roof of the store, and Jack Cooper could see the sun slant acutely through the window of the back room. It would be almost noon and he had not yet called the principal of Hal's school. The silent, dizzy dogfight whirled above his head beyond hearing. Most of the models were of World War I fighters, but he had also included planes from a later period: a silver Bristol Bulldog, a white Mitsubishi scout on floats, and hanging above all, the black, thick silhouette of a Breda 65. He had had to build the model from scratch, using plans found in a back issue of *Model Airplane News*. No kit had been available; none had ever been made. The plane had never been in demand, not even as a model. A thick pad of snow thudded to the ground behind the store. The day must be getting warm.

Ruth had surprised him in other ways. She hated teaching, hated the hundred or more composition papers that had to be corrected every two weeks, hated the sullen, defiant ignorance of her students, hated the shopping mall atmosphere of the community college itself. But she marched off every morning, prepared and determined, the radio in the VW Beetle playing Patsy Cline or Willie Nelson from a station in Albany. The old cliché, putting a shoulder to the wheel, came to Jack Cooper's mind sometimes as he did the morning dishes; and he would smile with the image of Ruth pressing her fragile shoulder against a heavy wagon wheel, yet that was what she was doing.

The struggle she waged every day with the dull chores of her junior position was partly a reflection of the battle she fought within herself to do these apprentice tasks and to do them well; and the two conflicts created a third energy. She took turns cooking, helped Hal with his homework, made curtains for kitchen and living room windows. One summer and fall she put up jars of fruits as they came in season, and Jack and Hal carried these glass jars, still warm, down to the small root cellar to place them on wooden shelves in neat rows: peaches, pears, cherries, and plums like fragments of the sun preserved, forever fresh and capable of lifting the dark.

The same energy affected their lovemaking. Ruth had never denied him but loaned herself with that curious abandonment he first experienced that day in the old bookstore. But the first year in Hammertown she turned to him with an intensity and frequency that astonished him; she found any excuse to touch and kiss him and her hands glorified him. Sometimes as he patiently fitted and glued a piece of the Vega model, he felt he was fitting together the parts of another perfect day, that the design of their lives had finally and miraculously come right, fit together right while he thought ahead to the night and to another kind of fitting, some suggestion she may have whispered the last evening taking shape in his imagination. The wing panel of the Vega pinned to the paper would extend, take shape, all of its pieces cemented together so it could be unpinned and lifted away, light and heavy all at once.

His father's sour voice would interrupt such daydreams. Ruth's sexual energy had not increased so much as it had, at last, been focused only upon him. At last he alone was getting, he could hear the old man grouse, what so many in New York had been enjoying on a routine basis, because there had been no one else when they first moved to Hammertown. He was certain of that: The late meetings or conferences with faculty advisors, as in New York, didn't start for a while. Ruth was not the sort of person to be engaged by the world's sense of duty and decency; Cooper sensed that about her from the beginning. She related to her own body as others might the seasons, and what her body told her to do was the only moral obligation she felt. Once this idea came to him, surprised him one afternoon as he looked over some old copies of *The Reporter,* it gave her behavior a distinction he used to confront whatever judgment the senior Cooper might have made.

The model of the Lockheed Vega was so large that he had had to borrow a couple of sawhorses from Clay Peck and use them to make a workbench of a hollow-core door. The 48″ WINGSPAN advertised on the model's cover became more real with the addition of each rib, so the bull-nosed leading edge and the wide knife blade of the trailing gradually shaped the wing into a ladder, rung by rung, a construction he might have trouble getting through the room's door. Cooper had thought of the man who built a boat in his basement. Maybe he'd have to tear out the back wall of the old schoolhouse to get the completed model out.

The fuselage was as long and as thick as his arm, thicker even, for if he could have worked his hand through the round opening of the engine cowling, he could have worn the fuselage like the intricately worked sleeve of an old costume. Almost every day Cooper would spend several minutes looking into the bare framework of the plane's body, marveling at his own work, how each piece and strip of balsa had been shaped and fitted and glued. It was spatial. It was like being in space and looking out on some magnificent, new constellation that he had made.

"Hal helps," the boy would croon behind him. Cooper had set up a work space for Hal behind his and gave the boy scraps of balsa wood and pieces of tissue to play with. He worried about the effect of the banana oil and acetone on Hal, and he would open the one window high up under the roof line for ventilation. He himself would feel slightly drugged after working on the model, trimming and sanding and doping the framework so that the grain of the wood acquired the glossy depths of fine furniture.

"But I keep the window open," he assured Ruth one evening. Hal had been given some hot chocolate that had warmed him and sent him to sleep with sticky thumbs plugged into his mouth and ears. Ruth lay face down on their bed as Cooper massaged her back.

"Oh, God," she groaned, going limp under his hands. "Mr. Magic Fingers. Ah, yes, there."

He worked his hands along the shoulder blades and then rotated them, as fists, inwardly toward her spine. He fingered the vertebrae, one by one, stretched them apart from either end of her spine, one hand pressed between her shoulders, the other cushioned against the swell of her buttocks. Small and compact but by no means a boyish ass, he gripped and kneaded the flesh. The sharp angle of waist compounded by the startling curve of hip clearly defined a female.

He told her about the day's work on the Vega, as he did every evening, and Ruth would half-listen but hear enough so that the model gradually took shape in her imagination as it actually did on the workbench in the back room of the magazine store. The framework was ready to be covered with red tissue. Cooper could not say why this step saddened him, but he always put it off, finding some part of the construction, say, the tail assembly, that "needed" a bit more finishing—put it off as long as possible, even though he knew that once covered, the whole rig became a magical volume that could fly. Her thighs were firm and resilient under his hand, and they tapered neatly at the knee.

"But something funny happened today," he said.

"If I were butter," Ruth groaned into the pillow, "I'd be in a pool right now." She had put her hair into pigtails. "What happened funny?" Her arms reached out to either side, the hands lolled slackly.

It was something Hal had done, he told her. They spent hours together, back to back, each engrossed in his own project in the room behind the store. Cooper could become lost in the geometric maze of balsa wood he constructed almost around himself, so when the boy said something or whistled out of the corner of his mouth—a peculiar arrangement of the heavy lips to make the sound—Cooper would be startled. Hal's preoccupation with the scrap balsa was no less intense. The two of them shared something more than the room.

"A dream of flying," Ruth said and raised her arms above her head to grip the brass rods of the bed's headboard.

"What?" Cooper had been as startled by the idea as he had been by Hal's whistling that afternoon. He fell upon Ruth, his whole weight a blanket that pressed her into the mattress. The resilience of her body in his hands, its texture and compactness, and the way she had fixed her hair, had begun to affect him.

"So what was funny?" Ruth wriggled deeper into the mattress, unwilling to surrender her own indulgence just yet.

Jack Cooper sat back on his knees and placed his hands upon her lower spine. His thickened penis bobbed over her buttocks like a peculiar divining rod. He told her again about hearing Hal's odd whistle and how he had been startled by it, so he had turned to look at the boy just when the piece of balsa wood Hal held in his hands snapped in two. It had been a block of wood that came with the kit half carved and meant to be finished into the plane's propeller by the model maker.

"No, don't worry about that," Cooper had spoken quickly to Ruth's groan. "I wasn't planning to use the kit's propeller in the first place. I have another one. I'm never able to do those by hand as good as the ones I can buy. But don't you see what he was trying to do? Don't you see?"

The balsa block had been precut into the rough shape of a propeller, the two adjoining blades angled to each other and the whole piece resembling a roughly hewn bow tie. Hal had found the piece in the box with the other parts of the kit and had been trying to twist it the other way. "Don't you see?" Cooper asked once more as Ruth looked at him darkly. She had pulled herself out from under him and leaned against the headboard as he described the incident, her posture and limbs apart, blandly vulnerable. "He was trying to straighten out the piece, like it was a mistake. He was trying to make it flat like all the other pieces in the box. Understand?" He laughed; his speculation became a joyful idea.

But the idea seemed to dismay Ruth Cooper even more and she continued to stare up at Jack until finally the radiance of his expression, his eyes bright and lovely without the clerklike glasses shielding them—a blind beneficent, she would think—warmed and won her over. She reached for him, rising to meet him to kiss his lips, unable to ignore the gift any longer, she fell back against the pillows, her heavy eyes lidded and her mouth shaped into something like a laugh to show the small, perfect teeth.

Outside the window of Kelly Novak's apartment, pigeons fluttered and fell like venetian blinds coming apart. Cooper sneezed. The sharp acetone odor from the assortment of nail polish she kept on the bureau top had caught in his nostrils as he had been about to put down the small model of the Curtiss pursuit ship. He counted a dozen bottles of nail lacquer, deep hues of maroon and purple—a funereal spectrum chosen, he supposed, to accent Kelly's flamboyant blondeness. Elena Underwood's plane was parked between columns of magenta as if it had landed there for a new paint job, maybe, the powder-blue wings and fuselage covered with a glossy royal grape color to disguise it. Disguise from what? Cooper's imagination toyed with the idea, because the composition of the nail polish and the paint he had used on the model were essentially the same.

"Something that has occurred to me," Kelly Novak said from the kitchen where she had been reading the new part of his manuscript. "Where do these people get the fuel for their airplanes? They fly all over the Pacific and they never seem to run out of gas."

The round, optimistic images of Kelly Novak's young relative stare at Cooper, so the young girl's placid regard undercuts the urgency in the older woman's voice. Mary Novak, bovine graduate, never worried about running out of gas—or so her several photographs suggested.

"Suspend belief."

"Suspend what?" The editor's laugh was hoarse, roughened Cooper imagined by the atmosphere in bars at the front of restaurants like the one they had just come from. "Where did you pick that up? You mean disbelief?"

"I've been reading some of Ruth's books. She's doing a course in criticism this semester." He nosed the blue pursuit ship around, facing out, so it would have room to take off from the bureau top if it had to. After the paint job.

"Alternative world." At eye-level, the P-24 looked amazingly real. He had done well with the details, the mud splattered around the wheel wells in the wing, the grime of exhaust fumes on the cowl. His paint work had been deft. Even the black lace that enclosed the wing tips was realistic.

"I think you've got it right. I'm not sure about the chapter with the orangutan. I mean, I like the idea of the ape suddenly losing himself in this island jungle, back in his old habitat—that's very moving. A stranger in a strange land, simian division. But I question the point of view. It's hard to identify with an ape, Jack." She had changed her clothes as soon as they returned from the restaurant. The sweat suit was gray with white letters on the shirt front: C.C.N.Y. "Having it all in his mind is troublesome. You can get the same effect, maybe, by having it in Flip Winslow's mind. Let him imagine his sidekick swinging around the coconuts, making out with the lady apes." She stood up. "C'mon, it's time you got to your train."

They walked to the subway on Central Park West, where she jogged and in the time it took to walk the two blocks, she told him about Mary Novak.

Ron Knox had left an hour before but Cooper could get no work done and only stared at the blank page of paper standing stiffly up from the Underwood typewriter. The store was silent, closing in on itself as the heavy snow pressed down on the roof. He found himself listening for the fall of the next batch of snow off the sun-warmed tin roof and made a proposition with himself; he would start typing at the sound of it, no matter what came out.

He would blame Knox for the impasse. He had been so eager that morning to get down to the store, to go through the window and into that never-never land, as Kelly called it; then, there stood the older man in the entryway of the store, waiting for him and wagging his arms back and forth as if to block, even more effectively, Cooper's entrance into his own place. The story line was still here, Cooper would be sure, perhaps, only wafting somewhere over his head, and he would even look up to the combatants of the silent air battle. He tried to put Winslow and his ape-gunner into the model of the black Breda 65. He could see the grim smile on the pilot's face as he put the fighter-bomber into a dive. Behind him, the ape's lips pulled back across his large teeth into a ferocious grin, as he faced the whining rush of the slipstream. The plane's controls hummed like a banshee. The powerful Pratt and Whitney shrieked in a crescendo that threatened to rip the heavens apart. Plunk. A curtain of snow had fallen past the rear window, briefly shading, abruptly ending the battle. It was no longer fun. Something was missing.

So he would call Hal's school and without directly asking the question, be assured by the principal that Hal was indeed in class; that he had been brought by their neighbor, Mr. Peck, and that they all thought Hal was a wonderful boy and a joy to have in class. They would all be sorry to see him graduate in May. He would have to talk to Clay about spending so much time with Hal. The boy must be in the way. And all the equipment and tools that the carpenter had in his workshop—well, that could be a problem.

"Not a bit," Ruth told him one night. He had given Kelly

Novak the model of Elena Underwood's P-24 several days earlier. "I've talked to Clay about it, and he is showing Hal how to make things. He's even taking him on jobs on Saturdays as a helper. Haven't you noticed that cap he wears lately? Wait a minute."

She went to her study and returned holding a crude windmill in the shape of a bird, perhaps a duck. The blades idly turned as Ruth passed it through the air to move the stubby wings up and down. The right wing trembled more than moved.

"He made this?" Cooper said.

"Yes." Ruth's expression was alert. "Clay helped him with the cutting and the hinges." She looked at the wooden windmill in Jack's hands. "He said he made it for me."

She had come home, cranky and rushed by assignments, by the schedule and demands of others—never her own work, never that, she had almost shouted all the way back from Green River, gunning the Beetle and twisting it around the potholes in the county highway. Now it was her turn to fix Hal his supper. She hadn't needed that this evening. Then, he was nowhere around. As usual. Or seemed not to be there, but he was. She could feel him hiding from her, playing some awful trick on her where he would suddenly pop out at her—"Hi, Mums," scaring her out of her shoes—all of his hugeness blanking the light and air around her, so she could hardly breathe yet sometimes find herself screaming, hands over her ears. "Ho, ho, ho, Mums," like a carnival mannequin looming over her all at once, menacing and ludicrous at the same time.

Oh, c'mon, she thought, no games tonight. An old teacher, still with a crush on her, had sent her a copy of Basho and she wanted to settle down with it in her study. But she was afraid to look for Hal. Then she saw the windmill on the table.

One wing drooped down to the checkered cloth, and the head and bill were only slightly defined from the block of wood they had been carved from. Enough. A hurt bird that had been able to make it only this far, to the table in this kitchen. "Oh, Hal." All of her anger and resentments caught in her throat like water swallowed from a wave that takes a swimmer by surprise. She had picked up the construction and had carefully pushed the broad blades of the propeller, which turned a worm gear that moved the rickety wings.

"It's beautiful, Hal," she said in a loud voice. He might be upstairs. "Thank you, Hal. You have done well." More likely, he was nearby, but she still dared not look for him. In what part of the afternoon had he hid himself, how long had he been waiting for her to come home and find this thing he had made for her? As she stood in the middle of the floor, she could feel him listening, breathing.

She lofted the windmill with her hand and the blades turned, the wings faintly trembled. The contraption might actually work! "Oh, see how the wings move," she said. It almost sounded like a line from one of her poems. Maybe, if she kept talking, he would show himself, slowly emerge from his hiding place. "This duck is going to go the whole way to South America. This duck is going to fly!"

Something about the pantry door, not quite closed. She had moved toward the storeroom off the kitchen. "Zoom. Here comes this big bird. Zoom! There goes Texas and the Gulf of Mexico. Zoom! Here comes Colombia, where the coffee beans come from. Zoom!" As she approached the closed door, the sounds behind it scrambled themselves, giggles and chokings and watery gurgles.

"It's beautiful, Hal. Mums thanks you very much." At first, he would not look up at her as she stood in the open doorway; then, his eyes rolled back, scared and eager all at once. Gleeful. He sat on the floor of the pantry, against the inside wall, under a shelf of preserves. He sat knees drawn up before his face and his hands beside him like packages come undone. He sat as if his excitement and joy had reached their limits; he could go no farther and so had sat down to wait for her to catch up, to find him there. The one small window in the storeroom illuminated his face, like a painting she thought, but his expression made her take a step back but not in fright, which was so often the case.

So, regardless of her school clothes, the cracked linoleum possibly snagging the good pair of hose she wore, Ruth sat down on the floor and leaned back against his raised legs, her back to him. "It's wonderful. Hal's done well," she told him and held the windmill before her face as if its assembly presented more intricacies to be studied than she had first thought. His touch surprised her by its gentleness. He lifted just one coil of her hair, slowly wound it around a thick finger, then let it slip away. She hadn't looked.

She didn't tell Jack Cooper about that. Instead: "You'll fix it up in the backyard? Along with that old birdbath. Next comes one of those mirror balls and a couple of pink flamingos. Jesus, we're becoming lower middle-class, Jack."

"I know just the place for it," he said.

"He's making something else, too." She leaned against the sink. "He and Clay are working on some project together. Hal is constantly breaking into giggles over the secret."

"Another windmill? A kite?"

"No, I don't think so. Something bigger. By the way, how's your windmill coming along? Do I get to see your little project?"

"Kelly told me the most amazing thing Wednesday. She is—was—Mary Novak. You know, the girl in the pictures on her bureau."

"When she was younger," Ruth said and looked out the

kitchen window. A male cardinal nervously pecked at something in the snow. "I forgot to pick up birdseed for the feeder."

It was more than just being younger, Jack told her. He tried to describe how Kelly's face had looked, as they walked toward the park, but then he also turned and watched the bird in the field across the road. Two more scarlet birds and a female cardinal had joined the first. He'd have to give Ruth just the facts. She had been more than bovine. "Fat Mary, was how I was known," Kelly had said. Her gloved hands were already posed pugnaciously for jogging though they had walked slowly along 75th Street. "Everybody's pump—that was me." One incident might get through to Ruth. Actually, Kelly had told him only one, the rest in general allusions.

"Junior Prom. Okay?" Cooper said to Ruth's profile. "A little town up above Amsterdam on the Mohonk. An old mill town, gone to seed. Her date pushes her around the floor all night. Everybody knows about her, right? Everybody's waiting. They have her number. Okay?"

"Okay, okay, I get it," Ruth turns back almost angrily.

He had wanted to be sure of her complete attention. Fat Mary. But prom night was different. They set her up in one of the old vacant mills, and the cars came and went all night long.

So she came to New York. Fat Mary had died; Kelly Novak was born. Starvation diets, exercise clubs. Her secretarial skills checked out. She moved on from job to position to appointment. All the time she read. She had always read; it had been the only thing that had kept her sanity, she said. From books, she knew there was another world that was different from the one she lived in by the Mohonk River. She would have jumped into the Mohonk if she hadn't believed that from books; she said.

"So I go back to the old place a few years ago." The filthy musk of the subway rose over them; the roar below overcame her voice. With all its huskiness, it didn't have much power. "I walk into this bar, a neighborhood place called The Jolly Dutchman. That's a laugh. A hangout. I recognize some of the guys. Older now. Gray. Beer paunches. They look me over. Who's this chick with four-inch heels that make her legs like Angie Dickinson's? Check out those tits, buddy. But, I have a glass of sherry. The best in the house. You can imagine. I'm cool." Kelly ran a few paces in place as they stood on the corner. She was eager to get to her five miles in the park, yet wanted to drag out the punch line.

"So I eventually finish the sherry, a perfect lady. Sipping it. So I get up; you could hear a feather break, and I toss a fifty dollar bill on the bar. 'Set 'em up,' I tell the bartender. 'Tell them Fat Mary was back in town,' and I walk out with a little twist of the ass."

He laughed alone. The story seemed to have offended Ruth. She had turned back to the window with a pained look. The cardinals had flown away. Her response made him wonder why he had told her. "Why have you never said anything?" Ruth asked him. The cardinals had flown away. Had she even been listening? Cooper was disappointed. He thought Mary Novak's story might be a profound parable; understanding and absolution all at once.

"What?"

"You never say anything. Never. Never get angry. Why don't you hit me? Beat me up? Say something?" All that time he'd been telling her about Kelly Novak, she had been thinking of that old professor who had sent her the haiku translation. Her affair with him, hastily enacted behind the locked door of his office, had been years ago—before they left New York. Jack must have suspected something. He must have known. Years back, yet, here is this teacher—he must be retired by now—still sending her books to read, the impulse to educate her all that's left of the old surge. What was there about her, Ruth often wondered? What scent still lingered in that emeritus imagination to sustain this remembrance and provoke such desire?

"Why are you so upset?" Cooper was dumbfound.

"Hear me," Ruth shouted. "Hear my story. Do you listen to my story?" She was about to say more when heavy steps sounded in the rear entry. Hal may have made the clumsy entrance on purpose?

Ruth had jumped up and opened the door for him, opened her arms wide for the huge boy who stood in the kitchen doorway, a curious, lopsided grin on his face. "Oh, Hal. Hal. Oh, Hal," Ruth said, her voice wet. "Da is going to put up your windmill tomorrow."

It made for a curious picture, Cooper thought. The diminutive woman attempting to enfold the oversized youth, but, who was comforting whom, who protected the other? Whichever it was, and for whatever reason, Jack Cooper enjoyed the picture the two of them made. He felt home at last.

So it would be Ron Knox's fault. It wouldn't be the first time the architect had ruined Cooper's day, just by showing up to go through the magazines for ideas. The pleasure Cooper had with his fantasy, of passing through the window as he thought of it, had become a need, so Cooper tried to assuage the ache and frustration of this morning's desire by small chores. He cleaned the typefaces of the Underwood. He tightened the screw on the half-spherical bell that warned of margins. He took a damp cloth to the machine's case, using some spray cleaner he'd brought down from the house. The white sheet of paper stuck up from the roller, a call for surrender or what, he did not know.

Moreover, urgency had been added. Kelly mentioned a power struggle developing between her and another editor, a young man who had come to Wilson Bean from another publisher, so Cooper felt it was important that he finish his manuscript quickly. He had to get to work, he told himself, and sprayed cleaning agent on the typewriter's keys. He couldn't let people like Ron Knox take up his time. He polished the keys. A few accidentally pressed against the blank white paper to print out something like a secret code. The ammonia in the spray cleaner cleared his head.

"What's the smell?" Ethel Knox had asked. "It's like Flora's House of Beauty in Green River in here."

"That's just paint," Jack Cooper had told them. "Hal and I are working on a model of Amelia Earhart's plane." Deafened by the concentrated silence of their project, yet somehow joined within that silence as they worked back to back as if a thread joined them, neither he nor Hal had heard the Knoxes in the store until the couple came dangerously close to the back room. Ron Knox could have opened the door and walked right in. He was like that.

"Anybody here?" The older man's voice had been just on the other side of the door; Cooper could see his hand on the knob. He jumped up and opened the door quickly and shut it behind him, raising his shoulders so Knox could not peer into the room and see any of the Vega's pristine skeleton ready to be covered with red tissue. He wasn't ashamed of making the model; Jack Cooper just didn't want to share the beauty of it with Knox.

"We're here to sign you and Ruth up for a little adventure," Ethel Knox had said merrily. She seemed too tall to laugh like that. "There's this perfectly cunning little inn over in Salisbury that's just hired a piano player for the dinner hour. We know you guys are just the ones to go with us some night."

Her husband grunted agreeably and nodded over a rack of *House and Garden*. He flipped through the back issues with a professional alacrity. Ethel Knox continued to talk, a long narrative about the personality of this piano player and how she and Ron used to hear him play at the St. Regis Grill years ago and how this pianist had retired to Connecticut— it seemed everyone had retired to Connecticut—and so here he was, and she just knew that the Coopers would *adore* the music.

Cooper would remember that morning, remember how he had finally moved away from the door to the back room, satisfied that Ethel Knox's jigsaw recollections of old musicals would confound her husband's curiosity about the back room. Knox became eager to quit the store and had stood in the aisle between *House and Garden* and *Fortune,* hands clasped behind his back, rocking on his heels and pulling his raw-looking neck up from his shirt collar as his head turned this way and that. He jiggled the change in one pocket, the grim, patient smile of a good husband fixed beneath the white brush mustache.

"Indeed, I do remember 'Lute Song,'" Ethel Knox had replied to Cooper's question. Perversely, he had looked for ways to prolong their visit, keep the older man suffering. "That lovely young Mary Martin. And who played opposite her? Do you remember, Ron? C'mon guess. Guess."

"Oh, I don't know, Ethel."

"Yul Brynner," she laughed, a tinkly sound behind one hand as she winked at Cooper. They shared her husband's ignorance. She opened the old program that Cooper had handed to her. A batch of magazines from an Albany estate sale had contained several dozen old New York theater programs. Ethel Knox seemed ready to re-create the whole musical, scene by scene. She hummed one or two of the songs as they appeared in the show's plot. Cooper had listened to her, keeping an eye on Knox's impatience.

At last the Knoxes had turned and gone, and the store settled into its musty comfort. Then he heard the whistling in the back room, that peculiar toneless sibilance pursed from the left corner of the boy's mouth whenever his attention converged on a single project. Cooper's feet had turned to lead; he couldn't move them, he told Ruth.

It had been too late by then anyway. The delicate splintering on the other side of the door sounded like fossilized cobwebs being pulled apart. Cooper sat down on the floor outside the door and listened to the purposeful whistling, the crackle and snap of a fragile dream, as Hal tore the balsa framework to splinters. It had been the same with the pheasant, Ruth said. He wanted to find out what made it fly. "Can you fix it?"

"No, it's finished. The last one I'll try."

The new sheet of paper in the Underwood would be crisp and primly white. Cooper could hear crows crying over the melting fields behind the store. If this day were ruined, he would have a fresh start tomorrow. The typewriter would be ready, the keys honed clean to chisel the words into the heavyweight bond paper. Maybe the day was meant for baking bread. He had not made bread in some time. Writing about Flip Winslow and his orangutan had become serious business because he was alone, without an audience, without someone to quietly observe him dreaming.

The day had become very warm and the road ran wetly with the runoff of melted snow that cut gullies into the shale-veined hill across from the store. About a dozen English sparrows perched on the telephone wires strung above the old railroad junction. The birds' casual arrangement on the wires looked like the notes of music on a page, and Cooper almost got some paper to copy the arrangement for someone to play the melody later. But then, the music was gone as the sparrows flew up and away. Perhaps it had never been music.

Red Schuyler's gray Oldsmobile made a U-turn right in front of the old schoolhouse. The U.S. MAIL sign on the roof glistened and seemed freshly painted but was only wet. "I got a package you got to sign for, Jack."

CHAPTER

SIX

"**B**UT why you?" Ruth sets the table for supper and looks annoyed. A small urn, about the size of a coffee can, gleams dully on top of the television in the living room. When Cooper put it there, he had to push aside books and a ceramic ashtray. "Listen, I've had a hard day," she continues as if Cooper has made an unusual request. He's said nothing. "You'll just have to eat beans and franks. I picked up a frozen apple pie on the way home."

"What about some of those peaches in the cellar? Hal likes those."

"Oh, please don't make a bother. Can't we just have an ordinary, bad meal once in a while? Does it always have to be some gourmet dish? I realize *your* editor may present a more interesting menu."

"Why do you say that? Actually, I like franks and beans very much."

"You're not supposed to say that." Her laugh was thin, then thickens. She perches on his lap and pushes his glasses above his forehead. "Ah, Jack, can I never disappoint you? Hurt you?" She kisses him and presses his face against her chest so fiercely that the coarse fibers of her sweater hurt him.

"What's the matter?" Cooper says at last. Her embrace had loosened. She is looking over his shoulder into the living room, a distance in her expression. "I'm sorry I brought that home." He strokes her arms. "For some reason, it didn't seem right to leave it down at the store, by itself."

"That isn't it," Ruth shrugs. She goes to the sink and begins to open two large cans of pork and beans. She works the wall can-opener vigorously, as if to wind a motor within herself.

Why, Cooper wonders, did he bring the ashes home and leave the rest—the journals, an old flying helmet and goggles, several tarnished medals—locked up in the bottom drawer of his file cabinet at the back of the store? These items represented the man's life, objects of the living and, he follows this kitchen theory, should be kept with the living—accompanied. Not those cinders in the living room, something you might buy at the co-op to put snap into your tomato plants.

Dear Mr. Cooper,
This box contains all the remains of this old cloudbuster's mortal coils and worldly possessions. Do with it what you will, but if it's no trouble, I'd like the ashes to be let fly from some high place. I see by the map that you are near some mountains. Maybe one day you can climb up one of these and let me go with a breeze. Downwind, of course. The rest is the kind of junk a person finds hard to throw away. The notebooks might interest you. Maybe you know someone who might publish them. Let me say, I've enjoyed our correspondences and your interest in the old days of flying. I'll be breaking ground soon, going West at last. It's been a long

breaking ground soon, going West at last. It's been a long and mostly sorrowful flight and I admit to being curious as to what I'll find up there. If anything. Hope this finds you well and continuing to prosper.

Happy landings,
Roy E. Armstrong
Capt. Army Air Corps, Ret.

Cooper realizes he's been staring at the space over the stove where the cuckoo clock used to hang. Cooking vapors have printed the clock's outline on the wall so it looks like a frame without the picture. Ruth finishes scraping the beans into a saucepan. "What was that?"

"I said, maybe I should give it up. It's no longer just sitting down and writing. It's a business. Po-Biz. Like these franks." She holds up a package. "See that stamp? That means these are genuine hot dogs with the correct amount of gristle, fat, and snout. Well, the same is true of poets now. You have to get certified."

"You can't stop," says Jack and looks out the window by the table. It was already dark outside. The shapes of the kitchen windows are projected upon the black snow by the light slanting through those same windows. Clay would be bringing Hal home soon. Ruth slices the package of frankfurters open and cuts them into different lengths.

All those long nights, the Saturdays and Sundays, working on her poems, her small person bent over her papers, her fingers smudged with ink like a felon's, fingerprinted for a crime. He feels bad. It seemed unfair to her. She was outnumbered; all along she had been outnumbered. He puts down the silverware for the three places set on the checkered tablecloth. Even old Armstrong had found someone to receive his journals and letters.

He knows why he left the old aviator's belongings at the store. He had glanced at a journal, one kept by Armstrong during his duty with the Escadrille, and without thinking, he put everything in the bottom drawer of his file—the one he could lock.

ITEM: 4 July '18. Skip Wightman, Harvard, brought back a Rumpler two-seater all by himself. He made the pilot fly over the field once, he close on its tail. The observer lay over the rear cockpit, arms flapping in the slipstream. Obviously dead. There was a smile on the German pilot's face. The war was over for him and he couldn't wait to get that two-seater on the ground in one piece. Skip waved him around to land, coming in behind him. Then, just as the Jerry had throttled back, Skip gave a three-second burst of the Brownings. The slugs must have all caught the pilot's skull because his head exploded like a red rose suddenly blooming. The Rumpler came in and landed itself, neat as you please, the headless pilot still spouting blood. Despite ourselves, we all applauded. What's Fourth of July, Skip says later, without fireworks.

Ruth has continued to talk about the poetry establishment and Cooper has resumed his chair, glasses in hand to clean them with a paper napkin. A pattern began to appear to him. He thinks of Ruth locking herself up to write her poems. Kelly Novak's shrine to her old self. There must be a closet full of diaries somewhere, mementoes of nights along the Mohonk. Now these old flyer's journals and diaries locked up in his office. Closets and locked files like this all over the world. Locked away for safekeeping. But safe from what?

"Who decides these things?" He puts his glasses on. "You make it sound like Russia—committees deciding on what's a good poem or what is good for poetry."

"Want to see my high kick?" Ruth says and turns from the stove. She surprises him. Her arched foot nearly reaches the ceiling light. "Not hard for a forty-year old modernist. I'm going to audition for Po-Biz. Want to see my routine?" She's begun a few dance steps and twirls in the space before the stove. Her diminutive figure lends quaintness to the parody and Cooper is momentarily caught up until he sees the hard light in her eyes. She takes the loaf of French bread from the refrigerator top and uses it obscenely.

"Ruth!" Headlights have just swept into the backyard. "Hal is here."

"Cut this up, will you?" She hands him the bread. Feet stamp into the back room off the kitchen. The voices are muffled, though Hal's balloons within the small vestry. When the door opens, Ruth is back at the stove, stirring the beans and Cooper is cutting the bread at the table.

"Oh, boy, franks and beans," Hal says.

"There's another one," Ruth answers but goes on her toes, and the boy bends over to kiss one then the other cheek. He wears a white cotton carpenter's cap stenciled in green with the logo for STOUT LUMBER AND OIL. Clamshell ears stick out pinkly. His mouth looks stained from cherry juice and the whole face, Cooper often thinks—the right number of freckles speckled the rounded cheeks—has not changed, never grown out of a childlike roguishness, like the face in a magazine illustration, something Norman Rockwell might fix forever in the imagination. But the body has become immense. They have to go to a special store in Albany to get his shoes.

"How about a drink, Clay? A beer?" Cooper knows Clay would not accept but makes the offer. The carpenter still stands at the kitchen door, holding his leather cap in both hands. The red mackinaw has been unzipped only part way.

"Coffee?" Ruth offers.

"No missus, thank you."

"Now go wash up, carpenter," Ruth tells Hal.

"Da," the boy says happily to Cooper, patting him on the head as he passes by.

"Thanks for getting Hal to school," Jack says.

"No trouble." Ruth measures oil and vinegar into a mixing jar for the salad. Jack makes one last cut and puts the sliced bread on a plate. Clay clears his throat. "Cold," he says.

"Is there a warming trend?"

"Not to speak of." He looks sidewise at Ruth. His face goes at a slant, the whole expression parallel to the diagonal of heavy brown hair that falls across his forehead. Perhaps, the years peering down the straight lines of his own joinery had set his features at this oblique angle.

Cooper tries to remember what Grace Peck looked like. He remembers her dog and how the countryside had been so disrupted. He and Ruth and the boy had just moved to Hammertown. Ethel Knox was alive. A long time ago.

"There's this job onto a house in Connecticut that Mr. Knox is redoing," Clay says abruptly and hunches his shoulders. "I can use a helper, which made me wonder if it'd be all right for Hal to give me a hand?" He had pulled a cigarette from a crumpled package as he finished and held it between the middle and ring fingers of his right hand, a manner not without elegance.

"What about the tools?" Ruth asks. "The saws and such things?"

The carpenter assures her that Hal would not use any of the power tools though, "He's more than handy." He'd already spoken to the school principal who agreed such a project would be good for him. They'd have to write a letter to ask that Hal be excused from the afternoon classes, mostly cut-and-paste endeavors, running and jumping. Clay could pick him up at the lunch hour and take him to the job. "He could become a good carpenter, that boy," Peck concludes and there's a glint at the corners of the hazel eyes. What Clay Peck is saying is that he could teach Hal to be a carpenter.

"There's hardly a house in the valley that Clay Peck hasn't put a nail into," Ethel Knox once said, winking and turning pink under the silver canopy of her hair. Doubtless, she'd heard some of the talk, probably Ron had told her some of the jokes. If Clay Peck had put a few nails into his own house, Grace may not have run off. Jokes like that were passed around with the pretzels at the Hollow Tap in Stout Falls, always good for a laugh, just after the carpenter sipped the last of his beer and eased out of the place with that peculiar sidewise motion.

He was still a stranger after fifteen years, and the Coopers had known him for ten of those. A developer up in Irondale had brought him to that village to restore the old general store and other buildings in that hamlet, but where he came from no one knew. The job in Irondale took longer than expected; each part of the restoration seemed to dictate another and then another. Peck's craftsmanship, his knowledge of wood, and his discretion with tools turned an ordinary job into a masterwork, making all around it shabby. "Get Clay Peck to fix your kitchen door," the saying went, "and you'll end up rebuilding the whole damn house."

He was alone at first, arriving in Irondale in a three-quarter ton Harvester pickup, the vehicle worn but as finely tuned as the tools carried in the back. The wood planes rode securely within a heavy chest made of camphor wood, the corners bound with brass. Cooper thought it might have been a sea chest that Peck had adapted for these tools, and he imagined old whaling ships whenever he saw it open in the carpenter's workshop; aromatic and orderly, each plane fitted into its own custom niche.

The job in Irondale stretched from winter to spring and into summer, then into fall and winter once again, as Peck's carpentry moved outside, from floor beams and sills to eaves and window units. To rebuild a porch column meant the other three or four would have to be done, though the others had looked all right until then. Grace Peck arrived in the spring, not the sort of harbinger for that season a person might expect, people would say later, but certainly not uninteresting. It wasn't that Clay Peck took work away from other carpenters in the area, some of them with crews and weekly payrolls to meet, but he never finished his own. Or rather the jobs never finished. Their completion never satisfied him; some detail always wanted attention—a porch eave made right by molding he had shaped long after in his shop. There was an organic effect from his carpentry, as if the raw wood had been restored to life by his cutting it and fitting it, had begun to grow again and his constant cultivation of it was required so the new summer porch it formed would not go wild.

"Oh, now, Clay, what are you going to do now?" Many a farm wife would say, a little apprehensively but excited just the same to see him angling across the backyard toward the fancy well house he had made the year before. Sometimes he'd already be at work in the playroom addition when the family returned from shopping. He'd have a small tool kit and usually a piece of wood, something he had shaped in his imagination and had made in his shop to fit a corner that had always bothered him. Something has been missing and it might be years bothering him as he worked it over in his mind. Then one afternoon, he'd show up with a cornice that fit just right—like the long-lost piece of a puzzle. "It's like milking in that there French palace," the farmer would tell his small audience at the co-op. Clay was no stranger to post-and-beam construction, and with the help of a couple of the farmer's hired hands, he had raised a sixty stanchion barn near Green River.

"But you should see the lintels on that baby," Ron Knox said. It was after dinner one time and, as usual, he was standing by his fireplace, an arm posed on the mantle. "All hand shaped and each one different. He must have got the designs out of some book. All mythical creatures. Bunches of grapes, pineapples on the pinions and around the windows; around the windows, he's made these casements right out of the *Arabian Nights*. Those old cows of Marshall's are going to feel like harem beauties."

"It sounds like you two are right for each other," Ruth had said.

"Oh yeah," Knox eyed her.

"I know what she means," Ethel said merrily. Her knitting needles clacked together rapidly. She was making sweaters that year for a small boutique in Sharon.

"You mean the harem bit," Knox said.

"No, no," Ethel Knox laughed, her high, tinkly laugh. "That the two of you are never finished with a job. There's always something you want to do to it."

Clay Peck enjoyed this distinction, enjoyed telling the Coopers by the back door of their kitchen, sometimes bringing the cigarette up to his mouth, as if he were about to light it only to talk through it—an important gesture even in his coveralls and red mackinaw—like that of a ward leader reviewing a list of registered voters. In fact, figures were the problem.

"So, there's this space of about three inches all around between the old house and the new wing," he's saying. "Now that don't seem much, but you take a tape and measure it three inches wide then wrap that tape around a building and you have quite a bit of gap."

"But can't you just—" Ruth gestured with her hands, "fill it in with something?"

"It's not like hardly a cake frosting you can put more onto," Clay says and laughs silently. Momentarily, the smile straightens out his face, as if a spring has pulled it right then let go. "Good for us, the owners are down in Florida, so we have time to fix it. I keep saying to Mr. Knox that the figures onto the joining don't seem right, but he just waves me away. So Hal and I have our work cut out." He pauses, blinks, aware that his words may have some extra meaning but then continues. "I'll make sure he gets fair wages." He hunches his shoulders.

"Won't you stay for supper?" Ruth offers.

"No thank you, missus," Clay replies and uses the invitation to leave, plopping his cap on his head. Suddenly, there is a wooden kitchen match in the other hand and the cigarette is presented to the lips once more. But he waits until he gets outside before igniting the sulphur tip with his thumbnail.

Cooper has accompanied him out into the yard, the crystal air polishing his breath, and he wonders about the carpenter's lungs; Clay has sucked on the match flame through the cigarette to draw in the heat, fumes and fire at the critical moment of the tiny explosion. Quickly, the black-and-white stillness of the backyard is restored as the match drops into the snow. Why he has come out with Peck, Jack Cooper isn't sure, perhaps a gesture toward some kind of formality—something Ron Knox might do, he finds himself thinking, wondering how he can turn and leave the carpenter in the cold without seeming rude. Peck continues to stand, taking deep lungfuls of smoke while sighting down the white barrel of the cigarette at the cement birdbath in the center of the yard. Then, he nods toward the windmill Cooper had mounted atop a length of two-by-two, set into the ground. It had taken him a whole hour with a pickax to dig through the frost, but the look on Hal's face had made the effort worthwhile. Whether Clay's gesture was to approve of this installation or whether it was to remind them both of his part in making the windmill, Cooper cannot tell.

"He wants to fly," Clay Peck says finally.

It takes Cooper a little time to realize the carpenter is not talking about the cherub on the dolphin's back. "Oh?"

"He's been making kites up at my shop. The missus has seen one of them."

"It's good of you to put up with him," Jack Cooper says.

"He's a good kid," Clay Peck says and walks to his truck. He drops the stub in the snow—three or four big pulls had burned the cigarette down to a nub—and swings into the truck. Cooper watches him back up and follows the taillights as they disappear around the road bend above their swamp.

It's a trick, like déjà vu, but just the opposite; this feeling he had when he stood outside his house at night and watched the lighted windows, watched Ruth and Hal moving past the windows inside. It was as if he weren't there, or had come back from somewhere, sometime in the future, and was observing them moving about getting along as if he weren't there, had never been there. Not even the cold of this night bothered him as he stood in the backyard, not even the snow edging over the moccasins he wore as house slippers.

"I sometimes think of the house as a spaceship," he would say to Kelly Novak several weeks later. She had taken him to a different place for lunch, a Vietnamese restaurant that had just opened. "Especially at night, in winter, looking at it—it seems so self-contained. I guess that's the word I want."

"I understand," the editor responded automatically. She

would seem nervous this day and kept fiddling with the silverware. Cooper would think it was because of the different place, not her usual haunt, though the same group of drinkers laughed in the raffia-finished bar at the front. They move with the restaurant, Cooper thought. "A spaceship."

"Yes," Cooper leaned forward to get her full attention, but he couldn't think of anything more to say. "Just like a spaceship." He would tell her about Hal. "Every night he goes over these magazines, but mostly an old *Life* magazine with pictures of da Vinci's inventions. The water mills, the airplanes, and the war machines. He and this carpenter he's working for are making them, I think."

Finally, the editor pushed aside her plate and told him she wasn't happy with the way his book was going. Yes, she agreed he had been writing to her directions. In the new installment before them, Flip Winslow was being hidden from the Red Tong agents by a family of orangutans.

"There's no humor in it," Kelly Novak would say. "There's an infinite opportunity for humor in this situation that you haven't realized. Did you read the Malamud novel I gave you? You should read that. He has his hero humping a lady ape."

"You're kidding," Cooper would say, putting down his teacup. "That's impossible."

His manuscript was only half of it, she would say, not even half of it. They had taxied to her apartment and Cooper would be sitting in the kitchen, the manuscript in front of him, as Kelly changed clothes and talked to him from the next room. There were different factors, she kept saying. An ironing board had been set up opposite the table, and it was piled high with papers: manuscripts, correspondence, and what looked like tax records. Cooper felt tired. He was tired of Flip Winslow and his ape—not the first time he had felt this way of late. The twists of the plot used to be spontaneous. He still typed in the back room of the shop on the old typewriter, but every paragraph had to be worked over now.

No, it wasn't just his manuscript, Kelly Novak would be saying as she returned to the kitchen, pulling in the sash of a red wool robe. He got the idea that the new man, "the twit" brought in from another house, had been trying to make her look bad to old Wilson. "He won't get away with it," she would say, but the more she talked, Cooper got the opposite impression. They had turned against her. The new man had turned them all against her. It sounded like Mary Novak all over again, only the site of the violations had changed.

She made more tea but Cooper could drink no more. These kitchen sessions had become workshops for her story—not his. He heard all about the new editor's schemes, the kind of books he pushed through. On the other hand, Wilson Bean and his wife still invited her to dinner at their small estate in Westchester. She would describe the house and how the evening went, the atmosphere in the publisher's library after dinner where brandy was served in large round glasses, she said.

"How much more . . . how much of this old flyer's journal do you have?"

Cooper would be relieved. He'd rather talk of anything but his own work. "Armstrong sent me several journal books. Mostly, they seem to be about his time flying for the Loyalists in Spain."

"Send them to me," Kelly Novak would say.

The sounds of Clay Peck's pickup have vanished and Jack Cooper feels enfolded by Ruth's shadow. It stretches across the snow in the backyard. He sees Hal come into the doorway from the living room. The boy is saying something to Ruth. His lips shape the words carefully and his expression is cheerful. But it is always cheerful, Cooper thinks. Ruth moves to the table, holding something. Salad, probably. Hal has opened the fridge and takes out a large glass pitcher of milk and brings it, on tiptoe seemingly, to the table where he carefully puts it down with both hands. Ruth comes back to the table with another plate and briefly puts her right arm around Hal to pat him on the back. She can reach no higher than his shoulder blade.

Cooper would remember the details of this homely scene—the way Hal's face suddenly went awry with fatigue, just a little boy to be tucked in soon after supper—as he stood in the dark across from Donald Jacobs's windows. The first two floors were dark and that was to be expected, for they housed the offices for the magazine and the writing program. Ruth had told him this and he had verified the information, to be sure he had the right place, before he took up his post in the stairwell of the brownstone across the street. *ARGUS: A Journal of the Arts,* and just below this panel, a newer plate screwed to the vestibule wall: QUINN COLLEGE MASTER OF FINE ARTS PROGRAM. But there was illumination above. A third floor was set back from the building's façade—almost a penthouse as Ruth had described it—so that the windows were not visible from street level and certainly not from the four steps below street level where Jack Cooper stood in the dark. There were lights up there.

Not the first time he had taken up such surveillance. Why, he didn't know. He wasn't even sure if Jacobs was at home, upstairs in his penthouse. What would he be doing, Cooper wondered? Reading manuscripts. Seducing women who had brought him manuscripts to read. Opening a bottle of wine, then reading the manuscript, then seducing the author. That would be the sequence. But what if the building were empty. Jacobs might have carried his seduction across town. Distance meant nothing. After all, he could manipulate lives as far away as Hammertown. Cooper had spent the whole day trying to place other lives. First, at Kelly Novak's and then later at Woodlawn Cemetery.

"Do you have any idea how many John Coopers we got buried here?" the registry clerk had asked him. The man's silver hair shone in the light. He looked like a retired policeman, Cooper thought, content to be out of harm's way at last. No, Cooper couldn't remember the exact date of interment, only the year of death.

"It was only meant to be temporary," he would say. "He was supposed to be taken out to Iowa, to Waterloo."

"You'd be surprised how many temporaries we got out there," the clerk said as he unfolded a large map. He began to draw circles with a red marking pencil at different points, while he thumbed through a card file. "We got several out there that's been temporary since before the Civil War. That's pretty damn temporary," he chuckled.

The map of the cemetery was pale green with intersecting lines in a darker ink as on a chart. Cooper expected the man to connect all the different points, some twelve or more locations circled in red, to trace the perimeter of something just underneath, something like an island sunk beneath the surface of the sea and which could only be glimpsed from above.

"So, here goes," the clerk said, handing him the map. "You got about an hour before it gets dark, at which time the gates will be locked; but it is my opinion to you to be out before that, as this place gets hostile and I don't mean ghosts."

But Cooper had not bothered to look for the grave, though several sites were close by the registry bureau. He had been in the Army when his father had died. He hoped he would recognize it if he saw the location, but he would come back when he had more time.

Ruth had been asleep when he got back from the city on the last train to Green River. Keeping watch before Donald Jacobs's apartment had made him late.

"Where are your people buried?" he asked the next day.

"My people?" Her mouth curved scornfully.

"The people who raised you."

"Oh, one of those places on Long Island. So why were you so late last night. Is that hunkie working you hard?"

He would tell her he had gone to the library to look something up and had got to reading and missed the early train. That was partially true, for he had gone to the library, but his research was done quickly and then he went back uptown, on the East Side. He had imagined his sentry duty outside the poet's apartment to be some sort of a game. Flip Winslow pursuing evil geniuses. But it wasn't a game, for he left shamed and wounded. A self-inflicted wound.

A warm breeze came off the East River, stirring grit off the sidewalk. It had gotten into his eyes as he stood in a dark stairwell across from the apartment. The taxi pulled up as if through water. Two couples had gotten out and he recognized Jacobs's stocky figure and bushy dark hair. When Ruth had introduced them years ago at the store on 23rd Street, the poet's dumplinglike physique had surprised him. He had thought, until then, that all poets were tall and lean, like Shelley. He had been strangely disappointed; all of her lovers were supposed to be tall and lean and good-looking.

The women talked and laughed loudly—nervously, Cooper would think. The other man said nothing, never seemed to pass through any area of light so he could be seen. Jacobs led the way up the steps of the town house.

One of the women looked like Ruth. Cooper would lean forward, peer above the level of the sidewalk, like a soldier looking out from a bunker; she was much younger than Ruth and when she turned briefly to her companion, the vestibule light defined a different nose and mouth. She didn't look at all like Ruth, actually.

The poet had unlocked the door and led the way; the two women followed, jauntily, arm in arm, and the second man came behind with his arms outstretched to hold the door open for them, though there was a protective, shepherding character to the pose, Cooper would think. If they had turned around, his arms would have blocked their way. First the lower-hall light went on, then the second-floor light. The illumination faintly outlined some of the office area of the front windows. Ragged pillars of books raised up behind the windows on the second floor. Then all went dark. Cooper craned his head back. He pressed against the back wall of the entry. He wondered if he dared risk climbing to the top stoop of this building where he might see some of the windows of the recessed penthouse. More lights had been turned on as others were turned off. Then more turned off while others were turned on. It was a pyrotechnic display. Some sort of a video game? Were the women turning the lights on as the men turned them off? The light pulsed. Once his father had sold some plans, for a very good price, for something called an "orgone box," and the undulating illuminations above reminded him of this sweatbox rig that was supposed to recharge the energy of the person who sat in it. How long he would stand there, he could not say. He had missed the early train. When he finally climbed the three steps out of the basement entry it was very late. The lights above continued to send out their throbbing signals, but Cooper would feel exhausted, drained.

"Aren't you going to share this humble repast?" Ruth calls to him from the backdoor. She looks like a black paper cutout pasted within the brilliant rectangle of the kitchen's light. Then she moves, crosses her arms. "It's freezing out here."

Hal is already seated at the table, a fork clutched in his right hand. The evening news unravels on the television set, and the voices of the commentators sound like guests casually waiting in the living room for their turn at the small table.

Cooper sits down across from Hal, and Ruth takes the chair between them. She passes him salad after helping the boy to some. "You may begin," she tells Hal softly. The boy's handling of fork and spoon is almost normal, and he no longer dribbles food from the left corner of his mouth. He sits hunched low in his chair, shy of his size. Drinking from a glass is yet a problem and the milk goes too fast for him to swallow. The muscles of his throat can't keep up and the milk backs up to spill out over his lips and chin. Ruth reaches out with a napkin and wipes his face. "Well, you're going to be Clay's helper? Going to build a house?"

Hal nods happily, chewing quickly, then smacks his lips. "Hammer and nail. Do all that," he says. "It's a *very* big house with lots of windows." He sounds sad, though his expression is cheerful. Sometimes, as with the milk, a word will get out of control, lose its place in the phrase, and pick up a momentum of loudness on its own so that the longer sentences veer wildly in volume. It embarrasses Hal when this happens so he usually chooses to speak only in monosyllables or short sentences except when he becomes excited and forgets.

But Cooper likes the sounds Hal makes. He told Ruth that they reminded him of old liturgical music, Gregorian chants, and she had laughed at first but then nodded. "Hal is getting so big, Ruth. He's becoming such a young man."

"He's our very own carpenter," she says patting the boy's hand. Hal looks at both of them. The light gray eyes switch from one to another, the small tongue flicks the corner of the mouth.

"What about these kites that Clay says you're making? You don't fly them in this kind of weather?"

"Uh, no. No kites now. I'm—I'm—" he chews and swallows. "I'm mak-*ing* something for spring."

"A kite?" Cooper asks.

Hal gives a sound that Cooper takes for the affirmative before the boy lowers his face to another forkful of beans.

"I'm going to have to give you a trim, young man," Ruth says as she ruffles the boy's thick hair. The blackness of it makes the flesh of his neck even paler.

"No, Mums, please not."

"Oh, yes. After supper."

"Oh, *no*," Hal's voice rises, a chorus of agony. His eyes roll frightfully. The weather forecast is on the news program. Cooper can see by the chart that a warming front was coming up from the Ohio Valley. In another few weeks, the snow outside would be gone, and the framed light from the windows would be erased, washed off with the thaw.

"You mustn't worry." Ruth leans toward Cooper, puts her hand over his, "I'm not going to quit. There's no way I can quit."

Later, she moves the high stool away from the wall phone and places it on top of some newspapers she's spread in the center of the kitchen floor. Mournfully, Hal takes his place on it, an old sheet tucked in around his shirt collar, so the boy's head and face is presented as if it were an object on display. Ruth clacks the shears with a professional flourish.

"I'm-a Giuseppe, the barber, with a bigga moo-stache," she intones, "and if you donna sit still I give you bigga da bash."

"Hoo-ho," Hal laughs. "Oh, Mums, you are a toots. Toot-toot!"

"Toot-toot," Ruth snips the hair.

Cooper hears these sounds as he sits in the living room, looking over the television schedule. At this hour, all three channels air game shows, but in a half hour there would be a comedy series he liked. It was the story of some people shipwrecked on an island and how they improvised. Hal enjoyed it and even Ruth would watch with them sometimes.

When they first got the set, she would never sit with them. Hal was little then, small enough to cuddle in his lap, as they watched Lucy and Desi, Beaver and all the different television families. But Ruth wouldn't watch. "It's that canned laughter," she used to say. "It's not real, you know. It's all mechanical, on a machine that some engineer plays out. So listen to Hal laugh. He's laughing with that machine. Like that machine. Listen to him sometimes when you're watching one of those crapolas. He laughs when that machine laughs, not because there's anything funny happening. That's funny? Lucille Ball opens a door and rolls her eyes? That's funny?"

Cooper waits for his program with the sound turned off, so the contestants on the game show turn and wave within the square screen like creatures within a tank. He hears Hal and Ruth chatting nonsense, hears the attendant clip of the scissors. On the burnished surface of the metal urn that contains Armstrong's ashes, amorphous shapes pass like images from another planet. The hour's contentment seems to shift the three of them into a different time, as if a switch has been thrown, in the same way he had turned off the sound on the television. They are preserved in this moment, kept safe within the small house as it is suspended and moves through the night, its windows piercing the dark with the profluent beams of a star.

The Sound of Wings
Accounts of Various Air Wars and
Personal Adventures Experienced by
Roy E. Armstrong, Capt. Ret.
U. S. Army Air Corps

Dear Kelly,
Here is the old guy's journal as you requested. I'll send you
more as I type it up; his handwriting is shaky, hard to read.
Do you think his fact and my fiction can be fit together? No
orangutans in his cockpit.

The weather has turned very balmy, maybe we'll have an
early spring. Hal busy as a carpenter's helper and working
on some secret project. Something for Ruth, he says. Wilson
Bean doesn't seem to publish much poetry, but maybe you
know of some editor that might look at her work? She's been
busy with the correspondence school but has put together
quite a collection of her own. Hope to hear from you soon.

Yrs to serve,

Jack

BLACK ACE MAGAZINES

Not even in Finland did any of us wear parachutes, and the planes were still nothing more than kites with engines bolted on the front; and here comes this Jew that used to make the circuit of the fields in France, huckstering these parachutes. I think a couple were the same ones, because nobody ever bought any.

"Well, now Izzy," I say to him. We're in this hotel bar in Helsinki. "You're still selling your umbrellas."

"Ah, Mr. Armstrong—of Yale, isn't it?" He has this professor way of talking down over his nose and mustache. "You have followed the sport here, have you. Which side are you flying for now?"

"The Whites," I say to him, though to be truthful I was never quite sure of the colors or what they meant. It could have been green or purple, all the same to me. When I got off the ferry from Stockholm, the Whites had just taken over the neighborhood, so I signed up with them. Now that's funny, to think how historical circumstances like that can change a person's whole life. What if the Reds had been in charge? "But I imagine you are working both sides of the field?"

"Of course," he shrugs and flags down a waiter. "Falling through space has no political distinction."

I should describe this place we're in. It's the restaurant-bar of a hotel that the Russians built for themselves when they ran Finland, and I mean the old Russia of the late, unlamented czar. So it's quite a fancy spa with big pots of ferns, gleaming brass, and skylights of colored glass as you might see in a cathedral. The place is also full of whores which is why von Loerzer likes to come here. I come here because I can hear English spoken. The Finns and Germans I fly with never speak to each other and certainly not to me, except for Klaus. The natives speak no English, only Russian or their own peculiar lingo. Some Swedish. Last week I came across an old *Century Magazine* in the library of this manor house where several of us bunk. I never read the magazine in the States, but I read it cover to cover. Even the ads. That must explain why the whores at the Metropole speak English, because a lot of them came from families that subscribed to magazines like the *Century* before the war. English seems to be the language of exchange here at the Metropole.

"So are you selling many of your chutes to the Reds?" I ask the Jew.

"Surely, you must have some estimate of that yourself, or has your marksmanship failed since you fly with the Hun?" He sips the tea this waiter just brought him.

"Lay off it," I say.

He looks at me for a minute, then slumps down into his chair. "Business is just as bad on the other side. All of you have this Icarus complex." Klaus has just come down the staircase into the lobby. He still has the gray, greatcoat with the fur collar draped over his shoulder, and I wonder if he kept it on while he did his business with the girl he had gone upstairs with. Seeing me with Pearlstein puts a crimp in his swagger, but he comes on, sits, and reaches down to flick at his boots as if he's just walked through a stable yard. I make the introductions.

"Vere do these chutes come from?" he asks Izzy.

"I represent a family firm in Akron, Ohio," Izzy answers. "They've been in business for twenty years, since 1900. Every parachute is guaranteed."

"This fellow has sense of humor," Klaus says to me and he smiles which makes the scar on his right cheek pucker. He claims that I put it there and I do remember a scrap with a white triplane with a green heart painted on the side—once over Neuilly about a month after von Richthofen went down. We had just lost Lufbery. But I never believed him. It was Klaus's way of being generous or of being friendly, saying you had taken a shot at him once and had just missed. Isn't that *wunderbar*? Meanwhile, he waves down a waiter and orders a beer.

"Why haffn't you sold one to Armstrong here? All you Americans should be *au courant*."

"Hey, it just occurred to me," Izzy says. "Are you *the* Loerzer?"

"Nah, nah. A distant cousin," Klaus says and looks away.

"So how many kills did you have?" the salesman asks.

"Eleven proved." Klaus shrugs and recrosses his legs. Like most of us, this kind of talk makes him nervous. A violin and piano have started up in the corner behind some greenery and there's a sound of big guns way in the distance, like summer thunder. Most of the heavy fighting is happening far north of the city. The music reminds me of the tea dances on Sunday afternoons when I used to trot with Sally. The waiter brings the beer and von Loerzer pays him with a combination of Swedish kronor and the script the provisional government pays us. It makes a small pile on the tray. The kronor is for the beer, the script is the waiter's. "So tell me," the salesman leans forward. "What was your most memorable shoot down?" Pearlstein should have a beard, I always think, a long bushy, black beard to go with the rest of his undertaker's look, though the lines of his face were rather delicate and the nose thin.

"That is an awkward matter for our friend Armstrong," Klaus replies after taking a drink.

"Ah, a friend?" Pearlstein looks at me with dramatic sympathy. "A mate, a wingman, perhaps."

"Not a friend," I say. "I knew Busch earlier in the escadrille but he was not a friend." Busch was from Colgate.

"Strange, isn't it," Klaus is saying, "how I attack someone with a countryman's name. Perhaps his father—yes?—vent to Stadz and dere a few years later over Chauny I set his son's Spad on fire."

"Burning Busch." Pearlstein says and looks at me.

"Vas?" Klaus doesn't get the joke and continues almost languidly. The details were already familiar to me. "We hear the one-thirty-ninth is across the way so I am up one morning hunting for your man Putnam."

"What are you flying?" Pearlstein asks.

"I haff mine Fokker tridecker und den I see this Spad at two thousand meters und I clumb into sun and roll over und down." His right hand has made the maneuver and Izzy's eyes follow. I can almost see the cloud cover through which the fingers dive. "He is a dummkopf."

"That was Busch," I say and signal the waiter.

". . . und never see me. He is flying like he fishes in a lake, just floating along." Klaus laughs loud and claps his hands together. "Den, I strike."

Bam-bam-bam.

"Just a little shooting and the engine goes up. No smoke but a flame, just like that. I must have hit the petrol. Then, the most extraordinary thing happens."

I remember Busch as a short, chubby boy, someone who was always writing his mother and passing around the stick-fudge she sent him. So I can see him crawling out of the Spad's cockpit, as von Loerzer tells Pearlstein, along the spine of the fuselage toward the tail assembly, away from the fire. All at four thousand feet. Anything was better than burning. We had all talked about that—what we would do. I picture Busch's short legs astride the Spad's fuselage as the plane continues to burn up front, miraculously keeping an even keel, gliding, Klaus is saying, with this small, round, bundled-up figure hanging onto the tail. Busch used to wear a scarf, I just remember, that his sister had knit with the Colgate colors. He probably had it on.

"Und den, he iss waving one arm at me."

"Ah, you're hanging around to see him die?" Pearlstein says with a strange light in his eyes.

"I keep company," Klaus says seriously. "It is—in English?" he looks at me.

"A point of honor," I say to the Jew who smiles ever so slightly.

"Yah, honor," Klaus continues. "I see him so clearly waving at me, then pointing at him—himself—und I see what he means. He wants me to shoot him. So I make one pass but I miss. The tracers go high. The fire is roaring past the cockpit now. All is flame. I come back. He is holding onto struts of the rudder now. I think that plane is staying up by its own fire, like a hot-air balloon. Oh, I have him so clean in my sights. He seem to smile und his eyes are closed. But the goddamn guns jam. I see his face become—how you say, all apart?"

"You just said it," I tell him.

"Yes, all apart. He guesses the problem. That ass of a mechanic have not properly cleaned the magazines. I beat his ass, you can be sure, ven I get back to the field."

"If you Krauts did some of that work yourselves, you wouldn't have had so much trouble," I say. "All of us were our best armorers. We knew everything about our guns. Took care of them."

"So, Armstrong—*my cher ami*, Roy—how can the world be so safe from your democracy if each of you knows so much about guns und how to keep them firing?" He has taken a cigarette from a silver case and lifted the candle from the table to it.

"But Busch?" Pearlstein asks.

"Oh, he jumps," Klaus says, blowing a stream of smoke straight up.

"Jump? How high was he?"

"Oh, about one-thousand-five-hundred meters. He disappear through a big white cloud."

"You see. You see that?" Pearlstein is on his feet and he is trembling. Then he sits down quickly. "If he had had . . . was this Busch with the Escadrille when I came by that time?"

"I can't remember." I really can't, but to make him feel better, I say, "No, he signed on after Wilson declared war."

This girl has been standing against a marble column where the lounge goes into a ballroom. There are a few couples moving about in there and I recognize a couple of my squadron. They wear civilian clothes as we do; this army has no uniforms for us. Her hair is a brilliant red, unnaturally red, and when she comes by the table, arm in arm with another girl, she throws her head back and laughs a little too loud. The skin of her neck and arms is very white, which makes her hair even more startling.

"Do you know how many of you brave airmen perished in the last exercise?" Pearlstein is talking like a professor again. "Almost sixty thousand. Sixty thousand. That's the entire population of the city of Toledo, Ohio."

"But how many were from this city of Toledo, Ohio?" Klaus asks. He rubs out his cigarette. The ashtray is made of green marble, and there's a hole through one lip where something had been bolted to it.

"Hello, sirs," she says. "I am full of thirst."

Without shifting his legs or, seemingly, his attention Klaus said something to her in German that made her white skin pink and her hair even redder. I caught the word *lutschen*.

"Jo," she says and looks toward the foyer. Her eyes are very dark, almost black. I wonder about her age. Plump arms and shoulders.

"I am good pleasure at that," she sing-songs, but her expression is flat.

But Klaus has already stood up and the two of them disappear around the stairway and into the unlit arcade of the Grand Salon. I note the girl is taking small, quick steps, not the long strides I saw earlier as she strolled past the table.

"Did you see that?" Pearlstein is saying, his forehead working up and down. "I can't believe it. He just came back and now he's doing another. But not you, Armstrong? You have no interest in a bit of fluff? The American, pure and . . . I watched you looking at that little whore. You'd treat her as a sister, I am thinking. You Americans."

"What are you? You're an American."

"Excuse me. Of course, my passport says it is so. But by birth, by life, by the treatment my family has enjoyed in America, well, perhaps I have no country. Just yet." He is smiling with eyes cast down. He sips his tea. "You must find this duty boring. An ace almost three times over and you just fly sightseeing runs over this marketplace?"

The duty is boring, I agree. We fly patrols of three ships, four shifts a day. Up and down, up and down. But the D-VIIs are fun to fly. I can see why we had so much trouble with them in '18, though the Camel could turn it in knots. But it's a stable ship, steady and with no spin to worry about. About six were flown here by way of Sweden because the Versailles treaty "outlawed" them. Too good. Good dive and can hang on its propeller all day.

(Jack, I think we can eliminate much of this technical material about the planes. To be safe, I've entered a copyright on these journals. You've got dynamite material here.)

Meanwhile, von Loerzer and the girl have returned, and she sits down in the chair next to me. Klaus takes up his former position, legs stretched out into the aisle so that waiters have to step over them. "Gut," he tells us. "Angel *lecker*," and he laughs more pleased by his cleverness, I think, than what his mixed-up language means. I am signaling a waiter.

"Something to drink?" I ask her. I figure she still might be thirsty.

"Yo, kytos. Thank you." She looks at me and then at Klaus as if there's a joke between them. "Limonaati," she tells the waiter.

Klaus and Izzy are talking politics and I am studying this girl as I pretend to listen. I'd say the clothes she's wearing are not hers, maybe an older sister's. The beaded top of the dress is cut for a fuller figure and hangs away from her as she bends over to sip her lemonade, so I can see her small breasts. Her shoes seem too large for her feet also. Up close, her hair is more startling. Scarlet. Her hands are squarish with plump backs to them, childlike. The nails are cracked and dirty. She could be sixteen or twenty-six. Somewhere between.

". . . this Herr Hitler." Pearlstein is saying.

"Herrgottsack!" Klaus explodes with laughter. "Dat little pimple. He's an Austrian and you expect him to move that mountain? Germany is no more, Jude—you have no need to worry about Germany again." He is smiling but the scar on his cheek has turned white so I guess he's more than sorry about the fate of Germany. Four years ago, if my Camel had slipped just a little to the left, Klaus would not be here. So he claims.

". . . true," he is saying to Pearlstein. Then he turns to me. "You remember Göring, Roy? He took over the Jagdgeschwaden when von Richtofen went down. *Ja?*"

"What about him?"

"Vell, the Jude is saying that some of the army is backing this adventurer, Hitler. In fact, I hear from Göring last week. He has been flying Fokker D-VIIs into Sweden to sell them. He is, how you say, a smuggler."

"What about?" Pearlstein leans forward. He is holding up the empty teacup, studying the leaves in the bottom. "What did Göring say?"

"Oh, he says nothing. Just about dogs he is breeding."

"But he is staying in touch," Pearlstein says still looking into his tea leaves.

"*Jawohl,*" von Loerzer replies, crossing his legs. "He was my rotten-kamerad and we have much to share."

"Even Herr Hitler?" Izzy asks.

"*Nein* . . . that joke. Göring is a fool about him. Politics spoils your aim. Isn't that right, Armstrong?"

"Right," I say. A violin starts squeaking in the ballroom joined by a piano and an accordian. "Dance?" I ask the redhead. She's finished her lemonade and is sitting on the edge of her chair, feet together and hands cupping her elbows. She jumps up. "I am good pleasure at that," she says in this baby talk.

We have the ballroom almost to ourselves. Sunken floor with tables set up and around on a tier. They all have tablecloths and small lamps on them, but nobody sitting there. The orchestra is sawing a foxtrot I recognize from before the war. I remember doing a few turns to it at the Hotel Taft in New Haven with Sally Emerson down from Vassar. So here I am turning to it on an empty floor in Helsinki with this little prostitute who hums out of tune. She moves like she was plowing. I've never danced with a more clumsy woman. Good pleasure at this she is not which makes me wonder if her other self-advertised specialties are similarly inept. She's all over my feet, and I have to shove her around the floor. She has this look on her face—sublime is the word. Holds her right hand out to my left with a kind of elegance, a kind of queenly crook to her arm that gives her the look of a swan gliding over the stream, if you don't look at her feet. I'm wondering if I'll ever see Poughkeepsie again. Nothing's black and white anymore.

Klaus and I have a good time with the Fokkers and he shows me a lot of tricks, but the two of us must seem like lunatics to Illka, our wingman. He's a sober, dour Finn who carries out the flight plan precisely while von Loerzer and I play tag all over the sky. From the air this country looks calm, lush. Many lakes, reflective. Spruce and pine forests as green as the small green heart Klaus has painted on his Fokker. The Grunherz of Bavaria, he says. Why don't I put the stars and stripes on my plane, he asks? Why don't I?

"Smitten with that little whore, are you?" Pearlstein says one evening. He has watched as I ask about Nikki. The waiter shrugs. Then a prostie, with a cast in one eye, comes over. She says Nikki is home visiting her parents. They live near Tampere, where all the fighting is happening. All the while she's telling me this, her one crossed eye is looking over my shoulder like she was keeping this eye out for someone. A customer, cops, what? I buy her a glass of beer.

"Your comrade, von Loerzer, doesn't make that mistake." Pearlstein is eating salmon and onions. He makes a thick sandwich and takes a mouthful.

"Business must be good," I say. He shrugs and continues to chew.

"You're funny," Pearlstein is saying through a mouthful of food. The orchestra is playing "There's Danger in Your Eyes, Cherie." "Where will you be flying next? Ireland? Do the Irish rebels have an airplane you can fly?"

Actually, Klaus has been talking about China. There's all kinds of little skirmishes going on there, different warlords squaring off. And they have the moola. My sister writes me that. . . .

(Jack, We have to cut a lot of this material. The China episodes and the South American part. That's a good sex scene in the sauna with Nikki, but it's not worth plowing through the rest of it. Also, the Hollywood section. Redford's already made a movie about World War I fliers making a movie about World War I flying. Even the affair with Jean Harlow, if we can believe Armstrong. Gossip column stuff and fifty years late. The stuff we can market is the Spanish Civil War. That's fresh material; no one's written about that from this angle. Sorry about your wife's poems. They had one good reading, but poetry has to knock us over. Here's what I've done—cut right to his arrival in Spain in 1936.)

The boys helped me celebrate my birthday the night before we docked at Le Havre. I'm the same year as the century and at '36. I'm the "old man" of the group. I look around the table. Frank Tinker only got out of Annapolis four years ago. Allison is a kid. Skinner is fresh out of VMI. Ben Lieder has knocked around a little—a journalist and photographer. But I am the old man, the only one with any combat experience too. And here we all are, heading for Spain. Different war. Last time, we were all Ivy Leaguers. Tinker has negotiated our deal: 1500 per month plus a thousand bucks for every enemy shot down. Sweet cakes, I tell you.

We're met in Paris at the station by these little guys who take us to a hotel on the Left Bank. I try out some of my parleyvoo on the natives and they just look at me like I was bedbugs. It was different in 1918 when they sweated their balls. They understood me then, you bet.

All of our belongings are taken and "checked" they tell us until we come back. I wonder how many of us are going to be coming back to pick up our suitcases. Jim Allison says he's left a package at the Illinois Athletic Club in Chicago also. He wears the metal check for it around his neck.

We are given Spanish passports and also new names. Tinker is now Francisco Tuejo. Lieder is José Lindo. And so on. I, Roy Armstrong, have become Juan Carrillo. *Olé*.

So I'm on the hunt again. All the while Lieder, or José Lindo, is talking to us about the Party this and the Party that. He's a red and makes no bones about it. Shut up, will ya, Allison says. How can anyone sleep with you shooting your mouth off. But it's good-natured.

It's cold in these mountains and sunny Spain ain't sunny. But it's warmer the next day and someone says we are near Barcelona. The word when we got off the ship was that Madrid had fallen to Franco and some of us said, good night, nurse. Close the door, Henry. But the word in Barcelona is that the rebels had got only as far as part of the University and that the front had stabilized along the Mansanares River. So, maybe things are turning out okay.

The Spaniards treat us like princes. Lots of wine and many toasts. Music. Skinner brings two girls back to the hotel but is too pissed to do anything with them. "We are no longer officers," Tinker says, "and none of us were ever gentlemen." "Except for Armstrong," Lieder says. He has a thick Brooklyn accent, so he sounds unfriendly but really isn't. I can take their joshing.

The next morning, hangovers or not, they drive us out to the field where we meet our Russian wingmates and see our little Chattos for the first time. The Russian planes are neat little ships.

Fixed landing gear, short stubby wings, and the open cockpit set just at the top wing, midway in the chunky fuselage. Technically, they are Policarus—some such sounding name—I-15s. "Park-your-carcass," Jim Allison calls them. The Russian pilots remind me of the Finns I flew with. They are shy, very solemn until they laugh, and then it's ho-ho-ho. Their heads and faces look skinned, close haircuts. Look like farm kids in the Midwest. We can't understand each other, except in the air. Tinker gives them names from the seven dwarfs in that movie we saw on the ship coming over. Doc. Dopey. Happy. And so on. They're a good-natured sort and just laugh and nod. They don't understand either. But in the air, they're something else. "Hot pilots," Tinker says. He's right. They show us how to handle these little fighters. These stubby little planes can move around like fleas on a hot plate. "Look at old man Armstrong," Skinner kids me. "He thinks he's back with the Lafayette Escadrille." I do admit to a certain pumping in the blood when I slip into the cockpit of these little green planes, and that big radial winds up. The wind in my face. This ship can turn on a dime. Very responsive. I can't wait to do a little shooting.

This field near Barcelona is where they put these planes together, the crates arriving by sea. After a week with Dopey and Company, we're ready to join the fray. Some of us, I'm not so sure about. Skinner and Allison seem a little hesitant. Lieder's a good pilot. So is Tinker. He says these I-15s remind him of the Boeing F4Bs he flew off the *Lexington* before the Navy pitched him out. You wouldn't think to look at him with his curly blond hair and long sensitive face that he'd be the sort of fellow who would get into so many fights. But one too many and the Navy says, good-bye Frank, hello Francisco.

So they call us *La Patrulla Americana*. For $1500 per month, they call us anything they want. We're supposed to fly down to a place called Albacete, south of here, where we are to be welcomed by the boys that have hired us. The Russians have been in this since last fall. November. Madrid had been a quilting bee for the German and Eytie bombers. Their Junkers would come in with crews eating liverwurst, drop their load, and get back to quarters for streudel. Then Dopey and Company show up in their little I-15s and it's close the door. They sweep the skies.

It turns out that Skinner taught French at Philips Exeter, and one of these Russkies also talks Frog so the two of them do all the talking for us. This Russian smokes with a black cigarette holder. He says the Germans have got their new dive-bomber going, the Stuka, but it is easy to get at. Clumsy and stiff. A lot of the German pilots have trouble flying it. He saw three of them go straight into the ground, never pull out. The German fighter is a Heinkel and no match for our Chattos.

"I flew one of the Heinkels," I say. All of my gang turn around. We're in Tinker's room at the hotel. The brandy's been going around and Allison has started a bridge game with a couple of our Soviet comrades.

"When was that, Pop?" Lieder asks.

"At the Cleveland Air Races a couple of years back."

This Russian—the one we call Doc—has kept looking at me the whole time as Skinner gives him the French words in one ear. Then he starts speaking slowly and puts the cigarette holder back between his teeth. "He is saying that the best pilots have been the Italians."

"You're joking," Tinker laughs.

"Best plane too."

"They wind up the spaghetti and let it fly," Tinker passes me the brandy bottle with a wink.

"All the weeping mothers in the world," Ben Leider says, "and we sit here making wisecracker jokes." He takes this outing a lot more seriously than the rest of us. On the *Normandie* coming over, he would lecture us—Professor Leider's seminars, Skinner called them—about this civil war. About Franco and the Fascists and about the Spanish Republic. He gave us a breakdown of all the interests involved and how the Republic was being blockaded by England and France, which is why we have to sneak into the country. Yet everyone else—save the Russians—is helping Franco. Even U.S. Texaco was shipping oil and gas to him. All them Heinkels and Stukas flying on Texaco gasoline. It's a mixed-up world. We were only there for the dough, he said.

"That's not true," Frank Tinker said. "I could have flown for Franco. In fact, I was thinking of doing so. But I didn't go in for bombing women and children."

"Ya got some principles, I guess," Leider says in his Brooklynese. "After all."

Skinner is on his feet, swaying a bit. "I noticed a couple of *muchachas* in the lobby a while back. Anyone want to see how they are in tight turns?" No takers. Leaves.

One of the Russians gets out a guitar and starts to strum it and they sing songs. They become very delicate when they sing. High tenors. We pass the bottle around. The hearts game is noisy. About an hour later Skinner comes back looking down. He couldn't find any companionship. We all start singing along with the Russians, not knowing the words. They teach us a song that has all kinds of languages—the languages of this war . . .

Ich came nach Spain in Januar
Yo hablar seulment English
But jetz I say, comment savar
Wie gehts, que tal, Tovaritsch

In return, we teach them "I've Been Working on the Railroad."

You couldn't ask for better flying weather the next morning, high and clear. Our heads are in bad shape. I don't think any of us has had more than an hour's sleep. Out at the field our Chattos are lined up like a picture on the tarmac. Turning over. The Russian, Doc, shows us on the map where we're going and gives us a compass course. He and two others will lead the way.

It's a small cockpit, compact, and I think of that guy who kept trying to sell us parachutes back in the war. We wear them now. Little flat packages that slap against your bum when you walk and serve as a seat cushion when you're in the plane. Roscoe Turner got me to wearing one after the last Thompson trophy.

It's a tight fit in the Chatto's cockpit. The Cyclone is seven hundred horses, and every hoof is kicking grit in my eyes before I pull down my goggles. The I-15 has good visibility. The top wing is set low over the fuselage on a kind of hutchlike construction. You can see through and over the wing. Then you can look over the side. Oh boy. Fun. If only I hadn't had those last few swallows of brandy.

The Russkies take off together. We six Americans, *La Patrulla Americana,* follow in pairs: me and Tinker, then Allison and Skinner, with Ben Leider and a guy named Len Green off last. We get up to 1000 meters in about a minute. It's a strange landscape. The colors are brown and red, gray. I can see mountains ahead. Lot of mountains in Spain. Where we're going in just beyond them. We climb another 2000 feet. The Ebro River passes below. A lot of fighting down there, I guess. Doc and his buddies are up another thousand meters, flying point. There shouldn't be any rebel planes around, but just in case . . . I feel real comfy. Knowing I'm surrounded by 9-millimeter sheets of armor plate increases my sense of well being. None of that between you and bullets in the Camel or the old Nieuport. Just painted canvas. Also, those wicker seats—like on a Sunday porch. This one is cast of metal. Oh boy. The slipstream stings my cheeks. I put my head back against the headrest and just enjoy the scenery, the feel of this little plane around me. Very quick controls—even with my hangover, I've never felt so good on the ground. I'm at home once again. The breeze in my face. I think of that time Jean Harlow and I flew up to Squaw Valley. We had "borrowed" that Morse Scout and it being only a single-seater, Jean sat in my lap. As usual, she wasn't wearing very much underneath. Some girl—well, I'll say.

My homey thoughts are intruded upon—and I mean intruded—by something I catch out of the corner of my left eye. It's Tinker's right wing tip. That son of a gun wants to have a little fun. While I've been enjoying my thoughts, he's crept up alongside of me and has edged in. He looks at me real solemn for a spell; he's so close I can read his name on his old Navy jacket. He has a little blue cloth fixed to the top of his helmet. He shapes his lips real careful so I can read the words: "I LOVE YOU." Why, that clown! I reach up and grab his wing tip poking into my cockpit and push him away. His long face seems to break into two parts when he laughs. Then, I see that Skinner is going to play the same game on me from the right. I get the picture. Two young pups, testing the old guy's reflexes. I'll have none of that. So I kick up the Cyclone and pull back on the stick. That little I-15 jumps up like a bronco, and at the top I do an Immelman and then go into a dive. Skinner has to skid fast to get out of the way, and at the bottom I pull up and the rest of them scatter fast. I could have got lead into two of them. Skinner would have been a goner. Then there's a flash over me. That crazy Tinker had come at me upside down, overflew, and came back in a tight turn that put him on my starboard. I rolled and dived away, but he came right down with me. We must have dropped 1000 meters because those mountaintops looked awfully big when I came out.

Meanwhile, the Russkies just flew straight ahead, as if painted on the bright blue sky. The lead plane—Doc's—waggles wings. Clearly, a command to cut the crap and come up with them. So we do and come up just under the three of them. If they want discipline, we can show them disciplino Americano.

Without any direction, the six of us get into a tight *escalier*, and I mean tight. You could walk up our six planes from wing to wing. Leider's left wheel is just over my right shoulder. It turns idly in my prop wash.

This is all Republican territory. The fighting's over around here. Doc and his three mates peel off and we come down behind them, still in formation. The city juts out over the plain to the south. We've been getting over mountains all morning. So this sudden flatness is very startling.

The Russians lead us in low, almost at house-top level over Albacete. I guess they want to show off their planes. Politics has a lot to do with this war—not like '18. We pass over this good-sized city. Signs of war. The big church is down. Burned. There's the airfield—and field is the word. I make out a whole bunch of people standing around. There's a platform with colorful flags around it.

The ground looks hard enough and Doc seems to know, because he just leads his other two wingmates down and they make a pretty landing together. Morning light flashes on band instruments. Oom-pah-pah . . .

Tinker dips his wings and leads us in by twos, staggered, and it makes for a more colorful introduction, you could say. Skinner bumps, then sets down smooth. But for him, it was the flawless landing of a wing. We taxi up to the line where Doc, Sleepy, and Happy are already out of their ships, the props stopped and shaking hands with the welcoming committee. We line up and dress right. I must say these planes make an effective sight all in a row. They seem ready to hop off the ground and give a scrap, and if I was one of these Loyalist guys, I'd feel encouraged by the sight.

(This will make a great scene in a movie. Maybe, even, start the journal here? I've talked to some people on the Coast. They're interested.)

It's hotter than hell. My feet start to sweat in the wool socks. It's like an oven door has opened and it's only January. What's it gonna be like in July? Tinker has already pulled off his leather jacket and I see the rest following suit. Coveralls, helmets, everything off. We're a motley crew inside our flying gear. Skinner and Allison wear turtlenecks. Leider has on a tie and shirt. I've got on my lucky Cuban shirt with the red lobsters. Tink is wearing his old Navy chinos, without the insignia, of course. Suddenly, these greasy little bastards are all over us, kissing us. It was making me sick. On the ground and in this heat. My head and stomach were doing barrel rolls. The rest felt the same. The crowd dragged us around, some of them put Allison up on their shoulders. The band was playing the "Star Spangled Banner" out of key and winded. I kept thinking, I get $1500 a month for this; it's not worth it. Leider looked like he was about to throw up, though he almost always looks like that.

Some more I-15s had got there ahead of us, piloted by other Americanos who had been doing their "basic" at a place called Alicante, over on the coast. Among these were Art Shapiro and Whitey Dahl. I knew Dahl before. His wife led a dance orchestra, and I met them both one night at the Coconut Grove where she was appearing. Shapiro was a funny guy: offhand, a loner. His Spanish name was Arturo Vasnit.

"Vasnit?" Tink asked later. "Is that Spanish?" Turns out *vas nit* is Yiddish for "I don't know."

So all of us are standing in a loose sort of military rank in front of this speaker's platform. Politicos standing up there with sashes around them, medals. Sun full blast now. I can hardly open my eyes. Everybody else felt the same way.

"Caesar, we who are about to throw up, salute you," Allison said next to me.

"How are you doing, Pop?" Leider asked. I guess I must have looked awful. That shirt with the lobsters didn't help.

Speeches. Like a Rotary Club but in Spanish. Skinner does the translating in patches. Victorious armies . . . heroes and brave men . . . forces of evil . . . fascism. . . . Familiar stuff.

Then this funny little guy with a big beret. The biggest beret I've ever seen, flops way down over one ear. He speaks in French and his voice sounds like a machine gun. Rat-a-tat-tat. I don't understand his parleyvoo but he means business. I'm standing in a footbath of my own sweat. Then, Sally bar the door. Who's that I see on the stand behind the guy with the beret and wearing one almost the same size? My old parachute-pal, Izzy Pearlstein. Can you believe it? This Frenchmen drones on, but Pearlstein seems not to mind. Does he sees me? Of course.

"Well, Captain Armstrong of Yale," he says as we are having some warm beer after the festivities.

"Like I told you before, I never finished at Yale; I wish you'd drop that, Pearlstein."

"Please, my name here is Marron." That figures. We all have new names. It's that kind of war; you change your name in order to be in it. Maybe all wars should be like that, so when you're through you can go back to being yourself. Nobody'll know.

"Who's the little frog with the beret?" I ask.

"That is Marty. He is the Commissar for the Madrid Department." His clothes look different. Pearlstein or Marron was never a fancy dresser, but the cut of his jacket and shirt look strange. European. "Ah, Señor Lindo," Pearlstein says to Ben Lieder, who's just come up and the two of them move off to one side. Pearlstein-Marron starts speaking quickly into Lieder-

Lindo's ear. The journalist has to bend down a little. Once his eyes go over me as he listens to the Jew. Then they go back to the ground.

"I'm glad to see you're on the right side this time," Pearlstein says to me. "I was wondering if I'd hear about you with the Condors. The Staffel 88 has some of your old adversaries. Sperrle commands them. Guess who has made an appearance with the Stukas?"

Our engines are being cranked up and Tinker is motioning to me. We're taking off for Madrid. Pearlstein has to shout over the roar of the Cyclones. Some of the planes are already breaking ground like angry gnats. "Von Richtofen's cousin—Wolf. He's over there too. You'll feel very comfortable here," he is laughing but not really laughing. "I remember those words of your German friend in Helsinki."

"Loerzer? Is he on the other side too?"

"Not yet." Pearlstein waves away my question. I can see he's not used to being interrupted. "I remember him saying to me you never have to worry about Germany again. Well, there they are," he said and points with his right arm in a northerly direction, where the first flights of I-15s have already headed.

Lieder has an unusual background. Born in Russia under the Czar. Went to the University of Missouri, became a journalist. Learned to fly. Strange world where a guy born under the Czar goes to Missouri University and ends up taking pictures from a little Cessna bi-wing for a New York newspaper. Well, I guess.

He's a hot pilot, though a little wild. He takes us into our first real scrap. Tinker is over in town, trying to get us better quarters than these tents we've been staying in. It's been raining almost since we got here. Anyway, word comes in that our side is taking a whipping just east of here from the Eyties and German bombers. "It's the Lincoln Brigade," Lieder tells us, his eyes flashing. "They are pinned down around Jarama"—he says it with a real *J* sound, but no one corrects him. So we take off. Fortunately, this field at Barajas has a concrete strip, so the mud doesn't bother us.

There are twelve of us and we make it to seven thousand feet in no time. Not long after we see the smoke and the little dots in the sky. I'm getting goose bumps the way I used to. The real thing at last. Like the old days. No cameraman cranking over my shoulder as I come down on some guy flying a Beechcraft made up to look like a Fokker. So long, Hollywood; hello, Spain. I cock my guns and clear the chambers. Boy, doesn't that sound good. I look over the side of my cockpit and down. There are dozens and dozens of planes down there and none of them ours. All have these large black Xs on them. Lieder has tipped his I-15 on its prop and drops like a stone. He's crazy. No one knows the stress these wings will take. But we're crazy, too, and follow him down. The engine is screaming. My head is pushed back against the headrest. I can feel my face being pressed out like pie dough. At about three thousand feet we pass through a flight of big Junker trimotors moseying along like dairy cattle. Below them, we jump down on Stukas just coming out of their dives. Bingo. Lieder seems to get one with his first burst. It just blows up. My guns are yammering on another. It staggers, then wings over and goes straight down. Skinner, Allison, and the others are just behind us. I can't see what they get on that dive, though Dahl took out a Stuka. They are ungainly looking airplanes. One wing and with fancy pants on the wheels.

We passed through and zoomed to come up to the trimotors. This was fine shooting. They began to veer off. I counted a mess of parachutes—all from Akron, Ohio, maybe? I couldn't tell which of our boys was doing it, but the formation was breaking off the bombing. I came up under one of them. The whole plane was on top of me. My bullets acted like a can opener tearing through the corrugated tin of the fuselage. As I passed up and around, I caught a glimpse of the pilot. He was very intent on his controls, and I could plainly see him working things furiously. The plane went into a flat spin. I must have cut some cables.

Meanwhile, I saw Lieder throw himself right into the middle of a bunch of Heinkels. They scatter like geese but then close in around him. I came over quick and so did a couple of mates. The Heinkel is no match for us in a dog fight, but with a five-to-one advantage they can be a problem. So three of us bore in to help Lieder out. He's holding his own with two of them. I come up on one from the right quarter. I let my sight drift up from the big X on the rudder until the hairs are just behind the cockpit. Then, rat-tat. The Kraut throws up his hands and then rips off his helmet and goggles. Tears them off as if they were stifling him. He has very blond hair. Another one down. If this war lasts very long, I'm going to be a millionaire.

If I live. The back of my seat rattles like rain on a tin roof. I look around. There's one of those little nasties on my tail. Blessings on that armor plate. I zoom, roll, and before he knows it, I'm polishing his tail. He breaks off. I go after one of his buddies. The sky has become smoky. I try to count heads. I think all of our gang are still in the air. I have to dive away from a big trimotor that is falling down on top of me, all aflame like a hay barn coming apart. Come around upside down and roll over. There's a Heinkel square in my sights. He can't get away. I let him go through his drill for a little bit, following him about in this splendid Russian fighter—comfortably. He starts looking back over his shoulder, wondering, I guess, when I'm going to give it to him. I decide on a placement shot and edge the stick back ever so slightly, so my sight is just behind the prop spinner. About where I figure his radiator should be. Then, rat-tat-tat. The propeller just falls away and smoke gushes from the cowling. Black smoke. He rolls over and slips out of the cockpit. Another parachute. There must be a dozen floating down. Whitey Dahl says later that he nearly ran one down.

Meanwhile, Ben Lieder is up alongside me and pointing down. All of a sudden we have the sky to ourselves. The Fascists have broken off and have hightailed it for their base near the Ebro. Later, we add up our score. We took care of twenty-three of those hombres and didn't lose a ship. One of us had to turn back to Barajas with a nick in his oil pump; the rest of us go downstairs on the carpet to take the pressure off the Lincoln Brigade. This was the first time I paid attention to names like this; I wonder if there was also a Washington or a Teddy Roosevelt Brigade.

Lieder leads us in low over the battleground. Our boys are up, arms up, and I guess cheering us. This is pretty country around here. Rolling fields like those in east Iowa but with olive trees.

There are farmers out in these fields, going about their business while men fight all around them.

I don't know about the others, but I figure I only have about a couple of hundred rounds left in my guns. But you figure 400 rounds per plane—eleven planes—that's about 5,000 bullets all coming in at nearly two hundred miles per hour. We can do a bit of damage to those ground troops before we're through.

Could you believe, guys on horses wearing red turbans and red capes? Well, I'll say. These are the Moors that Franco brought over from Africa to do his fighting for him. And they are on horseback and waving swords at us. I feel like I'm flying in the wrong film, like I overshot my perimeter and am in some backlot of MGM where they are filming *Beau Geste*. It's like shooting fish in a barrel. Some of us spook these horsemen into clumps and then a couple more come around and let them have it. It's a mighty colorful sight—these red capes and flashing swords and all the horses, everything just exploding and turning over together. I'm worn out with the fun of it. We chase them away. Lieder is balancing his wings, so we group around him and make a final pass over our lines. We're getting a standing ovation. I reach out and wave to the fellows down there. Then we climb to 6000 and head back to the base. It's 11:10. The whole thing took about 45 minutes. A good morning's work, and I'm hungry.

(Jack, I'm having some meetings in the next week or two that have to do with the future of Wilson Bean. Nothing to worry about. I have lots of support, and the old man has more or less promised me the position. But we have to go through a certain number of steps just to make the dance look interesting. So I won't be able to meet with you for a while. I want to put the Flip Winslow book on the back burner for a time.)

Tinker and some of us moved to a field just west of Madrid. There's only one radio at the hotel. The British want the BBC. The Russkies have their programs. The French tune in on Paris. Sometimes we can get a shortwave from Atlantic City. Every group tries to get control of the radio. This is never going to work.

Flying here, I get my first look at Madrid. A big city with wide boulevards. It's fairly quiet now but you can see it's taken a terrific pounding.

Just last week, I earned another thousand bucks. We had a quick scrap south of the city with some Heinkels. I caught one of them at the top of a loop. That Kraut must have thought he was stunting for his *mutter*. I turned right inside of him and wasn't he surprised to find me on top. But, rat-a-tat-tat. Katie, bar the door. I saw him duck down inside the cockpit coaming, like he was trying to get away. The plane just kept on flying level for the longest time. A stable ship. Then, it flipped over and straight down. All this took about twenty seconds.

When I fly back over the field, I waggle my wings to show I got a scalp, and I see these different planes lined up. "Wait until you fly these babies, Pop," Allison says.

"Park-your-carcass-sixteen," Tinker says as we walk down the line.

"But it only has one wing," I say. I thought the two of them would never stop laughing. Now, of course, I'd seen planes like that, flown them before these kids were off the tit, but I meant this new plane looked like someone had taken an I-15 fighter and cut off the top wing. Same big, round, flat nose. Same high dorsal behind the cockpit that smooths into the rudder. But there are differences. The body is made of wood, plywood. And then there's the landing gear.

"It folds right up," Allison says almost dancing. Under the wing there are holes cut out that fit the pattern of the wheel assembly, struts and all. Well, I'll say.

"Wanna take a spin?" Tinker asks me. I really would like to have a bath but I say sure. He checks me out with the controls. The ailerons are split so they can be used for flaps when landing, because you have to land this brick with the power on. Other details like that. The radial is about the same horsepower as the I-15s. But the ship seems lighter. It breaks ground very quickly and with a little leap. The crank for the wheels is between my feet and it feels like I'm winding up an awning. There's an appreciable difference with the wheels up. Frank has said to take her up a few thousand and do some rolls. Oh, boy. Not the turns of the I-15, but can she roll over!! And loop. The stick has the same kind of spade grip, and just the slightest pressure and she rolls like a Milwaukee beer barrel. Whoopee! Two guns, mounted in the wing. Tinker says two more are to be added up front. Four guns. We'll give those Fiats of the Asso Bastoni a little fight. Especially speed. I can't believe my airspeed. I translate the kilometer readings again in my head. At one point, I'm doing better than 300 miles per hour. Good night, Salvatore.

I buzz the university grounds. The lines are close down there. Parts of the campus, building to building. Some of Franco's troops captured the science labs and ate the lab animals; all of them came down with terrible diseases. Meanwhile, the Loyalists captured and still hold the Philosophy Building. That seems only fair.

After amusing myself with the new I-16, I bring her back to the field. The sound of that big radial pop-popping as I throttle back makes me forget. I'm not in a 15. I almost forget to crank down the wheels. This is going to be a chore, raising and lowering this gear. I'll get used to it. She almost stalls out on me, and I gun the throttle, drop the flaps after finding the lever Tinker showed me. Then crunch. I'm down in one piece. A decent landing. Cheated the grim reaper once again.

It always amazes me. To be up there with nothing between me and oblivion but some yards of varnished canvas and pieces of basswood. Somehow it works. It's magic and genius and imagination all put together. Who would have ever thought this body could be carried away from the earth so easily.

Bad news from Barajas. Ben Lieder was shot down. The report is that he jumped into a mess of Heinkels, crazy as always. Outnumbered by about ten to one. Before his mates could get to him, he was going down in lazy loops, first one way and then the other. Sounds like a dead man on the stick. "All the weeping mothers of the world," he used to say. He took this war seriously, that it was supposed to be the last chance for freedom. They say his I-15 crashed head on into one of those hills around Jarama. No body recovered yet. So long, Pal.

Isn't it always the last chance for someone's freedom? This small city near our field—Avila, it's called—is completely enclosed by a high stone wall, built about 1100. All sorts of towers and angles the defenders could shoot from. Drop rocks and boiling oil or whatever. And I guess it worked. But now we can get over those walls at 200 miles per hour, 300 in the new fighter. But that proves nothing. There's a "last chance" for every generation and that last chance has to be defended by the machinery of the time. Except here and now in Spain it seems that, but for us in our Russian planes, this last chance for freedom is about to be overcome by machinery from the future. Like flying over these walls. Somehow, freedom has not kept up with the inventions thrown against it.

Avila's only about sixty miles west of Madrid. A good road and Tinker has commandeered a big Rolls-Royce touring car that Skinner calls the *Puta Express,* and we can put a beeline on Madrid whenever we steal enough gas to make the trip. I'd like to come back to this city when the war's over. It must be beautiful. It's a mess now but still keeps going. The Stukas and the Junkers had had a field day until last fall. The fight around the University meant heavy shelling. But all through it they kept working on a new subway. Went to the races at the dog track. Dances. Soccer matches. "Better to die on our feet than live on our knees," this woman called *La Pasionara* says on the radio. Skinner makes a lot of dirty jokes with that one.

Some of the boys head right for the Florida Hotel where there is a guy who lets anyone use his bathtub and drink his brandy. He's a correspondent named Hemingway and has written some books, too. I leave them on the Grand Via and walk around the city. You'd hardly know a war was on but for the bombed buildings. I mean the songs and the gaiety of the neighborhoods. The cantinas.

I find myself in the middle of a big crowd of people marching along the boulevard, waving banners and singing the "International." They come to a park where there's a speaker's platform. This war is full of speeches. I wonder if the Rebels talk as much. Maybe the Loyalists are making up for their lack of armaments and fuel by talk. Trying to talk and sing their way to victory. Like that old wall around Avila, but their words and music are their stone and mortar.

I've never felt lonely at 6000 feet, all by myself, but in this park in Madrid, surrounded by hundreds of people, I feel very sad, very cut off. Dad died a year ago and mother still lives in the same house outside of Hartford, but that seems far away. More than distance. I mean like on another planet somewhere and I'm over in this park in Madrid looking down as if from outer space. I wish the night would pass quickly, so we could get back to the field and I can get back into the cockpit of my Polikarpov. That's where I belong. I ought to sleep and eat in that cockpit, never get out of it.

I kill time in a bar with a few beers while I watch a couple of guys play a game with dice. As soon as they find out I'm American, the beer is free. That's embarrassing, so I leave. I walk over to the Grand Via and toward the Florida, where I hope to meet the guys. Some boulevard. I hate to have to cross it in peacetime with normal traffic. Bad enough now. Like Wilshire Boulevard. I'm on the Grand Via across from the Florida Hotel, an ornate structure. Behind me is the Telefonica, at fourteen stories it is one of the city's highest buildings. They keep the lights on its aerial tower burning to challenge the Fascists.

When I see her come out of the building, my first thought is that it can't be her. Then when there's no doubt that it is, I look away not wanting to see her. Or her see me. Too late. She leaves the other women, all of them telephone operators off their shift.

"Is it you, Roy?" She rolls the *r* as I remember.

"Hello, Nikki," I say. We're standing on the curb of Madrid, Spain's biggest avenue. Just then the air-raid siren goes off. A false alarm.

A tam of light-blue velvet is perched over one ear and the red hair is smoothed down over the other. She looks alert. A bubbling light in her eyes. "I am so happy to meet with you," she says and hugs herself. "You are flying for the Republic?"

Her coworkers from the telephone company eventually drift away as we talk. "So what is your name these days?" I ask.

"Oh, the same," she shrugs. "Nikki Raismuninen is not easily translated into another language." We are in a café and ask for some coffee. The nightlife seems to just go on, no matter that Franco's boys are just up the avenue—in parts of the university. When we drive down from Avila, the University is on our right, at the city limits, and we always hear gunfire.

"I was there," she says. She tells me about last fall when she fought with a machine-gun company in the School of Architecture. They finally had to fall back to the Philosophy Department, and then only hold the second floor. "We would start the elevators up and throw grenades in them so that when they reached the top floor where the Fascists were, they would explode. Then, they would do the same, sending them back down." She put one of her hands before her face as she laughs. "Boom." The whole thing sounds like a prank. Halloween. In fact, she looks a little like one of those cute halloween pumpkins the five-and-dime sells. "We fired our guns from behind stacks of books," she says. "We used the library from the basement. Stacks and stacks of books. See, that's where I get this."

She pulls her blouse away from her skirt and I see a pinkish red scar across the white flesh just below one breast.

"*La guerra es asi,*" she says when I make a grimace. (I remember her small plump body in the dim light of the sauna built by that lake. Her skin a silvery satin, not a blemish on it.) We take a horse buggy to the Salamanca district where she's living. This area doesn't have a scratch, because most of the embassies are located here and Franco doesn't want to make enemies. She stops the driver and hops out to what looks like the back wall of a garden. There's the outline of a mansion inside. "Next time. You call me at the Telefonica next time." And then she slips through the iron gate and disappears into the garden.

On the way back to the Florida, as the horse clip-clops along, I play a numbers game. I'm trying to figure out just how old Nikki must have been when Klaus von Loerzer took her into that darkened dining room fifteen years ago in Helsinki and when I spent the night with her at that summerhouse that turned out to be her family's old estate. She looks to be in her twenties now. Well, I'll say.

Skinner went down yesterday, also Sleepy and a French pilot who had just joined us. Eight of us were cruising over Carabanchel Alto when about fifty, it seemed like, Fiats jumped on us. Sleepy didn't know what hit him and just went right in, full out. I caught a glimpse of Skinner working his way through a couple of the Fiat units, his Chatto turning like a broken firecracker. I couldn't help him. I had all I could do to get away from a couple that had me coordinated and pumping those big twelve millimeter slugs from a distance. When I looked again, I saw Skinner in a spin off to the left; then his top wing folded up. I kept waiting for a chute. *Nada.* Good night, Mabel. *Adieu,* old Pal. We broke off as fast as we could and made it back to Avila at three top level. That night Frank Tinker auctioned off Skinner's address book. It went for a bottle of Old Grand Dad that a new guy named Flip Winslow had brought with him. He's a funny sort but a hot pilot. Doesn't say much but has rugged good looks. Carries a picture of a monkey in his wallet. Kind of humorous, I guess.

We hear the Germans have brought in a new airplane that is much superior to the Heinkel and maybe even better than the Fiat. These Messaschmids, they're called, have shown up near Aragon, north of here. Single wing and retractable landing gear like the I-16s. But here's a funny thing, their cockpits are all enclosed. A canopy closes over the pilot so he can't feel the wind. The word is: fast.

Hemingway is a pleasant guy and we hit it off pretty well, mostly because we are about the same age and so feel a little odd among all these kids. Also, when he found out I had gone to Yale he asked me a lot of questions about Butch Jenkins, who I didn't know personally but had seen around the campus of course. "He was one son-of-a-gun footballer," Hemingway says to me. We're sitting on his bed in his hotel room. There's a crap game going on over in the corner and Frank Tinker singing in the bathtub. "Roll Me Over." The writer's brandy is especially good—he brings it down from France—and he's very generous with it. I'm killing

time before I meet Nikki across the street. He wants to know how
the Mosca—what we call the I-16—is going to stack up against the
new German fighter. Everyone's been talking about it lately. The
real name is Messerschmitt, from its designer.

"We can handle it," I say.

"That's the ticket." He grins. I like the way he smiles. "How
many do you have now?"

"Four," I say. "That I can prove anyway."

He laughs at that. Then he asks me about the war. He was in it,
it turns out. But he wants to know if the flying is different. What
does it feel like? It's like shooting at ducks, isn't it; that is, you
have to calculate the speed of the target and make allowances? He
knows a lot about hunting and guns. I get the feeling that he's
interviewing me. He says he wants to introduce me to this fellow
Merriman who is running the Lincoln Brigade. I tell him we've
already met, in a way, and I describe the engagement at Jarama.

"Sounds like a turkey shoot," he says.

"Neat," I say.

We've been moved back to the fields at Barajas because it's
raining like hell and this field has a paved landing strip. There's a
big fracas over at a place called Guadalajara. You ought to hear
the Russkies try to say that! The Italian Legion has put on a big
offensive with tanks and planes. Never saw so many planes in the
air at once. Guadalajara is only about 50 kilometers from Madrid,
northeast of the capital, which is the object of the Fascist push.
The attack led by Mussolini's famous Black Shirts. A fearsome
bunch. We have everything in the air that can fly. If we could put
wings on bathtubs, we would.

Keep looking for this new German fighter. Only Fiats and
Heinkels. The Fiats are bad enough. We break into two wings.
The Russians keep the Fiats busy upstairs while Tinker leads the
rest of us down to go after the Black Shirts. They are easy to find,
marching along like Duce was reviewing them. Oh, boy. It's like
bowling. We have four guns on our Moscas now and they really
do the job. The Italians break and start running. Their own
armor gets in the way. Never saw anything change so quickly. The
Loyalist brigades took over. It's a rout.

I wish Ben Lieder were still around so he could explain to me why we are losing this war. Madrid is saved. We win these battles like Guadalajara, yet we seem to be losing. Ben would know why.

In a café one evening, across from the Telefonica where I'm waiting for Nikki to get off work, Ernest and some of his friends sit down. One of them asks me a lot of questions because of my 1918 doings. They seem to make quite a bit over me and Hemingway looks kind of proud like I was a younger brother he's just discovered. So I try to throw him off.

"Did anyone ever tell you, you look like Roscoe Turner?" I ask him.

"As a matter of fact," when he laughs the resemblance gets even more so, "I met Turner once." He used to work in Kansas City on a newspaper, and one time around 1934 he went back to visit old friends. He also wanted to have his hair cut by the barber who used to do it—he has this sentimental streak in him—but the shop had been moved out to the new airport, just built in the middle of the Missouri River. "I'm sitting in the chair. Turner comes in and takes the next chair. He's wearing a light-blue uniform and boots."

"That's him," I say. "Designed it himself. Your mustache is different."

"He was on his way to some airshow and had just landed in Kansas City to refuel. Took the time for a trim. Very neat hombre," Ernest says.

"That was the year he won the Thompson," I say. "I was flying right behind him, lap for lap, and was about to take him when the oil pump on my GeeBee blew and I had to drop out."

The others have started talking among themselves. When I look up, he's smiling almost sweetly at me. "How come you are here, Armstrong? What's in it for you besides the dough? The flying?"

"Yes, that," I say. I hope to see Nikki running across the street, her cheeks puffed with excitement. But no luck. I can tell he's serious.

"But you could fly almost anywhere. On the other side. Why here? Why on this crummy side? Don't you know we're losing? Do you know what this war is about?" He's still smiling, but I feel uneasy. It's like the kidding I take from some of the guys. "Everyone in this scrap has a reason, both sides."

"So why are you here?" I ask.

"I'm losing my innocence," he laughs and slaps the tabletop like it's a big joke. "What's left of it."

I look up Nikki and we got to a hotel called the Society. She's full of fun this night, a little drunk from much brandy and wears her light-blue tam the whole time. Nothing but that.

"Now, you are thinking, Roy," she says at one point. "What do you think?" Her childlike hands massage my neck. I am thinking. I'm still trying to figure out how old she must have been in Helsinki that time Klaus took her behind those French doors. And what did he do with her? Was it something I haven't done with her. I never understood the German. I want to ask her what von Loerzer did that time in Helsinki when she was only about fourteen, but instead I tell her about meeting Pearlstein, how I've seen him around Madrid. In the street or at these rallies.

"Comrade Marron," she says. She starts getting dressed. She has become serious, distant. She has to get back to her rooming house.

"But who is he?" Her slanted eyes become slits. Sometimes in certain half-light, like in this hotel room, she can look almost like a Jap. "Who is this Comrade Marron— Pearlstein?"

"He is like a policeman," she says finally while buttoning up her blouse. She throws on a cloth coat that has a funny looking fur around its collar. "Come, Roy. Find me a buggy. You don't have to escort me home."

But I do anyway, to the same back gate of what looks like a big mansion. It's all dark as before. She says she has a room in what used to be the servants quarters. "You give me much pleasure," she says and hops down. "That there are man like you—still." Then she's gone into the shadows of the house garden.

We've been very busy lately and have taken some more losses. Notably, Jim Allison got shot up but managed to bring his Chatto down near Alcala. He had lost a lot of blood but he'll be okay. Doubt if he'll be back. Dahl says Alcala is where Cervantes, the author of *Don Quixote,* was born. "Did you know he died on the same day as Shakespeare?" he asks.

"No, I didn't know that," Frank Tinker replies, using his regular tone of voice. "But I'll tell you one thing, Whitey. The next time you break off an attack before I do, I'm going to ram your fucking tail." And they start arguing about the afternoon's foray. I leave them and go into the lounge with the radio. Some of our English boys are listening to the cricket scores on the shortwave. I nod to Doc and Happy who are relaxing in a corner. They're okay in my book. Some pilots. I wish we could speak easier. They make me understand they are glad Allison is going to be okay. We all have a drink on that. Foul brandy.

Then the evening courier putt-putts up the driveway with the mail. The English and the French always get most of the mail. Letters and newspapers, magazines. But there's a letter for me. All stamped with different, important-looking markers. It's already been opened and read by several different sets of censors. I don't know why I have to read it; can't someone just call up and tell me what it's about? It's from Klaus von Loerzer.

"Don't you remember him?" I ask Nikki that night. She's like a kid on her first merry-go-round. All I've done was to take her to the movies, for gosh sake. The Royalty Cinema was playing *The Gay Divorcee* with Fred Astaire and Ginger Rogers.

"Could you teach me to dance like this Ginger?" she asks. We're having a sherry before going over to the Society Hotel. "You were such a good dancer in Helsinki. Come, show me Fred Ah-star-ie . . ." and she was twirling about the café. Her dress stands away from her.

"Truly, you don't remember Klaus?" I ask her. I describe his overcoat. That night in Helsinki when we all met. That he spoke German to her, said something that made her blush at first. She couldn't remember. Or says she can't. So how was I going to ask her what they did behind those closed doors? I wonder if she remembered any of the men. Was she working more than the telephone switchboard? Don't the Spaniards have their own telephone operators. What is Nikki doing here? What's her reason?

"But really, you don't remember this German?" I am following her. She is skipping with her arms out, trying to imitate Ginger Rogers. Her clumsiness is cute. "He said something to you in German and you blushed, and then the two of you went into this ballroom that was all dark and when you came back, I bought you a lemonade. Don't you remember?"

"R-r-roy. A long time back, *jo? Ich ficke muchos. Monta.* Many mens. Come dance with me like Fred." And she starts sing-songing this tune from the movie and twirls, stumbles a bit. I catch her. "Do you know this Ginger R-r-rogers?"

"No."

"Do you know any movie star?"

"As a matter of fact, I do." We are sort of waltzing down the avenue toward the Society Hotel. Some people notice us and applaud. Others walk by without looking up. That's the kind of city it is.

"Is she *kaunis?*"

"Not beautiful so much as—"

"Sexy."

"Yes."

"Am I more pleasure than she?"

"Yes, more pleasure." Years ago this skinny blonde comes up to me—hello, she says—I'm Jean Harlow. Can you teach me to fly.

Dear Roy Armstrong,

Our Swedish friends have said they can get this delivered through the lines to you. All-American Boy, old comrade. We now fly opposite sides. Enemies? How can old rotten ka-merads like us be enemies? We are old warriors, Roy, and should be sitting in sunny cafés, telling lies to pretty girls. Alas, not so. You would enjoy this Messerschmitt 109 I am flying, and I am sorry you may see me coming toward you in it. It is a far thing from our old Fokker D-VIIs. I can say no more, you understand, but your Russian ratas will be hard put to keep up, I can promise you. I am not in your area, but maybe someday soon. Look for me, Roy and, as you used to say,

Happy landings.
Klaus von Loerzer

So far, I've made seven thousand dollars in this war. I've set ten as my limit. One way or the other, when I reach ten, I'm clearing out.

The papers are full of the Germans bombing this little town on the northern border. Big black headlines. They bombed it all day with everything they had, including the sleek new Heinkel bomber, a twin-engined monoplane with a body like a cigar. Many civilians killed. Nobody knows why they bombed the place. It has no importance to the war at all. They even used firebombs on it. We hear the city has been totally leveled: *La guerra es asi.*

"You see why I'm not flying for them?" Frank says in the lounge. The radio is being switched from one language to the next. The French win out. Tinker is very angry. His long face is pinky white and his hands shake. "Can you imagine those bastards bombing people like that all day long."

Never seen him so upset about anything. He gets up then sits down, then stands up again. "Lets fly up there and get a few of those bastards."

"Sit down. Relax." He's suddenly calm. The tight line of his mouth goes soft and he gives me an Errol Flynn smile.

"You're right, Pop. Wise old head. Lie back and enjoy it. That's the wisdom." Our English mates have their turn at the radio.

". . . the casualty toll in the Spanish village of Guernica continues to rise. Latest reports . . ."

When I get to town a few nights later, the Madrileños seem to be similarly changed. The cafés are opened, the weather is warm, and there's been a lull. The place seems quiet. The newspaper kiosks have big posters of a magazine cover. Two cartoons side by side. One shows a sky full of planes with Fascist markings dropping bombs: *"Duchas de abril."* The other is the same ground

with nothing but crosses all over: *"Flores de mayo."* That was a big
hit for Al Jolson. Jean did a great imitation of Jolson for me in
her dressing room once, wearing only her skivvies. Well, I'll say!

I can't locate Nikki. The people at the Telefonica say she has
been sick. I take a streetcar out to where she lives. It is still
daylight, the first time I've seen the Salamanca District in daylight.
Handsome neighborhoods. All these big houses set back within
gardens. Most of them have flags of the different countries. I get
a lump when we go past the American embassy. The Old Stars
and Stripes looks pretty good. But I'm not supposed to be here.
I'm Juan Carillo, and my American passport, my American name,
is locked up in the baggage room of a Paris hotel. Tooey Spatz
warned me I could lose my commission. "But, I can't say I blame
you," he wrote. "I share your ideals." One thousand ideals a kill,
Tooey.

This big mansion is set back behind a lot of hedges. I
recognize, in the daylight, the iron gates that Nikki slips through
in the dark. But there's a big blue-and-white flag floating over the
building. This is the Finnish Embassy. She's living at the Finnish
Embassy!

I get back to the center of town and go to the Florida to
Hemingway's. There's a note pinned to his door: NO BATH TODAY.
But I'm not after a bath, so I knock. Come in. He's sitting on the
bed as usual, this small portable typewriter on his lap.

"Where have you been, you fucker?" he says. "Take a look in
there." He nods toward the bathroom door. I open the door and
catch my breath. I look out on open space. The Grand Via is just
below. A Stuka put a bomb along the side of the hotel, and it
sheared off his bathroom neat, just like the stroke of a chisel. A
couple of open pipes stick out from a wall. That's all.

"I have to go down the hall to take a dump," he says. "I
thought *La Patrulla Americana* was supposed to be flying cover
over Madrid."

Hemingway has been doing a piece about the Guernica
bombing and I tell him about Frank Tinker's reaction. He's
looking at me close and then says, "Just an excitable boy. Not like

· 207 ·

a couple of old horses like you and me, Jack. He's still looking for right and wrong."

"My name is—"

"I mean, Roy. Sorry. Are you sure you don't have a brother named Jack?" He smiles. He's made this mistake from the beginning. I tell him about Nikki and what I have just discovered. He seems interested and hands me a bottle of Rioja. He has one also. It's the early part of the evening, too early for the brandy. I brought her to a fiesta he and some of his journalist buddies threw at a restaurant near the Segovia Bridge. Nikki had just cut her hair—almost cut it all off—and Hemingway couldn't get over it. Kept looking at her and patting her on the head, calling her little daughter. I didn't quite like it.

But he's not really interested tonight. "Have you run into these new 109s the Germans are flying?" he asks me.

I say not yet, but we've seen them up close. Very close. One morning last week, we heard this heavy sound coming over the field from the north. We just had our flight plan and our planes were ticking over on the line. It was already hot. This new guy, Flip Winslow, buckles his parachute on over his underwear.

"They sound a lot different," I tell Hemingway, "not just that they have closed canopies; hell, old Roscoe Turner had one of them on his Wendall Williams Special."

"Sure, I remember that," Hemingway says and tilts the wine bottle for a long sip.

"But it's somehow different in a fighter." He looks at me. "You have to feel that air in your face, feel the turn. But these bozos come in low. There are four of them. The sound is not the usual rackety-rack of a radial or even the whine the Stuka makes. It's a steady, low throbbing, like the low rumble a shark might make."

"That's a good one," the writer says and nods.

"It's a serious sound."

"Rolls-Royce engine, I hear," he says.

"No kidding. Like the old car we're driving?" But what I didn't tell him was how this kette of Messerschimitts came in low and we all hit the deck. But they're not shooting. Just dropping an invitation, you might say. Want us to know they are the new kids on the block and won't we come out to play. I haven't seen anything like this since '18, and then when they pull up, the lead ship does this offhand snap roll. I could have spotted that pilot anywhere—even if I hadn't glimpsed the green heart painted on the cowling as the 109 flashed by. Klaus von Loerzer.

Tinker is running like a crazy man toward his I-16, and a couple of the Russians go after him and bring him down. They are good-natured about it. Pat him on the cheeks and dust him off. Then they waggle their fingers under his nose and lecture him in Russian. He takes it well enough, knowing the rightness of the reprimand even if he can't understand the words. I tell Hemingway none of this.

That night I bum a ride back to Avila on an ambulance. Nikki never showed up anywhere. When we go past the University heights one of the sawbones, an Englishman, tells me that the Fascists have been pushed out of the Institute of Hygiene and Cancer. What a nutty war! How can anyone take it seriously, with armies fighting over hygiene schools or sniping at each other from behind busts of Aristotle and Spinoza.

This little town up north that gets wiped off the map. Someone, turn on the lights. Can't wait to make my ten grand and clear out. Wonder what Harlow is up to these days?

The numbers are beginning to be worrisome. Last month up in Aragon, almost eight hundred Fascist aircraft against only eighty of ours. It's a tough fight, ma. And we're losing. It's not much better around here. Franco's boycott and the blockade is working. Our I-16s are holding up, but we can't get parts for the Chattos. All kinds of strange craft showing up. The other day over Brunete, I saw this French Morane being shot to pieces by a Fiat 32. It was a pretty looking airplane but no match. Someone later said it was Morato, their big ace, on the kill. I couldn't help our guy out. The Fiat's heavy cannon literally shot the plane to pieces. The wheels dropped off, the tail is Swiss cheese, and the pilot is halfway out of the cockpit. One wing folded up. The pilot had the canopy back and was climbing out when he got it. Then he went to pieces, like a marionette coming apart on its strings.

This woman they call Dolores—*La Passionata*—is on the radio all the time with her deep, rich voice like an opera singer but in Spanish. There seems to be more sandbags piled on corners in Madrid, and the streetcars don't run so often. I run into Pearlstein-Marron in the Retiro, not as big as Central Park but with a lot more atmosphere. An orchestra plays in the ruins of an old church. There's a tap on my shoulder. It's the parachute salesman turned cop, but I don't let on. A word to the wise.

"Ah, Captain Carillo," he says. No more of Yale.

"Comrade Marron," I give it back to him. We walk to a small pavilion with colored lanterns. The night is warm. Couples at tables. Old men with young women. Waiters bustling about. Who says there's a war on?

There was this morning at ten thousand feet. We mixed with some Messerschmitts. They are no match for us close up, but they are fast as hell. Tink scored almost too easily. I looked quickly at the Condor plane. No green heart. The flames took over. The pilot bailed out and then I saw one of our boys in a Chatto, I think it was Doc, roll over and follow the chute down, pumping lead into the body that dangled in the straps. Bloody fine sport, old man, pip-pip and all that. Comrade.

"What about this fellow Tinker?" Pearlstein is saying. He is talking into his teacup, which I seem to remember him doing in Helsinki. "Was he really expelled from the United States Navy?"

"I guess so."

"He had an offer to fly for the Fascists."

I tell him I didn't think it was an offer. He liked their planes, the way they organized their squadrons. Then, I told him about Tinker's reaction to Guernica.

"He seems sincere," Pearlstein says and sips his tea but he doesn't sound all that sure. "And your Helsinki girlfriend?" He wipes his mouth on the napkin. It must be the clothes he wears, but he no longer looks American.

"You don't have to worry about her."

"Who's worrying?" He shrugs and looks and sounds like the old parachute salesman. I get a warm feeling about those old days—him, me, Nikki, and Klaus all sitting at the same table in Helsinki. Now, here we are, all going in different ways. "You know, you're quite dangerous," he says and laughs, but not funnily.

"Me?" I think he's talking about my score. Eight as of yesterday.

"Even your old wingman von Loerzer has joined up—on the other side, to be sure, but he's following a star." This is beginning to sound like the malarkey Hemingway's been handing me. "You don't have a star."

"Listen," I give it back to him. "If there were more guys like me who just do it for the money, for the fun of it, there'd be fewer of these blowouts. The world could go about its business. It's you politician guys that make it ugly."

"Don't try to be profound," Pearlstein replies. "You don't have the papers. You see this girl called Nikki some?"

"What's it your business?" For Christ's sake, I've tangoed with one of Hollywood's biggest stars and I got to answer to this little creep about a telephone operator?

"You might be safer in the air, Carillo, than you are with her. In this park for instance, anything could happen." He has looked around like he expects anything to happen.

"Cut the baloney, Pearlstein. I knew you when you peddled umbrellas around the escadrille." A couple of guitars start strumming inside the casino. What a war!

"Precisely my point, Captain Armstrong. You never permit anyone to change. It all must stay the same for you. No progress beyond the status you have assigned them." He laughs and I get a whiff of onion. I smile. He still eats raw onion, doesn't he? But I see this is a serious discussion. He's talking. "This little Finn, for example, you yet believe her the whore from the Hotel Metropole in Helsinki because she lets you enjoy her at the Hotel Society in Madrid . . ."

"How do you know about that?"

". . . but you remain the same All-American boy, meat and potatoes. By the way, I have a nephew at Yale these days, perhaps you can recommend some professors. Have you kept in touch? But this little Nikki is not the same girl-harlot of 1920."

"Oh, come off it, Maroonie." He does smile. "She's just having a little adventure, like all of us. Hell, she even stays at the Finnish Embassy. Nothing fishy about her."

"Does she indeed," he says, like he's making a note of it. "That explains a good deal."

"Like what?" A falsetto voice sings flamenco inside the pavilion.

"Do you talk about your flight plans with her?"

"What flight plans? You think this war has a plan of any kind? We just jump when we get poked."

"But you are jumped quite often. Lately, you lost several comrades—the man you call Skinner and others, for example."

"For God's sake, we're outnumbered almost one hundred to one sometimes. We're jumped on when we get up to take a piss."

"Ah, for the elegance of the Ivy League." The song inside becomes frantic, the beat blurs, then everything quits. Applause.

"What's she supposed to be—some sort of a spy?" A great part for Jeannie! I'll drop her a note with the idea. I can see her wearing that little blue beret Nikki wears—and nada. Olé.

"You've heard of the Fifth Column?" he says.

"Oh, that. That's ground war stuff. Nothing to do with me."

"They could be here tonight. In this park." He rolls his eyes and I almost laugh. Who can take this clown seriously. "They are inside the city, waiting to cut us down."

"Boogie-woogie," I say. That makes him wrinkle his brow a few times.

"How secure you must feel in your lack of affiliation," he says. "You're a wild card. Any suit, any value. No value." Then, he seems late for an appointment, and he gets up and runs off.

Somehow he forgets to pay for his tea and cake. Someone always takes the check, that was his manner. Well, I have $7000 in my account in Paris and can afford to be generous. More guitars, an accordian. Glasses and silverware tink. Laughter.

This morning my ears burst with different sounds. My sides are sore from being thrown around the I-16s cramped cockpit. Now a few hours later. Wine, the perfume of women on the breeze. Trees softly swaying. This morning I nearly got my ticket punched. I had just got a bead on an Eytie Breda 65, one of those hump-backed fighter-bombers, was giving it to him good. Flip

Winslow, the new guy, used to fly one of these for some outfit in China. Here goes another thousand claims, I'm saying when my whole plane pushes to one side. This 109 was practically sawing off my tail. They have a nose cannon as well as machine guns. I rolled away but he held on. I kept rolling until I got dizzy. My hand slipped off the control grip, and the plane went into a dive. The Kraut was still there. Could it be old Klaus? Hey, comrade, it's me. I looked around. The 109 had pulled up too early and I immediately zoomed. No plane I've ever flown can respond like the Polikarpov. I was coming up under him very fast. No green heart. He saw me and did a snap roll that would have taken the wings off of most planes and made it into a cliff of clouds, heading for the sun.

At the far end of an alley of tall trees I see several figures. A waning moon makes for a theatrical setting. Looks like two men and several women. Even in the moonlight, the hair looks red. It is the one spot of color in a black and silver picture. I had waited for her at the Telefonica, but she hadn't shown up. What had she been doing? Where had she been?

Why do I follow? Do I hope to catch Nikki in the act? Behind the French doors? After all these years? It's a spooky place. Overgrown hedges. Big gum trees. Statues appearing whitely at every turn. Ruins, but I can't tell if they're old ones or through the courtesy of the Stukas. Maybe I'm a Peeping Tom. I want to see her in action, maybe. Maybe I want to see her doing whatever she and Klaus did fifteen years ago. Would that cool this burn I've had all this time?

It's a maze and I'm deep into it. Lost. I can make out the roofline of the Prado off to the right. Trains toot in the same direction. The Tocha Station. Then this statue, where the hedge curves, moves. It's her, of course, but the hair on my neck is standing straight out. She's wearing a draped, white frock and looks like one of these classic statues. But for the red hair.

"Where are the others?"

"What others? There are not others." Before I can say I saw her with the others, she is kissing me. Close the door, Katie. "I saw you with Comrade Marron and waited until he left."

"You afraid of him?"

"I'm not afraid of him. Come, I have found something that I think will interest you much." She kisses me again and looks up, her slanted eyes narrowed as if the moonlight was too strong for them. "Come, R-r-roy." She has me by the hand and begins to run.

She seems to know her way around this park pretty well. We pass the Crystal Palace and then into more maze and hedges behind. I hear water spilling over. Suddenly, we're in an opening, like a Roman theater. A colonnade, curved seats but where the stage should be is a pool of water. A grotto behind in the shadows.

"See?" Nikki says on her toes. She has kicked off her shoes. Now she starts slipping out of her clothes. "Just like Suomi. You remember? The sauna by the lake. We give each other much pleasure."

She's running down the steps toward the pool. Silvery and pink. Not even the boy's haircut can disparage her womanly form. She jumps in with a squeal and splashes. She jumps up and down and her breasts glisten, the tips like strawberries in the moonlight. The water in this pool looks slimy. No telling who might come on us. She's still jumping around like a pink seal. "Come, *kommen, avanti, venez, venid.*" I sit down on one of the benches and watch. "Oh you, you stone in the mud."

I start to shiver but not with cold. Pearlstein may be right; perhaps I'm safer with the Condors shooting at me than I am here on the ground. Who is this girl-woman? Who is Pearlstein? This is a screwy war. It's not enough to have guys on the other side shooting at you. There are people on your side after you. Even generals are being shot dead by some of their own people. One of our own Russian pilots—the one we called "Happy"— disappeared the other night. He'd been with us since Barcelona. Some guys just woke him up and drove him away. Doc let us know that questions about his whereabouts were not welcome.

So I'm sitting here in the moonlight with Nikki, who I don't really know. A Mata Hari who has maybe lured me here. What a target I am. I'll never collect my seven thousand dollars. There could be some guy behind the hedges taking a bead on me. Maybe there's a price on my head?

"Kom, give me fooking, R-r-roy." But I'm halfway up to the top of the theater. She's pulled on her dress and is running after me, barefoot, holding her shoes.

I feel a lot better out of that park and cross the avenues to the railroad station, where there is a cantina open. The station has taken some Stuka hits, but it's still operating. I buy her a coffee and a brandy and she sulks. When she pouts, Nikki's round face becomes even rounder, more childlike. Especially with the short hair. Cute. She points at the big station clock. Midnight. By the time I've grabbed the waiter and paid him, she's halfway across the station. Running. She's jumped into a hansom cab and the driver whips the horse; it's all like he was waiting for her.

The carriage heads down the paseo and all I see is the round top of her red head. I keep looking, expecting her to at least wave. *Nada.*

"Look here, old chap," Flip Winslow says to me. We're in the Rolls-Royce the next night, going into Madrid. A message from Nikki that she had to see me. "We have to allow these girls their little sprees. They are built differently from us. Overlook their ways and be happy. That's my motto."

His rugged good looks give his words a ring. His background is sketchy. Something about being thrown out of the Army Air Corps and he's been freebooting around China. Swapped a lot of stories. He's one helluva a flyer.

I ask him to come with me to the Telefonica to meet Nikki. When we get there, there's a crowd outside the entrance. Gendarmes. Qué pasa? Some anarchists and reds are fighting over the telephone exchange. We're all supposed to be on the same side? Oh, yeah, but they're holding the telephone operators as hostages.

"It's Nikki," I say to Flip. "She's in danger."

"Right," he says, his handsome mouth set grimly. "We must find and rescue her, old chap. Lead the way. I'm right behind you."

We start running up the stairs. Fourteen flights. The elevators are stopped. Flip is right behind me. The .45 Colt automatic that is always tucked into the waistband of his Danforth trousers, is held almost negligently in his right hand. The weight of my Barettta 7mm comforts my palm. On the twelfth floor, we can hear weird signals, see flashing lights. Colored lights that keep changing like a pulse, a strange code maybe being sent. Women are screaming. I look at Winslow. His eyes have become dangerously dark. "Miserable vermin," he mutters through white, even teeth. We rush on.

Together, we burst through the frosted glass doors on the fourteenth floor. Pandemonium. Winslow's Colt barks once and then again. Two figures in blue coveralls buckle, fall. Papers, wires, and chairs are all over the place. Women operators are huddled behind desks. Going through their rosaries, some of them. Winslow and I walk, back to back, through the place, our pistols blazing, taking their toll of the evil-looking desperados. Anarchists. Reds. Whoever they were, they're jumping like rats. We make a quick reconnoiter of the outer room. No Nikki. Flip nods toward a pair of closed swinging doors at the end of the room. We push through.

They had tied her to a big post in the center of the room. Her dress is torn. Her eyes are puffy and her mouth looks bruised. What had they been doing to her? "Oh, Jack, it's you," she says, "I knew you would save me."

"Not Jack—Roy," I say. "This is Flip." I untie her. I don't want to think of what those brutes may have done with her. She's in my arms, her hands clasped tightly behind my head, her lips on mine.

"Oh Roy," she says. "It was terrible. Never leave me."

"I won't, kid. Why don't you and I skiddoo this madness and get back to Omaha."

"Hey, wait for me." It's Flip Winslow, grinning from ear to ear. "Is there room in this dream for me?" The elevator is working and the car doors close.

"You can believe it, pal," I say and push the button for the ground floor. Nikki's smallness fits perfectly against me. I have killed for her and would do so again. Flip seems to hear what's going through my mind and he smiles. He pokes at the bill of his old Corps hat with the muzzle of the heavy automatic. The cap pushes back and he winks.

Down on the street, there's a newstand and a guy hawking the evening papers. There's a picture on the front page. It's the same picture they always use, the one from *Hells Angels*. I have stopped at the stand.

"What iss, Roy?" Nikki says. Flip is getting a taxi for our first stop out of this place—the Finnish Embassy to get her belongings. "Someone you know?" The headline is big and black: *JEAN HARLOW ESTA MUERTE*

I hold Nikki close, like I plan on holding her for a long time to come. "Someone I used to see in the movies."

CHAPTER

SEVEN

COOPER would remember the light in Ruth's eyes when he pushed the call buttom in Don Jacobs's foyer. All that morning as he took off the storm doors and hung window screens, she had hunched over the keyboard of the computer that took up most of the space in her small study off the living room. All that morning, the whir and scrape of the machinery accompanied him on the usual tasks that came with the first fine weather of spring. He even hung the clock back up over the stove and set it going.

The computer sounded to him as if it were clearing its throat, if it had a throat; as if someone reached far back in his head to pull down a lot of matter, but this image was unfair as much as it was disagreeable, he thought, for the matter that was being pulled down was poetry filed into the terminal bank by the far-flung candidates for the Quinn College Master of Fine Arts Degree.

For two days Ruth had been pulling this poetry, by the stanzas, from the electronic memory of the computer and punching the keys to reproduce it on yards of printout paper. She hardly looked at any of the poems, but tore the paper into neat lengths of letter-sized manuscript. Earlier that spring, soon after Jacobs had sent technicians to Hammertown to hook up the computer, Cooper had asked her if the work coming in was interesting. Ruth had shrugged her shoulders and turned away.

The machinery seemed to affect her, to process her as it processed the commands she gave it. She had become more angular, but it was a different angularity from that awkwardness he used to collect and somehow hold together in his arms in the old store on 23rd Street. Her body had become sinewy, as if the pale green screen she looked into cured her in some way.

The backseat of her Beetle was often piled to the windows with the small cardboard mailers containing the magnetic disks on which the world's verse seemed to have been encoded. Moreover, the success of the program had increased her importance to the community college so there was talk of moving her into an administrative post with larger office space for the computer and the Quinn program's files. Her own poetry was written late at night— sometimes she would get up at three or four in the morning to go to her study—he found her at her desk once; looking drugged. The obsession, the extravagant urge to write, remained like a fever, untreated.

When he met Kelly Novak for lunch, Cooper would remember the whir of the computer in Ruth's study; the restaurant's air conditioner made the same sound. That morning he had set the clock going, excited by the way all the parts had fit together and worked, even with the article in the 1952 issue of *Hobby and Craft;* his success with the repair had surprised him. It was an old clock and once they had been offered three hundred dollars for it by an antique dealer, though the bird made only a little sound when it poked from its cubby.

"If you think I'm going to listen to that asinine doo-doo, you're out of your gourd," Ruth had told him.

So, years before, Cooper had taken it down to his shop behind the magazine store and tinkered with it and managed to disconnect the mechanism that drove a small wheel which, in turn, rotated a shaft that sent out sounds that might resemble a birdcall. But he had not made it completely silent; it had still uttered a defiant rasp on the hour, a wooden clearing of the throat, as it were. Each time it sprang through the tiny door above the clock's face, little beak parted and ready, it would seem to freeze with embarrassment, and the painted eyes almost looked around to see where the sound had gone. It had been there, on the other side of the door. That is, until Hal had wrenched off its head.

"What's so funny?" Ruth had asked. She handed him the folders he was to deliver to Jacobs.

"The clock. Where's Hal?"

"He went off early while you were in the shower. He went up to Clay's. His project, I suppose. Clay will take him to school. He'll see you've fixed it when he gets home." She sat down at the kitchen table and pulled the housecoat close. The mornings were still cool. "Why did you fix it?"

"It was broken."

"But it's been broken a long time. Why start it up now?"

"I don't know," Cooper had replied truthfully. He fit the folders into the briefcase, beside the envelope with the rest of Roy Armstrong's memoirs.

Ruth had studied him. Her eyes seemed larger, more prominent, due to the cut of her hair. The two salons in Green River had introduced this style to their part of the country. Farm wives began to look like schoolboys, though the style was not all that different for them, minus a few dozen pink and green plastic curlers that used to wind their hair, skull tight. Did they ever let that hair down, Cooper wondered? But, it looked just right on Ruth.

Yet, he was a little upset with her for letting Hal slip away. She had seen him bring the clock up from the store the night before and knew he planned to hang it this morning. He had wanted the boy there so he could show him the thing had been fixed, after all this time; good as ever. Not a ceremony so much as a renewal, Cooper would think, and he had wanted Hal to be there.

It had been a long time since Hal came down to the store, sat behind him as he typed, reading comics as Flip Winslow took off into the pure, blue sky. Maybe, it was no longer fun for the boy either. As Kelly Novak became interested in the story, he and Hal had lost their interest in it. Or maybe these projects and helping Clay Peck may have made Hal more serious too. Perhaps Hal was growing up.

So, Cooper mused, he would be left with the cuckoo clock or some similar fix-it that he could look up in the magazines. Weekend projects for the rest of his life, to be glued or tacked together with no one to admire them or do them for. Ruth had her own work, and lately, she even had Hal. That barb turned in the wound of his own making. Cooper was jealous and felt a little ashamed by it.

But last night, Ruth and Hal had begun dancing in the kitchen, spontaneously. Maybe it was a routine they had rehearsed sometime. The boy had been drying the larger plates and pots, when suddenly they were doing this peculiar waltz, woodenly taking the different points of the circle they turned in like those life-size figures that parade across the face of town-square clocks in Europe. Ruth hummed the tune, her hands stretched out to hold Hal at the elbow. Stately, they turned. The boy's head was thrown back, eyes closed, and his pink mouth and large, black nostrils opened rapturously to breathe this flash of happiness.

When they saw him leaning in the doorway, watching them, they quit—at once and guiltily, like children interrupted in a fanciful game by an adult.

"You're funny," Ruth had been saying. She helped him close his briefcase.

"How so?"

"You want everything to come out right. Like the movies. The way things are supposed to come out." Across the road, sparrows picked through the dark, moist mats of last autumn's leaves, looking for grubs. They reminded her of housekeepers at a resort, turning mattresses, getting beds ready for another season. "What's happened to Winslow and his monkey friend?"

"Armstrong's memoirs have taken over, I guess."

"You haven't shown me any of that story in a long time," Ruth had said wistfully. "He was looking for that girl on an island. She was captured by evil agents." She laughed and looked even more of a street urchin, cocky and presumptuous.

Her manner and appearance aroused Cooper. He wanted to take her up from the chair, to place her on the nearest surface and, there, make love to her. The urge had been as sudden as it was strong and it shook him, for they had not been close like that for some time. Her work with the computer seemed to have dampened her sexual desire. The late conferences and extra office hours that used to last past midnight were things of the past; he was pretty certain she was seeing no one.

Lately, she suggested an almost penitent quality, which Cooper found strangely exciting. But the clock on the wall behind him had begun to scrape and pull itself together, the trap clicked open, and the muted sounds of the bird scratched at the hour.

"I'm taking the eight-thirty train," he had said as if it were an excuse, and, in fact, Ruth had looked a little scornful as she stood up and pulled the sash of her robe tight. It was that old expression that always made him feel peculiar, mocked him for denying himself a pleasure that was readily available and his for the taking. So she kissed him with affection.

"This is a better place than it looks," Kelly Novak said as they sat down at the table. The menu offered Mexican, Italian, and some Chinese dishes, and the drinks, beer, and wine were carried in from someplace in the rear. None of the old comrades in cocktails that used to take up the front of the other restaurants had joined them here; mostly young couples sat at the other tables. They all had knapsacks at their feet and read to each other out of guidebooks as they ate. "Also near my apartment. I have an appointment tomorrow morning with Hal Easton in L.A. and I'm lunching with Alex Brown. Spielberg is supposed to show up. He'd be a natural for this. I have a call in to Benny Siegel."

The names meant little to Cooper, though he had discovered that she did not use them to impress him so much as to verify herself. She and those people she used to introduce him to in the other restaurants did it to each other. Litanies of names that sanctified their daily rounds. Nor were all the names famous, even recognizable. They didn't have to be. Indeed, Cooper often wondered if some were not made up, on the spot, to authenticate a particular, humdrum event. "I was picking up my laundry and ran into Benny Siegel." No one asked, who is Benny Siegel? For the answer might be, he's the guy you run into when you pick up your laundry.

"I see you've been having fun with Armstrong's memoir," Kelly continued. "Flip Winslow to the rescue."

"Well, I have the rest of the memoir with me." He aligned the plastic placemat before him with the edge of the table.

"I think it's great! I should have thought of it myself." She tapped his hand. Her nails were fire red. "This is the sort of wacky adventure stuff that those guys on the Coast are looking for. No. I think, Winslow should be in it from the beginning. Maybe put him together with Armstrong—one character!" Her eyes opened wide with the size of the inspiration. "But just for the record, what really did happen to Nikki and the others?"

"She was murdered by KGB agents." Somehow, telling of the girl's death fifty years ago—she would be almost eighty today, Cooper thought—was inappropriate for this audience and this place. How she must have fought and struggled as she had been dragged to the edge of the open elevator shaft. Then, down all fourteen stories, that soft, pink body falling and falling to its sudden concussion at the bottom. A neat little gal, was the epitaph Armstrong had given her. "I guess she was a spy of some sort," Cooper told Novak.

"And the German? I kept expecting him and Armstrong to have a showdown."

"No, they never encountered each other. Armstrong did keep track of von Loerzer. He was shot down on the Russian Front later on." Their sandwiches had come and Kelly Novak was already eating. "What's happened at Wilson Bean?"

She was out. She had lost out to the other candidate but, she wasn't unhappy about it. Certainly, the first shock of it but now that she had time to think about it—well, the possibilities were limitless—for her and therefore for him too. The word had got out, she said. "Just yesterday I had a call from Janet Emory at MCA, and the phone has been ringing off the hook. It's not my fault if old Wilson wants to hand over his empire to a ninny, is it?"

She had bitten into her sandwich and tucked a stray sliver of chicken back between her lips. "None of this will affect you. I still want to work with you and I'm taking Armstrong's journal to the Coast, because I think, I know, I can sell it. I'll have more free time now to give to it and other projects I have." She took another bite of the sandwich.

Maybe she would gain weight on the Coast, become the old Mary Novak. Her appetite seemed to have increased. He sensed she needed the Armstrong memoir almost as much as food and probably chewed it up, digested it in the same tasteless fashion. What did it matter? He had never believed those inflated figures she used to toss around anyway. He had hoped it might happen, but didn't expect it. Now she was a loner like Armstrong and Winslow and even Ruth. So, it was like passing on a legacy, giving her this material and not expecting anything from it. Old Armstrong would understand, probably.

Two more couples had entered the restaurant, unshouldered their knapsacks and sat down at a table beneath a large poster picture of a bullfight. Cooper wondered if the restaurant were on an old hiking trail, paved over by Amsterdam Avenue but still listed in the guidebooks.

Some of the people in the restaurant didn't seem much older than Hal, and their earnest concentration over guidebooks and menu had put his mind back on the track that he had followed on the train down to the city. He had been sorry that Hal had not been there to see him hang up the repaired clock.

Each trip into the city had added to the distance between him and the boy, and he felt the intimacy they used to share in the back room of the magazine store pull away. Those times when he would make up the stories about Captain Winslow as Hal read beside him seemed far away and desolate, like the abandoned stations of the old Harlem Railroad.

The trips down to the city reversed an older route that had once taken others deep into the wilderness and returned them to civilization to regard their neighbors, even their wives, differently, because of the strangeness or the wickedness they had witnessed deep in the woods. Cooper wondered if evil was to be found any more at all. Was he hoping to find it standing in a darkened stoop to spy on Jacobs from a distance? If come across in an old journal; it could be smoothed out to accomodate a trend for happy endings. A young woman thrown to her death in Madrid a half century ago, because she believed too fiercely in something, could easily fall into a happy ending. Or happy landing, he thought, and his abrupt laugh startled Kelly Novak.

"Let's give Nikki a parachute," he said and Novak looked at him wide-eyed, an all-purpose expression that suggested amusement, recognition, and wonder all at once.

But with the trails paved over, the old boundaries and sites were hard to find—not even with a map, Jack Cooper mused, as he wandered through the vast desolation of Woodlawn Cemetery. The late afternoon sun struck the chart he held in his hand, so the long rays of its light slanted across the sea-green surface of the printed paper. He set off down an alley of small mausoleums, shuttered with iron grills and looking like beach cottages closed up for the season. Their tenants never got beyond the city limits; Cooper laughed, just as he caught a flash of color outside the rim of his eyeglasses, but it was not a bird. He looked. Two figures, one of them wearing a fluorescent orange cap, moved through a distant marble thicket.

Far above, a jet liner flew into the western sun. Perhaps Kelly Novak would be on that plane. Looking up, he admitted that he had never really believed his Winslow adventures would become the book and then the movie that Kelly had promised. She had not deceived him so much as fooled herself. The sky had become dark blue. Another jet had passed over. Maybe the pages of the Armstrong journal would flutter down into the cemetery like so many birds landing. Maybe Kelly Novak had so annoyed her seatmate that the man or woman had grabbed her attaché case and thrown it out the window. Over the side of the cockpit. Cooper laughed. Even now Armstrong's words were flying west faster than the pilot had ever flown, perhaps being changed at this moment by the very speed itself. "I can see Scott Mellon playing Armstrong, can't you?" Kelly had said with dessert. "How about Winslow?" Everything comes out right.

"I am sorry," Cooper said aloud. He addressed the worn stone face of a figure on top of a nearby tomb. Films like that—all the flying and stunts required—are expensive, so nothing would come of it. But, in the meantime, it would be passed around—Nikki, Armstrong, von Loerzer, even the Russians—would be passed around with the hollandaise sauce. Then, he feels different. There, flying west in that tiny plane was Kelly Novak with Armstrong's memoir in her attaché case safely under the seat—and she was still Kelly Novak. For a little bit longer, and that might be more than just something. He had done that, at least. Cooper wished her success—happy landing. "No, I am not sorry," he said.

He walked down into a small vale and referred to his chart once again. The stones here were modest, some hardly peeping above the grass. Well, Dad, is that you? The question was not spoken, scarcely fashioned. The marker bore the correct dates: JOHN A. COOPER. It is a long way from Iowa, but he would get him there somehow.

He was a simple man, Cooper thought, and wanted very little. It's not so easy now, Dad. Sometimes, a thing will happen that will make you wonder why everything is complicated. We make it so. Last week, Hal had brought him the skull of a bird in pieces. It had become dry and very fragile, and perhaps the boy's clumsy handling had broken it. For the past year, he had been collecting such specimens, studying the sketchy wings and vertebrae of birds in his room almost every night. Humming. Cooper had helped him suspend some of these tiny, white bones from the ceiling on silk thread.

It was in three pieces, Dad, and looked like it may have been a Canadian goose. They never fly south anymore, never leave in the summer now; for that matter, they don't go north either. They stay on local ponds the whole time. The center part was made of a straight piece of bone with sections going out from it. Some of these sections had been cut out in the center, filleted, to make them lighter, he supposed. The two side pieces that had broken off had holes for the eyes and flared out in the front to form the top part of the bill. The holes for the nostrils were clearly seen.

Now here's the funny thing. He took the pieces down to his workshop and when he started gluing them back together it was like when he made those models. Everything fit. Made sense. It was like putting together one of those models where the plans for it had become lost but it didn't matter because the parts had been designed to fit only one way. They explained themselves. They could only fit one way, and it was wonderful to see how they did fit. He knew nothing about birds, but he could put this one back together, or at least this part of it and so then why not the whole thing if need be—because everything was so clearly logical. Simple.

"Oh, Da, you do it," Hal had said, then kissed his cheek with blubbery lips, and they were both a little embarrassed for a bit—Cooper mostly, because the boy had to bend down a little to reach him and it was like he was suddenly the child.

Then Hal became impatient and began to shift his feet as Cooper pointed out how a former, the one just before the eyeholes in the skull, had been scalloped just so with no loss of structural strength. Cartilage that shaped part of the eye socket agreed perfectly with the top of this former, on either side. That's the place he had laid down a neat line of glue. Not so much a dovetail, he told Hal, as a goose skull. The boy took the repaired head bone, so strong and fragile at once, and clumped upstairs to his room. Cooper could hear him humming, the same noise he himself had made as a boy to accompany the swoop and climb of a model plane held clumsily in one hand. He was sure Hal was doing just that with the restored skull.

But here's the thing, Dad. Even if we had all the parts and put them back together we couldn't make it fly. As a boy, he had made models like that. There was that Stearman trainer, remember, and that Fairchild 25 that looked so beautiful but just wouldn't stay in the air. It would be the same thing. Looking at this bird's skull, he had wondered where the flight had gone. There had been something in there, perhaps in those spaces that he thought had been hollowed out for lightness—maybe that's where this unique flying part had been located, not cemented, otherwise it would be there—but maybe just floated in there of itself, giving off buoyancy—something that had made the whole thing work. Fly. If he could have found it.

That's what he had been trying to say to Hal, Dad. That in those spaces where a bird keeps the matter that lets it fly, some of us keep the dream. Both disappear into the thin air, become one. Like mist rising.

But he could not hold the boy back. He was too big for that, too large to sit under his arm on the sofa as when they watched Lucille Ball. "Poor kid," Ruth would say. "You're turning him into an automaton. Laughing with that canned laughter." But what's the difference now? Who is being manipulated now? Who's the robot? Do you remember Red Skelton, Dad? Red Skelton was a favorite, and Cooper had got letters, when he was in the Army, about Red Skelton. He should have seen the last program, the man is a genius of comedy. Hope this letter finds you well and warm. Korean winters sound as bad as those back in Iowa. The store is doing well. Have had some good orders from college libraries. Have you thought more of college when you get back? I see you will have the G.I. Bill. And have put something aside too.

"Hey, man. You got something for us?" Both wore plaid hunting jackets of dark red, and the one with the orange cap had spoken.

"Something, man," repeated Orange Cap. His voice was soft and soothing. His companion looked behind them and then around. A light breeze, still with a wintry edge, roved through the cemetery. Both men turned up the thick collars of their jackets.

"What would you like?" Cooper asked.

"Some of this and some of that. Mostly that." He had pointed to the briefcase in Cooper's hand.

"What's this jive?" the other said. His voice was high pitched. He looked over his left shoulder. "We got the mark. Let's deal and scat."

"So what you got?" Orange Hat nodded toward the briefcase.

"Poems," Cooper replied. The cemetery slipped deeper into dusk. Far off, a crow called, and Cooper thought that peculiar, to have crows inside the city limits. But then he remembered that Poe had lived nearby and he also remembered, looking at the two men facing him across sunken graves, his father telling him of Poe walking all the way from his small house in the Bronx down to Wall Street, every day building up the fire so what-was-her-name would be warm while he was editing that magazine. Way down-town. Every day.

"Aw, c'mon now, man," Orange Hat said pleadingly. "We got no time to be humored." The other came up close be-hind him and said something into his ear. Both hunched their shoulders, like part of a routine, and regarded Cooper almost sadly.

"Here, let me show you," he replied, unfastening the briefcase. "I have nothing but poetry, but you are welcome to it."

"Cocksucker. Keep your hand out of that bag." The other had stepped to one side. He pointed a small pistol at Cooper. The gun seemed to have slipped from the heavy sleeve of the mackinaw. Orange Hat has not moved but still stood with his hands deep in his jacket's pocket and with the same sad, quizzical look on his face. "Just put the stuff down nice," the youth with the revolver said.

"You mean right here?"

"Oh, my goodness," Orange Hat said, his voice turning mean.

"No, I mean, right here?" Here, on Dad's grave, Cooper wanted to say but he sensed that would only confuse mat-ters more, and then he thought it funny to come all this way to put this poetry that Ruth had printed out from the disks she had received from all over America, to put it down now on his father's grave. It was like an offering of some kind, hundreds of tributes written for this unknown man and now delivered. Here, Dad.

Orange Hat had begun to come forward, stepping care-fully around the outlines of graves. His companion kept the pistol aimed at Cooper. The crows called again and the horns of distant traffic sounded. People going home, Cooper thought. Something else. Another sound he couldn't place but the men before him did, at least saw where the noise came from, for they quickly turned and fled. They ran in tandem, leaping over the gravestones like Olympic hurdlers and then, with Indian war whoops, took separate routes and disappeared.

A squad car with a squeaky fan belt coasted to a stop behind Cooper. One policeman got out, followed by the other.

"Gee, I'm sure glad—" Cooper started toward them.

"Go for it and you're a dead man," the younger cop said. Both pulled their revolvers and kept him covered.

The sergeant at the station house later apologized to Jack Cooper for the younger cop's behavior. He was only on the beat a couple of weeks and also, his dad was a lieutenant on the force and he probably was eager to prove himself. Cooper would understand. He had told them that he was married and had one child, a son, himself. Send him the bill for the glass frames and he, the sergeant, would personally compensate him for the damage. It didn't look like much anyhow, just bent a little. When Cooper had been thrown across the fender of the police car to be handcuffed, his eyeglasses had spilled off in the struggle. The two officers almost fought between themselves to cuff him first. He had put up no resistance.

"It's like a jungle out there," the sergeant had continued as he took Cooper's arm like a comrade. "Can you imagine dealing dope on holy ground like that? Anyway, you really had us, pally." The policeman laughed loudly, the sounds coming out as round as the face behind them. Other officers in the room took their cue and joined the hilarity. Cooper was reminded of the time he and Ruth had gone to Town Hall to hear the Cossack Chorus. "You really *did* have poetry in that briefcase." The sergeant bent double with the pain of the revelation.

"Jesus, poetry. Think of that!" another policeman repeated. Another shook his head and dug a companion in the ribs. "Poetry!" the third man shouted. Their wonder was unbounded. Several shook their heads, still not quite believing what they had just witnessed. All of them had thought the sergeant would have a stroke when he opened that briefcase and pulled out all those pages that really did have poems typed on them. Honest to God, actual poems. His face had turned the color of tomato soup. It really is poetry, he had said, to make it official.

Oh yeah, let's hear some of it, one of them asked, and so the sergeant read some of it out loud—not a bad voice for it either, Cooper reflected, a little like Charlton Heston's in *The Ten Commandments*—bringing the whole squad room to a standstill. A hush closed down but for the continual clicking of a teletype in the corner and a phone ringing outside somewhere. He finished the one page and became silent, casually leafing through the rest of the manuscript, whether with interest or bewilderment, Cooper could not tell.

"She-it," an officer finally said. "You call that poetry? Where's the fucking rhyme?" The room had turned on Cooper, once again, with suspicion. Heads went together.

"Okay. Knock it off," the sergeant shouted. "What do any of you turds know about poetry?" He returned the manuscript to the briefcase and handed everything back to Cooper. He even walked him to the door of the precinct and looked unhappy when his offer of a ride was refused. "It's no trouble," he urged. "I got a guy going off duty who's got a girl living down near where you want to go." He squeezed Cooper's arm and winked. "Are you sure? He can give you a lift."

Sure of the address only, Cooper said to himself, as he rang the bell beneath the printed card: *QUINN MASTER OF FINE ARTS D. Jacobs, Director.* Who was Quinn? He imagined a slim, well-knit Irishman who had immigrated to Boston, worked on the docks, became owner of a tugboat, then several more. Then founded a small college that had gone broke in the slump of the 1970s.

There must be someone there. Cooper pushed the bell again. First, he had stood across from the building, in his familiar post beneath the house stoop, and seen the lights in the penthouse give off that peculiar pulse. Scouting the terrain before landing. He had been expected. "Don will be glad to get these," Ruth had said that morning when she handed the packet to him. Her eyes had glistened with pleasure, with the measure of Don's gladness. He pressed the bell once more.

"Who's there?" The voice came from the small speaker next to the bell panel. He sounds tired, Cooper thought. Weary. "What do you want?"

"Jack Cooper, Mr. Jacobs. I'm delivering—"

"You've been pushing the wrong button," the voice said. "See, over to the left, the button with just my name on it?" Cooper looked at the other button. "That's the button you should have been pushing," the voice continued patiently. "You see, it's after business hours, so there's no one on the second floor. It is fortunate that I happened to hear the buzzer down there."

"Yes it was," Cooper agreed. He spoke as if to a deaf person, into a hearing aid, and he thought he might have spoken too loud. He lowered his voice. "Should I push the other button?"

The speaker was silent, considering the question. "No, that won't be necessary," the voice finally said. "Now, wait for the door buzzer."

The interior surprised Cooper. The first floor of the old townhouse was like a warehouse; cardboard cartons were stacked almost to the plaster moldings around the ceiling. The banister up the stairs was shaky and the wallpaper had come off in patches. The place smelled like the back room of the old magazine store on 23rd Street. On the second-floor landing, a dim light burned. He could barely make out the hand-penciled sign on the closed sliding doors: *QUINN MFA*. The magazine *Ajax* was represented by a handsomely printed brochure, with pictures of its contributors. He looked for Ruth's name among those poets who were not pictured. "Among others," Cooper read. She would be included among others. He took out a pen and neatly printed her name on the poster: RUTH COOPER.

The stair up to the third floor narrowed, only wide enough for one person, and, as if to correct this limitation, a small chair had been mounted on a track fastened along the top of the banister. It was the sort of mechanism used to transport the infirm from floor to floor. At the top was a closed door with a large mask carved of wood and painted in primitive colors, decorated with shells and fiber, illuminated by a small spotlight.

Curiously, he found himself listening for some sort of sound from the other side of the door. He wasn't sure what sort of sound, maybe the hum of a dynamo or the crackle-static of a secret transmitter. But, it was dead quiet; nor could he hear anything when he pressed the button beside the door. It was painted red and jutted out from a cone of molded plaster.

"We're working late." Jacobs said. His small eyes looked intently from beneath the short bill of a small black cap pulled down to his ears, a Dutch sea-captain's cap. "But come in, now."

Watch-spring coils of dark hair sprung out from beneath the cap and around his ears. Cooper thought the rest of Jacob's dress suggested that he had been preparing for bed. The poet pulled the tasseled sash of a maroon bathrobe around the circumference of his middle and shuffled ahead of Cooper in worn leather slippers. He wore pants but no shirt, and his chest was thickly haired. When they had met years before, in the old magazine store, the poet had seemed older than Cooper.

Cooper followed him down a small dark foyer. Within, the apartment seemed to be but one large room, the dimensions of the building itself; yet there must be other rooms, Cooper figured, certainly a kitchen since Ruth had told him that Jacobs also liked to cook. And, in fact, just as they came into this large room a young woman pushed backwards through a swinging door holding two mugs.

"It would be agreeable if you could join us in some hot chocolate," he said as he took the package of poems from Cooper. He put it on a table and then took the two mugs from the girl, for, close up, she seemed much younger than Cooper had first discerned. She seemed unused to her dress and its accessories, as if this wardrobe was worn rarely, only on certain dress-up occasions. An older sister's dress and a size large. She walked uncertainly on high heels. Jacobs had nodded, and she went back through the kitchen door.

"It is pleasant here," the poet gestured toward an area between two small sofas set before a mantle faced with dark-blue mirror. Before he took his seat, he had flipped a switch beneath the mantle, which activated a circular device set into the hearth. The machine's round face had several smaller round openings each with a colored gel, hues of red and orange and purple were rotated before a bare light bulb. This was the source of those power pulsing lights that had radiated their mysteries into the night—that Cooper had observed several times this spring from across the street; even tonight before he rang the bell.

"Where have you been?" Jacobs asked as he faced the fireplace. He even held one hand out, as if the colors would warm it. He looked back closely. "What's wrong with your glasses? Have an accident?"

· 236 ·

Cooper made up a general excuse for his lateness. He even pulled down one sleeve of his jacket to cover the raw, red line left on his wrist by the handcuff. The young cop had been very eager. Cooper had never been handcuffed before. Maybe the girl was Jacobs's daughter and she might be doing her homework in the kitchen now. He imagined her sitting at the table in the center of the room, pencil in hand, studying her lessons. One leg tucked beneath her.

The poet continued to smile at Cooper's fictional account of his day. The mundane details he made up—a museum visit, a movie—apparently fit into the man's casting of how Jack Cooper would spend a day in the city. But his smile was pained and only stretched toward the right ear, giving his amusement a curious importance, an amusement that would never be wholly stimulated so a complete smile would be impossible to do under any circumstances.

"And how is Ruth?" Jacobs asked. He sat down and raised the mug of hot chocolate as if to toast her.

Cooper felt he could answer the question on many levels, but chose to make up, again, an ordinary answer. As he spoke, he tried to see her in bed with the poet, doing things they did. Did the man smile then, too—the superior recognition of a sexual cliché. Ah, you do that also, do you?

"It's a tough business, this poetry racket," Don Jacobs had been saying. "I'm glad Ruth is still hanging in there. Think of all the people who want to write poetry and can't." His eyes beneath the cap bill twinkled as he leaned forward and tapped the thick package Cooper had delivered. "That's only a tiny fraction. It's like counting stars."

"She works very hard at it," Cooper heard himself say, suddenly overcome by an anger that surprised him. Jacobs's amused look, filtered by the revolving display, seemed to see his thoughts. Cooper had become her purveyor. He heard himself hawk her dedication to her poetry, her sincerity, and he wondered if he had also offered her body to Jacobs years back, without knowing it. It was a disagreeable idea, and it passed through his mind as the device in the hearth turned from magenta to cyan. Why don't you get angry, why don't you hit me, she used to cry? Which always startled him, that she never understood that his tolerance was a measure of his love for her, his respect for her work and her temperament. All these years she must not have wanted this patience, but had asked for something else, a gesture so simple as to be missed.

Jacobs had stood up to flick off the hearth display. Enough for tonight, his gesture seemed to say. Cooper felt that something horrible was about to happen. Surely, turning off the colored lights had been a signal for him to leave. It was as if Ruth had been there but had left this room that resembled the art deco lounge of an old ocean liner. Had the engines stopped, turned off by Jacobs just now? Were lifeboats being put down as the vessel wallowed in the swells? Would they really look for her small body in the immense sea? Or just pass on. Cooper was stunned; he had been looking about the room for something he could hurt Jacobs with.

"I shall continue to do all that I can for her," the poet said. It sounded like a promise, he did the same for all of his old mistresses, an arrangement as genteel as the smile on the man's face.

Someone was rising to the penthouse on the mechanized chair lift. The two men listened to the machinery's whine. Cooper guessed it was another woman, and simultaneously, he knew the girl in the kitchen was not Jacobs's daughter nor was she studying anything. Was it even a kitchen?

"She's here," the poet said in a loud voice and stood up. "Come, I'll show you the view from the terrace," he said to Cooper who got up quickly and followed, still holding the mug of chocolate—feeling awkward.

The view from Jacobs's parapet was spectacular. Cooper could see across the East River and far into Queens. He watched a large jet make its approach to LaGuardia Airport and it looked close to coming down among the apartment high rises clustered on the other side of the Queensboro Bridge. Traffic moved along the highways. A couple walked a small dog along the sidewalk below. A perspective reduced the dog to the size of a mouse.

Jacobs obviously waited for him to comment on the view. Cooper got the feeling everyone brought out here was supposed to say something about the view before he was ushered out. The patio was such a jumble of broken deck furniture, and stacks of old newspapers, trays of sooty dishes that Cooper wondered if the area was only an exit route for unwanted guests. "Nice," he finally said.

Inside, he watched the young woman go from the kitchen, open the door, and greet another who looked older. The two embraced, pressed their cheeks together in a sisterly fashion, and then disappeared through the swinging door together. Perhaps to talk about shoes or fashion, Cooper reflected, for the newcomer had also been dressed with a curious chic.

"Some of my students," Don Jacobs explained. "They help me proof the magazine. We're meeting a deadline for the new issue tonight."

"Are they poets?"

Jacobs moved away from Cooper and lifted his head to smile at the sky. "They hope to be. They are a great help to me," he said. The phrase was smooth with usage and his laugh was as much a sigh. He glanced at Cooper from the sober side of his face, then took two steps, then one more away. "You silly man. Thinking of throwing me over, were you?"

The accusation uncovered the impulse. Cooper reached out to place a hand against the cool wall next to them.

The poet had been leaning against the parapet, casually, like an old friend, and then with a grace that belied his portly build, he eased himself up to sit on the wall and, then, to stand upon it. A breeze off the East River fluttered the hem of his robe. Cooper sat down on one of the rusted chairs.

"Push me over," Jacobs said. "Be a hero. That's what you're thinking, isn't it?" He had begun to walk along the top of the wall, pacing back and forth. Cooper suspected the act had been performed many times, a feat to impress young women. Certainly, the trick must have been done for Ruth, one more clever sleight of foot to fascinate her.

He felt sick and foolish. There was no way to win against men like Jacobs, because the Elenas of the real world did not want to be rescued, however many poems they might write in anger about their servitude. That was the arrangement, he guessed, the understanding between men like this and women like Ruth. And when men like him and, yes, Armstrong, tried to pull their rescue stunts, it was always the women who suffered, who fell to their deaths. Rescue operation a success, all hostages killed.

All of them had been flying at the wrong altitudes on useless errands, infatuated by the sound of their own wings. It *would* make a good movie, Kelly had said, and maybe she had been laughing at him and Armstrong and Winslow all the time. She should know about this. That's all it would make—a good movie. None of them had asked to be rescued and maybe all the talk they heard about getting their wings only raised their fear of falling. On the other hand, men like Jacobs gave them helplessness and security, comfort in captivity. How stupid Cooper felt.

Another airliner turned the night sky on the lathe of its engines' whine, like one of Clay Peck's machines smoothing out imperfections. Then, the night reassembled itself again.

A dog barked from below. A siren left a wake in the distance. A radio was turned up loud and then, just as suddenly, turned off. By now, Cooper had fixed his glasses, all the while straightening them as he sat on the terrace roof. He fit them to his nose and around his ears and stood up and walked toward the apartment's front door. He heard Don Jacobs call something to him which sounded sympathetic. Like an apology.

"What's all this about getting into space," Buckminster Fuller had said. Jack Cooper had heard the architect speak at Hunter College, and he repeated the words to Ruth one night. They had been standing in the backyard, he remembers, looking up at the stars. "Doesn't anyone realize we *are* in space. We don't have to get into space; we're there already."

"You don't have to tell me about living in space." Ruth had said. "I know everything there is to know about living in space."

Then, Cooper thought, she had been making another crack about moving to Hammertown, about being lofted out of the scene in New York. But on the train back from the city, he now wonders if she hadn't been talking about something quite different. "Do anything you want," he remembers her saying sometimes in the early days of their marriage; this was a metaphor for something much larger and more complex than sexual desire.

If he had misunderstood her, his imagination must have disappointed her, for she had been asking, he thinks, for some kind of definition, some ending to a space she felt lost in. So, on the last mile or so before Green River, he walks the train aisle as if his footsteps might hasten the trip, speed his return to take her in his arms and hold her captive.

All the house lights are on, though it is near midnight. He

sits for a moment in the rusted Skylark, counting the sounds in the swamp. Even the lights in Hal's room are on. Maybe they have planned a party. A homecoming. He remembers something in the freezer, a dish that might be warmed up for such a feast. The birdbath glows in the house lights. The arms of the windmill are still. Hello, hello, he says to the boy on the dolphin's back and gets out of the car.

Ruth sits at the kitchen table. She had been drinking coffee, and she must have heard him drive up but she hasn't moved. He studies her through the window, and in that perverse effect a glass pane may have, their positions are reversed. It is Ruth who has come back, Ruth who has just returned. She doodles with her spoon on the tablecloth.

"Here," she says when he comes in. She doesn't get up. "Here, come sit beside me." But that isn't enough closeness for her, because she puts herself on his lap, takes off his glasses, and kisses his eyes. All this day and most of the night, he had been trying to see things clearly, distinguish one thing from the other—even straightening the bent frames of his glasses himself so that he could use them, see better; and here she was taking them off. That's funny, Jack Cooper thinks, as he turns his face up to hers to receive her caresses, as her face looms large above him and all edges become blurred and light is diffused—which might be true vision after all. Her face is wet, and, close up, he notes the lips taking his are tremulous. Then, she tells him about Hal, about the boy's triumph which they would have to share and endure.

AFTERWORD

"So this morning the boy, Hal, comes up to my place and we start to put all of it together. Mr. Cooper has gone down to the city on business, and the missus is in there with that there machine of hers. Wired to it almost. Her eyes popped out more than ever. What about school, I say to the boy; you're going to get into trouble, but he just nods and gives that big grin as the good-natured boy he is.

"All last winter he would bring me these drawings out of magazines and books showing these constructions that the ancients had made, but not really made, mind you, but only drawn out. One time, one of those model kits of a weird contraption. Plans that were meant to be made up, but for some reason they never got around to building them, like they had gone onto more practical matters such as forts and cathedrals and strange-looking war machines. Some of them, I swear to you, looked like the work of children trying to imitate something they had seen but meant to be made out of materials other than what they could find at

· 243 ·

hand; so they went ahead and made the thing anyhow out of planks and rude fittings, hammered together with spikes, whereas the prototype used a kind of glue that's been lost, if you follow me.

"Now look, I say to him, it's not going to work. If it had worked, someone would have done it before, but he just keeps bringing me more pictures and then he sets down in my shop and starts cutting and chiseling and just to protect him from losing his fingers, I say—Let me do that. And that's where I got caught up, don't you know. And, together, we make up the story of him helping me with that house in Connecticut, which he did do sometime.

"Because the damn thing made sense, and it was beautiful besides. It was a lot more complicated than the kites we had been making, and it had this arrangement in the middle of straps and pedals that set it apart right away from anything else. Say, kites were like an old species; here was a whole different breed. I swear it was just a beautiful piece of work. All that time he had been studying birds—taking them apart, you might say, to see how they worked.

"Oh, we used ash for the frames. Earlier, he had dragged up bamboo from the swamp. I got the silk for the coverings over to that remnant store in Great Barrington. Hal started giggling to himself almost all the time we worked on it, all the while I'm telling his parents he was helping me on houses over in Connecticut. The whole construction was jiggery but strong, and if you put your hand on it in a certain place you could lift it like a feather. I began to think that them ancients, as smart as they were to dream up this rig, couldn't put it together because they didn't have someone like this boy, Hal, to work it. He was the missing part they couldn't find and couldn't make. He just had to come along on his own, you might say.

"So this morning, him and me carry this contraption up

to the top of the Knob where I used to find Grace sometime, staring off into space. You can see into Massachusetts,
and Connecticut, too, from up there. I sometimes go up to
look the other way, at the sun going back behind the Catskills, for it makes me wonder. There's more than common
sense here, I think. There's more than what I can measure
and cut and fit even if most of the time I think that's all
there is to it. I guess that's how I got so fired up with the
boy's project. It didn't make sense but then again it did. It
should. So this morning the two of us are up there on the
Knob on either side of this machine made out of sticks and
a little cloth and a bicycle gear and pedals, and I am all at
once in a sweat because now it's not just measuring and fitting smooth pieces of wood together but something else
quite different. It's like the sun was coming up from behind
the Catskills and not going down; but it wasn't backwards
either, but like a different world where that direction was
the rightful one. So I try to dissuade him, but he's already
crawling backwards into the rig, snuffling with a pleasure
that makes the wings of the piece vibrate like those of a
moth outside a window on a summer night.

"Then he is standing, the whole business wearing on his
back and shoulders. He's a strong boy, don't you know,
more than most men. Why I've seen him lift a hundred
weight—there's this old birdbath I let him have, I took from
a place across the line—lift it like it was no more than a jar
of preserves. But I say to him, Now, Hal, just take a run
down the meadow there and no more,' and he nods and
faces the backside of the Knob, which flattens out into that
savannah. Be satisfied with that, I say to him. You have
done this and it will work, so be satisfied that you have done
this. There is no one who has done this, I say to him and
thinking that not even those ancients whose idea he is wearing on his back, that sprouts out of his back like some pecu-

· 245 ·

liar angel—peculiar, I mean, to this other world where the sun rises in the west, and so I am worried because the sun is clearly coming up in its usual way, over from Connecticut.

"So, like I say, he turns and starts running down through the meadow, his feet getting less traction as he goes until he's all in the air and he pulls up his feet and puts them into the fittings and pedals fast. He pulls his arms in and out and the wings slowly bend and push out and I think it's them plastic pulleys, the ones with the aluminum casings that is doing it. The ancients never had pulleys like that or they would have made one of these themselves instead of just sitting around doodling them on pieces of sheepskin. But, I don't really believe that.

"Because the boy was flying. The wings moved slow but taking powerful cuts at the air, and his feet moved fast on the pedals, which was a right comical difference to the slow way the wings moved, though it only showed his determination to stay up there. That's enough now, Hal—I'm calling to him because he's gliding way down at the end of the meadow and just before he reaches that stand of white pine, he turns it around—just as easy as if he done it all before—and starts back toward me, rising to follow the contour of the ground as it rises up toward the Knob. That's just fine, Hal—I say to him, talking to him as easy as I'm saying this to you because he is just overhead, feet pumping and the great wings rising and falling. I could almost reach out and touch him and maybe I should have done so, reach out and take hold of that curved piece of ash that bowed down underneath like the breastbone of a bird and pulled him down.

"Then he says, I can hear him plain as day, 'This duck is going to fly.'

"It was like looking up and finding an owl or a hawk had been gliding over you all that time, quiet and observing you all that time. Hal then said, 'Well, hello there,' and he smiled but his face was still serious, and the soft whir of the cycle sprocket as he pumped the pedals and the faint creak of the wings was all the noise he made.

"So then he had passed out on over the Knob, before I could stop him or maybe before I could want to stop him because my ownself seemed to be flying with him there too. I had built the contraption hadn't I? If I could have sung something I would have. He should have had a song to go along with him, because now he has gone way out beyond, and the ground has suddenly dropped way down below him, going from the few feet above the meadow on one side of the Knob to the valley floor way down on the other. But it made no difference to him. He had actually flown no higher, only the ground had dropped away beneath him. Come back—I said—only talking to myself because I knew it was no use to shout. He kept going, turning and making circles in the most wonderful manner. How long I watched I cannot say. I wondered about his legs, strong as he was. How long would he be able to keep them pumping? But he rose higher and dived and then rose higher again, doing tricks that I have only seen on birds. And like some ancient bird, he began to call something out—just one sound—over and over, and I finally caught the sound of it as he turned my way. It was her name, over and over, her name. Ruth. Ruth. Ruth.

"So then he swooped and flew down the valley, turned like he had become tired not of staying aloft but of staying in this one place, circling and circling like a redtail waiting for something to appear on the ground that would release him from that endless band and though he was distant now, I got the sense that he, too, had been waiting for something or for someone to appear so that he could fly over them and say—Well, hello there, and so be released in some way. I could still hear him call for her. No point in crying after him. He would not hear even if within earshot. I kept him in sight as long as I could. The meadow behind me emptier than ever. He flew in the large, lazy circles that had a sense of watchfulness onto them, and I would catch a flash of something between the great wings that must have been his face as he turned this way and that, looking for whatever it was he hoped to find on the ground. Then he was gone. But his search not over. Only carried farther on. Later, of course, he was to come down."